I0596092

WHERE HAVE ALL THE ELVES GONE?

Christian Warren Freed

Copyright © 2020 by Christian Warren Freed

Excerpt from *The Lazarus Men* 2021 Christian Warren Freed
Cover design by BrozeDesigns
Cover copyright 2021 by Warfighter Books
Author Photograph by Anicie Freed

Warfighter Books
Holly Springs, North Carolina 27540
https://www.christianfreed

Second Edition: January 2021

Library of Congress Cataloging-in-Publication Data
Name: Freed, Christian Warren, 1973- author.
Title: Where Have All the Elves Gone?/ Christian Warren Freed
Description: Second Edition | Holly Springs, NC: Warfighter Books, 2021. Identifiers: LCCN 2021930765 | ISBN 9781957326252 (hardcover) | ISBN 9798313026237 (trade paperback) ISBN: 9780578474762 (ebook)
Subjects: Urban fantasy | Fantasy | Dragons and Mythical Creatures

Printed in the United States of America

10 9 8 7 6 5 4 3 2 1

HAMMERS IN THE WIND:
BOOK I OF THE NORTHERN CRUSADE

"I love this book. This book hooked my attention on the first page and it was hard to put down. There is darkness in this book, you know something is going to happen so you keep reading to find out what. The author writes it so good, it's like you are there experiencing what the characters are. And I love it."

"I purchased this book to read to see if it would be suitable for my daughter to read. She is advanced in reading, but some books for kids older than her can be a little too much content wise. I think this one will work out great for her and she would enjoy it as much as I did. I'm glad I came across this book and can't wait to read the rest of the series."

THE DRAGON HUNTERS

"Excellently written. The author is able to really capture the stress, fear, and panic of life and death situations such as combat. Greatly looking forward to the next installment in the series!"

"Mr. Freed weaves the parts of this tale together smoothly, keeping the story moving at a good pace. He uses his own military background to paint powerful battle images and then he moves on. With only a little background, he makes the reader care about the members of the band - to worry about them and want them to do the 'right thing'. He adds depth to the characters through their actions and his dialogue is very realistic."

DREAMS OF WINTER:
The Fractured Universe #1

"Steven Erikson meets George R.R. Martin!"

"THIS IS IT. if you like fantasy and sci-fi, you must read this series."

"The writing style is absolutely beautiful, and made me want to keep reading. The writing makes the story and its characters real. They're not just people that I'm reading about; they're true fighters that are hanging onto their last hope. It makes the story compelling and a pleasure to read."

Other Books by Christian Warren Freed

The Northern Crusade
Hammers in the Wind
Tides of Blood and Steel
A Whisper After Midnight
Empire of Bones
The Madness of Gods and Kings
Even Gods Must Fall

The Histories of Malweir
Armies of the Silver Mage
The Dragon Hunters
Beyond the Edge of Dawn

Fractured Universe
Dreams of Winter
The Madman on the Rocks
Anguish Once Possessed
Through Darkness Besieged
Under Tattered Banners*

Where Have All the Elves Gone?
The Lazarus Men
Coward's Truth: A Novel of the Heart Eternal*
Tomorrow's Demise: The Extinction Campaign
Tomorrow's Demise: Salvation

A Long Way From Home: Memories and
Observations From Iraq and Afghanistan+

Immortality Shattered
Law of the Heretic
The Bitter War of Always
Land of Wicked Shadows

Storm Upon the Dawn

War Priests of Andrak Saga
The Children of Never

SO, You Want to Write a Book? +
SO, You Wrote a Book. Now What? +

Forthcoming   + Nonfiction

For everyone who has ever had the suspicion that the world
is not what it seems. Keep looking in the shadows. Who
knows what you might find?

ONE

Daerdalon roared in agony as the crystal spear stabbed into his heart. The Dark Elf clutched desperately at the haft, trying to dislodge it before it was too late. Enchanted, the crystal spear was like poison. Smoke and steam issued from his pores. Viscous fluids leaked from the corners of his thin eyes and drooled from his ears and nose. His mouth twisted in pain as he clawed at his slayer. Hatred blazed in those red eyes, silently damning the man who had killed him.

Tavis Halfhand took a step back and watched as his lifelong enemy started to dissolve. Running the crystal spear through his heart had been exhilarating and climactic. The great plague of the world was ending, all in one fell swoop. Justice had come to claim Daerdalon, justice long in coming. His evil had turned the surrounding kingdoms into mockeries of life. Trees and bushes had died. The people, those foolish enough to remain, were downtrodden and beaten into submission by the seemingly endless cadre of ogres and trolls. Not until Tavis and his band of brave heroes had sought out and found the crystal spear had anyone dared to hope.

This momentous day restored hope to a broken world. Tavis struggled not to smile. Proud of his deeds, his thoughts turned back to his beloved Annisha. Once the most beautiful woman in the eastern kingdoms, she was now little more than a decaying corpse in an unmarked grave. His quest for revenge may have been satisfied, but it left a hollow pit in his heart. He was nothing without her.

The ground began to tremble. Fires erupted from a hundred fissures. The air turned dark with smoke and ash. Tavis wrenched the crystal spear from the defeated Daerdalon and fled before he became the dark elf's last victim. Powerful legs carried him into the open ground, and he ran for his life. Much of the surrounding countryside collapsed in on itself, scant meters behind him. His breathing was ragged. His lungs burned. His legs struggled to move faster. Tavis knew he was going to die.

The gryphon swooped down low, coming in from behind, and snatched Tavis into the air a moment before the ground beneath him dropped away. Tavis looked down and watched the ruin he had caused with a sense of satisfaction. It was over. He had won. The darkness of Daerdalon was ended, and life had the chance to prosper once again.

The End.

Daniel Thomas leaned back in his chair and cracked his knuckles. He exhaled a long, slow breath; staring at the words he'd just finished typing. For the thousandth time, he almost wished he were Tavis Halfhand, swashbuckling his way across the worlds of his imagination and rescuing as many maidens as he could. Well, maybe not that last part. He was sure what Sara, his wife, would say about that! Daniel chuckled softly. The thought of having a few adoring, scantily clad women hanging around desperate to prove their gratitude lingered just a while longer.

Unfortunately, real life wasn't quite so glamorous, or dangerous, as his imagination. Oh, he'd had his time in life-threatening situations. A brief stint in the Army had been enough to send him to Afghanistan and then Iraq with the 101st Airborne Division. Sara constantly got on him for having old Army memorabilia in the house. She argued that it influenced their kids too much. He always shrugged and asked, "What do you want me to do about it? It's part of who I am."

The rigid structure of Army life was not for him, however, and he got out after his six-year enlistment. Besides, combat wasn't what he'd imagined when he was a kid playing with his brother in the backyard. Stick guns and running around yelling *bang, bang, bang* wasn't even remotely close to the horror and fear he'd felt when the shooting was for real. The feeling of when he'd killed his first enemy soldier was incomparable to anything his mind could conjure. There were simply no words for the mixture of raw emotions colliding in his heart and mind when he envisioned the man pitch backwards in death. It still bothered him, from time to time. That face would never leave his dreams.

Daniel had tried his hand at a few odd jobs here and there, but nothing called to him. That listless feeling was the most infuriating he'd ever had. Always having an overactive imagination, it was no stretch for him to make up fantastical stories to tell his children when he tucked them in at night, and they loved it. Soon, he did too, and the first inklings of turning those stories into a novel had popped into his head. That was all it took. He'd toiled day and night, much to Sara's admonishment, until he had more than one hundred thousand words finished.

That novel, *Rise of the Dark Elves*, was quickly picked up by one of the bigger agencies in New York City and then a major publishing house. Daniel relished how greedily his first book was consumed by the strong fantasy base across the country. *Rise of the Dark Elves* went on to become a New York Times bestseller for nearly six months, and Daniel became one of the most sought after authors in the country. His book tours were resounding successes followed perpetually by speaking engagements, writer's workshops and even a stint as a guest judge in a few of the more well-known amateur competitions. Daniel Thomas had finally figured out what he wanted to do with his life.

He followed up his first breakthrough novel with three more, all set in a mythical world filled with elves, dwarves, dragons and wizards. His fans couldn't get enough, nor could the publishing world. His success was a goldmine for the big timers in the City.

Then the dark times fell on the fantasy world. Elves just weren't popular anymore. The dramatic decrease in sales left him reeling. All people wanted to read about, it seemed, were vampires and silly teenage girls falling in love with monsters that should be depicted as tearing out throats. No one cared about elves.

Daniel found himself in a dying market, and it was unsettling. His name no longer took top billing at events. Lines at book signings dwindled to all but the most diehard of fans. His agent continued to try selling his latest novels, but each consecutive one was harder and harder to get off the shelves. Residual income from his string of successes shrank, forcing him to find part-time work at the local grocery store stocking shelves at night. It wasn't much, but it helped pay the bills and take his mind off the steadily devolving market.

Still, no part of the situation was strong enough to dissuade him from pursuing his one true love. New stories and characters sprung into his mind at random, so fast he could barely put the words on paper. Sara didn't understand it. He couldn't properly explain it. Writing was the best form of stress relief, taking his mind off his problems, the stress of being at home during homework time with the kids, keeping the house clean, and so on. That, and, not to brag, he was damn good at it.

Hitting save, he drafted an email, attached the file, and fired it off to his agent. There. All done. Daniel slid the chair back and left his study. His back hurt a little from being hunched over the keyboard for so long, but the satisfaction of putting those two most magical words on the last page filled him with euphoria. It also left him hungry. A quick glance at the dark cherry grandfather clock showed that it was close to six thirty. Dinner time. And hopefully, he'd missed homework time.

He smelled dinner long before entering the kitchen. Fresh tomatoes and basil mixed with ground Italian sausage. Fresh Italian bread warming up in the oven filled the hallway with the most pleasant aroma. The only thing better was a fine cigar with his bourbon after the kids went to bed. It had become a ritual. He'd take the page with scribbled notes on storylines dand word counts and burn it the night he finished the rough draft. That, a cigar, and some of Kentucky's finest finished the night properly. Of course, there was always the chance Sara was feeling a little frisky. He broke into another smile and entered the kitchen.

Coming up behind Sara, he slid an arm around her waist and leaned in to kiss her neck. "I love it when you smell like that."

She smiled before pushing his wandering hands away. "Dan, I'm making dinner, and the kids are in the other room."

"You're no fun. What happened to the risk-taking girl I fell in love with?"

She snorted, stirring the homemade red sauce. "She got married and had kids. Now, if you're finished, I could use some help getting dinner on the plates."

"No rest for the wicked, I see," he chided and went to the cabinet to pull out the plates. He couldn't pass up the opportunity to give Sara a light slap on her butt. After all, she was next to irresistible in the plum shirt and black skirt. They may be pushing forty, but she was doing a superb job of maintaining her figure.

He frowned, looking down at his steadily developing belly. Not that it was big, but he wasn't the scrawny hundred and fifty pound kid that had joined the Army anymore. His workouts now consisted of walking their two Bernese Mountain Dogs, and that was more than enough. They were well over one hundred pounds each and capable of pulling his arms out of their sockets if they wanted, and they wanted quite a bit as far as he could tell. He loved those dogs and was willing to suffer a few strained muscles for the enjoyment and adoration they showed in such a simple act.

"All right spill it. What's got you acting so strange?" Sara asked suddenly. Her hands were on her hips, and she gave him a cross look.

Daniel turned. "What? Can't a fella be happy?"

"Not without an ulterior motive," she replied just tartly enough to get a rise out of him. "Let me guess, you discovered the cure for cancer."

"If I could be so lucky. No. If you must know, I finished my latest book today," he fired back, pretending to be a little hurt. "I sent it to Ariel already."

"What did she say?" Sara turned back to stirring her sauce. A quick taste told her it was ready. She pushed him out of the way and started to serve.

"I won't find out until tomorrow. I'm hoping this one will be easier to sell," he told her and shrugged. "We'll see. I've got my fingers crossed."

She nodded. "Well, uncross them and call your children. It's feeding time at the zoo."

TWO

Daniel -
What can I say? As usual, your prose is clean and easily readable. The story flows and is well written. Unfortunately, I can't sell this. Fantasy has changed. I'm sorry, Daniel, but this just isn't what people want to read anymore.
Cheers,
Ariel

Daniel frowned and angrily hit the reply button. His fingers flew across the keyboard, writing a scathing email that would only put him back on the market for a new agent. After the initial fury started to fade, he read through it and realized he would essentially be committing career suicide if he sent it. Instead, he decided on a much more traditional approach.

"Wastrel Literary Agency, how may I help you?"

"Stella, its Daniel Thomas. I need to speak to Ariel," he answered sternly.

He could almost hear the hesitancy before she spoke. "She told me to expect your call, Mr. Thomas. Let me see if she is busy."

Daniel started to pace across the living room, suddenly glad he was dressed in an old glow-in-the-dark Halloween t-shirt that said *I am the treat* and a pair of black shorts. Getting dressed up to go to her office would only have infuriated him more. As it stood, the longer he waited, the more he stewed. This was the first-time Ariel had ever written and said she couldn't do it. Normally, her pleasant attitude and mild demeanor led to a very amiable work relationship between them, but now it served to fuel his anger.

Realistically, he should have been mad at the current market, not Ariel. She needed to make a living just as badly as he, putting her in the dubious position of alienating authors that just weren't in demand anymore. As angered as he was, Daniel wondered how she must feel. Friends of quality were hard to come by, especially now that the younger generations chose to sit behind their computer screens like slaves to technology and send emails rather than speak to their friends in person. He had always enjoyed the work relationship he and Ariel had established. She was a good agent and an even better friend. Being mad at her didn't suit his purpose. Not that that helped much.

"Mr. Thomas? She's ready for you now. Thank you for waiting," Stella said with a tone he didn't quite understand. A moment ago she had sounded hesitant now he could almost believe she was relieved.

"Daniel, I know what you're going to say, and believe me when I tell you that it wasn't an easy decision to make." Ariel immediately went on the defensive.

He felt his cheeks flush. "You have no idea what I am going to say. I poured my heart into this story, and you barely skimmed over it. And don't try and convince me that you read it in a single night, either."

"Daniel, calm down."

He paused. "Give me a good reason to."

A sharp breath and then a beat. "How long have we been friends?"

"Close to ten years. What does that have to do with your last email?"

"Everything! Look, I'm trying to make this easy, for both of us. Do you think I like having to come back to you and tell you no like that?"

Daniel had his doubts but kept them private. The last thing he needed was to incite her further. Nothing good would come from both of them flying off the handle. Daniel decided to let her vent and, hopefully, convince him that his world wasn't crashing down around him while he stood by helplessly.

Her voice was naturally song-like but with an aggressive undertone he found discomforting, as if she were trying to dissuade him from being angry. "None of the houses are buying *anything* to do with elves or dwarves. Not a single one in New York wants to touch that subject. We're running into a brick wall on this. Your name isn't the draw it used to be, and there is nothing I can do to change that so long as you continue to turn out traditional fantasy. Our best approach is to sit down and try to figure out another direction for your work — unless, of course, you want to crank out some humdrum take on vampires or such?"

The last was said with more mirth than he was ready to accept. Daniel frowned heavily. *Goddamn vampires. If I could only get my hands around the necks of the people responsible for this craze!* His mind raced, struggling to come up with viable alternatives. Nothing came to mind, further deepening his emerging depression. Anger flushed from his body so quickly he was left with a chill.

"What are my options?" he asked as calmly as the gnawing feeling in the pit of his stomach allowed.

"Think outside of your comfort zone. You're a very talented writer, Daniel. There has to be some other sort of inspiration that you can use to create a different type of fantasy world. What about some sort of alien world?"

"Oh, God, Ariel. What hasn't been done about aliens? Hollywood and amateur filmmakers have sunk the alien genre into the mud. I can't reduce myself to that. How much free time do you have today?"

This time the pause was a little too long for his liking. He immediately became concerned that she was going to try and duck him. Some of the anger returned.

"I'm really busy today. There's no way I can fit you in to my schedule," she started to protest.

"Nonsense. Everyone has free time during the day, especially you agents," he replied aggressively. "How about I come down and we do lunch?"

Her frustration bled through in the terseness of her tone. "Daniel, I really don't have the time. Why don't you go sit down and try to come up with something I can sell?"

She knew exactly what to say to put him over the edge. "You're not getting out of this so easily, Ariel. I'll be down around six. We'll do dinner, my treat, and you can explain why you can't turn my story into a successful sale. See you then!"

He hung up before she could reply, feeling rather good about himself. Being non-confrontational was a bit of an issue for him, so being able to successfully tell Ariel off went far in bolstering his self-esteem. Curiously satisfied, Daniel looked around his living room and realized he had almost nothing to do for the next seven hours. Both dogs sat patiently on the ends of the two couches, staring up at him expectantly.

"Sorry, boys," he told them, "but I'm going back to bed."

Daniel yawned and stretched. His heart jumped as the heavy thump at his feet startled him. Slowly, he opened his eyes, wiping the gunk from the corners. Wagging his tail and looking at him with that odd stare was the oldest dog, Zeus. He had one of Daniel's sneakers hanging from his mouth. The other had fallen from Daniel's chest when he awoke, making the thumping sound. Apparently, the dogs had his day planned for him.

"You want to go for a walk, eh?" he asked. Zeus dropped the sneaker and jumped onto the couch with uncontrolled excitement.

An hour and a half, two cups of coffee, and a hot shower later, Daniel got dressed and sat down in front of his computer, intent on getting some work done. A pair of new stories had sprung to life over the last few weeks, and he wanted to flesh out the basic concepts. Unfortunately, his mind couldn't focus. Every thought strayed back to his latest novel and subsequent rejection. He likened the feeling to being trapped in a shark cage and not knowing how to swim. Nothing about that situation suggested safety. Come to think of it, he'd never learned how to swim. Total failure all around.

The black screen stared back, mocking his inability to create. Daniel hated his computer then. Restless and frustrated, he powered it down and went back to the living room to watch a movie. Like most writers, he had trigger mechanisms that helped spark his imagination. More than six hundred books and three hundred movies lined the shelves of his library, a feat he was quite proud of and made a point of bragging about when he could. Lost among the endless tomes and films dating back to the original Universal horror movies of the 1930s were the three films that had started it all.

He'd seen Star Wars close to a hundred times. It was the first movie he'd ever been old enough to see. His fondest memories were of his father taking him to the drive-in back in upstate New York when he was only four years old. Star Wars was by far his favorite movie and left him feeling inspired enough to crank out a few thousand words. Or at least it normally did.

Daniel threw the old pot on the stove and poured some vegetable oil on the bottom before dropping a scattering of popcorn kernels. The microwave stuff just didn't do it for him and making it on the stovetop left him with so much more than a small bag of Orville Redenbacher's finest. The smell reminded him of his childhood. A few minutes later, he was nestled in his favorite recliner with a cold beer and bowl of steaming popcorn.

After two hours, he still wasn't feeling motivated. He couldn't help but think about his conversation with Ariel and her dismissive email. There had to be more going on. There had to. She'd never told him no before. Never. Daniel decided to get dressed and head downtown a little early. He threw on an old North Face jacket and headed out the door.

He had barely made it to the front of the car when a pair of what could only be described as brutes stopped him cold. Two thugs of men; Daniel couldn't help but feel dread. Both had thick arms, almost too thick for their loose flannel shirts. Their foreheads were heavy and stuck out over their eyes, giving them a devious appearance with exaggerated features and small eyes. Their steel-toed work boots were scuffed and overused and absolutely the largest shoes he had ever seen. Daniel thought the brutes could pass as stand-ins for the Hulk. And they were leaning against his brand new BMW 3 series.

"Can I help you?" he stammered, doing his best to sound tough, although none of the group believed he stood a chance if things got physical.

The bigger of the two, if that applied, pushed off the car, leaving a dent in the door just below the side mirror. He clasped his massive slabs of hands together and cracked his knuckles. The dark hairs stood out against the bright red and yellow of his shirt. His stride was brutish. Each footstep was a quiet earthquake. Daniel could hear the bones snapping.

"You need to stay outta things, you hear me?"

His voice was so thick Daniel had trouble making out the words. Daniel stared at the brute more closely. The man had an almost grayish pallor and teeth so large he had trouble closing his mouth. Daniel's first instinct was to think one of his friends was playing a joke. There was no way two such extreme looking people could be so nearly identical.

He decided to be a little bolder. "Stay out of what? Who are you? You need to get off my property before I call the police!"

The second one began to laugh. A dark, menacing sound that rippled through the hundreds of pounds of muscles bulging obscenely all over his body. His right hand drew back and slammed into the door. Daniel looked in dismay. The brute didn't seem to notice he'd actually hit anything. He went right on smoking the foul smelling cigar drooping from the corner of his mouth.

"See that, puny man? You don't mind yer business, and that's you," the first one threatened and took a lumbering step forward for effect.

Daniel struggled to swallow his heart as he dug into his pocket for his cell phone. He'd barely put the thing to his ear when the brute charged. Never in a million years would he have believed such a monster could move so fast. Even seeing it happen didn't help soothe his fractured psyche as the brute closed the ten-meter gap so fast his figure nearly blurred. He snatched the phone from Daniel's hand and crushed it like it was made of Styrofoam, knocking Daniel down in the process. Pieces of cheap metal and plastic scattered across the lawn, reminding Daniel of death's touch.

"Let's kill him!" the second snarled. Thick ropes of drool spilled from the corners of his mouth.

Daniel swallowed nervously. The prospect of being crushed to death by these monsters was more frightening than nearly being killed during the invasion of Iraq.

"Naw. Boss wants him alive." He turned back to Daniel. "We warned ya. Don't make us come back. Next time won't end well," the brute sneered and spun away. He took the time to smash in the Beamer's back window on the way out of the driveway.

Daniel lay on the cold pavement, staring at the casual devastation the pair had caused with minimal effort. His arm hurt where the brute had grabbed him. His mind reeled from the shock of the assault. Who were those men, and how had they managed to move so damned fast? Breath coming out in plumes of mist thanks to the early fall chill, Daniel failed to make sense of it. He couldn't think of anyone who wanted him dead or threatened. And just who was the Boss? Irritated and more than a little scared, he picked himself up, brushed the stray pieces of grass and dirt from his jacket and headed to his car.

After a closer inspection of the damage, he reluctantly turned away from the ruined vehicle and went to the car to get the old stand-by. The 1965 Mustang had been a gift handed down from his father. Dark blue, the rebuilt engine purred when he turned it over. Soon enough, he was heading out of his neighborhood towards downtown. He briefly considered going to the police, but with no leads or believable stories, Daniel doubted they'd put much effort into it. He chose going to see Ariel instead. Maybe she would have some answers. Besides, it was already starting to get dark. He was late.

THREE

One of the things Daniel found most annoying about fall was the sun setting so fast. Daniel wasn't a big fan of the night, especially during the winter months when it seemed to dominate the world. This stemmed back to his Army days when he was expected to be at work no later than 05:45, rain or shine, and stayed in the motor pool until well after sunset. Factor in the fact that the Army liked to do most of its training at night (he never did get the hang of wearing nods), and he'd vowed never to work outside at night again.

Shadows stretched across the streets, the sun blocked by the high rises and smattering of skyscrapers. City lights warmed up, the dull glows slowly illuminating the encroaching darkness. Everything looked more ominous to Daniel. Perhaps it was in reaction to his assault earlier or maybe just because he imagined sinister forces waiting impatiently for the sun to go down.

He knew the notion was ridiculous at best. The world wasn't anything like the settings of his books. Everyone knew that elves just didn't exist. There were no dwarves toiling endlessly in mines of unending jewels and wealth. No dragons scouring the skies in search of easy prey and piles of treasure on which to make a bed. Daniel often filled his spare time with idle thoughts of fancy. He wondered what a world with those fantastical creatures might really be like. Would they be dead set to kill each other simply because they were different? Or would there be some sort of high king crowned with representatives from each race to rule the world?

Daniel liked to think it would be a better world. Every day, the world was inundated with increasingly dismal news. He got the impression the media was more concerned with trying to sell a poorly written story designed to scare the viewers than in inspiring them. He couldn't remember the last good news story he'd read. Occasionally, the major networks threw in fluff pieces that had no relevance to life, a thing that infuriated him and almost made him stop watching the news altogether. He had better things to do with his time.

One positive the news did have for Daniel was providing inspiration for his stories. It was almost too easy to skim through the pages and take a particularly juicy story to turn into magic. Thinking about it soured his mood. *"I'm sorry, but I can't sell this."* Daniel ground his teeth while he drove. That old anger resurfaced, directed towards Ariel. Rationally speaking, he knew it wasn't her fault, but he was anything but rational. He wanted to know why, needed to know why he was no longer good enough to warm people's hearts or become a part of their lives. It was insulting. It was maddening. It was….it just was, he was forced to admit.

The Mustang grumbled into the parking garage. The lower levels were still fairly crowded. It was dinner time, and with all the quality restaurants downtown, he didn't even bother trying to look for a spot on any level lower than five. Zipping up his jacket, Daniel snatched his laptop bag and headed for the elevator. His subconscious made him nervous. His blue eyes scanned the shadows for any possible hiding places for those two brutes to wait in ambush. He could feel the soldier instincts struggling to resurface. They wanted to take control, to put his life back on track.

Those days were over now, a fact he was reluctant to admit despite every attempt at turning his life into something normal and what the average citizen who had never served would consider respectable. Still, it was no easy thing to simply stop reacting to drills and tactics that had been beaten into his head for years on end. He shook his head. Mild paranoia was settling in, making him jump at shadows. He didn't like that at all.

Daniel got down to the crosswalk and waited for the light to bring him across. He briefly glanced at the blonde beside him. Her navy blue dress clung to all of the right places, and her matching heels made her legs a sight. Stopping himself before his thoughts got him into trouble,

Daniel refocused on what he'd come here for. Ariel had answers to give.

The elevator music helped stoke his anger. It was one of those unanswerable questions that plagued most people. Who selected the music to accompany an already awkward ride up and down the guts of a building? Standing so close to strangers was a thing that took getting used to. After all, you didn't know if the man standing beside you had a severed head in his bag. Or if the little old lady humming a church song had just finished poisoning her husband. Maybe the music was designed to calm them down? He didn't know but guessed that irrelevant artists were lining up to get on those tracks.

The thirteenth floor was dedicated to the Wastrel Literary Agency. Thankfully, it was emptied out. Halloween weekend had arrived, and no one with sense wanted to stay trapped in their offices and cubicles any longer than necessary. There were too many scantily clad women dressed in inappropriate costumes and men dressed as gladiators, or worse as far as he was concerned, about to roam the streets and bars in search of a good party and possible company later.

A single light from the back of the floor beckoned him. Ariel's office. He straightened his shirt beneath the jacket and barreled towards the light. Daniel wasn't sure, but he thought he heard muffled voices followed ominously by a wet smack and a stifled groan. His mind had to be playing tricks on him. First the brutes attacking him in his own driveway, and now this. It was time to get into his comfort clothes and pour a nice stiff glass of Woodford Reserve. A little bourbon would do him some good right about now.

A cut-off scream was followed closely by glass breaking. Old, repressed instincts suddenly took over as his mind decided it was real. Daniel ducked and searched for an attacker. A slender shadow spilled across the beam of yellow light angling down the corridor between cubicles. He briefly considered chasing but knew he was in no condition to. He lacked intel and, more importantly, anything that could be used as a weapon.

Daniel decided his best course of action was to wait until he was sure the way was open and then investigate. He only prayed he would be in time to rescue whoever had screamed. Anxiety got the better of him much sooner than he wanted, and he started to creep forward, using the faded blue cubicle walls for cover. Every sound was amplified — his heartbeat, his footsteps across the spackled tiles. He winced with each new sound, certain the assailant was lurking just around the next corner to silence any witnesses.

Old courage suddenly emerged, from where he could only guess. He circled around in order to get a better angle on the office door. There might be another attacker still inside waiting to spring a trap. Taking chances was pointless, and he wasn't willing to needlessly risk his life. He wasn't a hero, despite the latent desire to live out his novels, but that was just fantasy. Anything foolish now might only serve to get him killed. Truth be told, a quiet life stuck in the midst of anonymity held the most draw. That had been reduced to a fragile dream.

Daniel finally got into a position where he could see directly into Ariel's office. What he saw confirmed his worst fears. The outstretched body lying in a spreading pool of cooling blood could only be Ariel's. His anger died, replaced by immeasurable sadness and confusion. Why? A pointless question but one he couldn't help ask. Daniel scanned her body for injuries. The rise and fall of her chest was shallow, but it was still there. She was still alive!

"Ariel?" he whispered.

Agony crippling her, she slowly turned her head his way. The pain in her eyes was so intense it made his stomach roil. Dark blood leaked from her nose and mouth. She struggled to speak, but the words came out a strangled hiss. He was no medic, but all the signs suggested she didn't have long to live. Cursing himself, Daniel dashed the final few meters across the open area and entered her office. Using his right foot to shut the door, he positioned his body to block any intruders.

What he remembered from the various combat lifesaver courses during his career gave him a rudimentary understanding of what to do. He took a deep breath and recited the fundamentals over and over. ABC. Airway, breathing, circulation. Her chest rose and fell in shallow movements. A good sign but not one guaranteed to keep her alive long enough for EMS to arrive. He absently reached for his cell phone before remembering the brutes had turned it into tiny specks of trash drifting across his yard. *Shit!*

"Daniel.... you must leave!" she finally managed to gasp after he placed her on her back and elevated her head above a stack of books.

The truth being too dark, he decided to lie. "Shhh, save your strength, Ariel. It's going to be all right."

Her right hand weakly grasped for him. "Listen to me…not much time….is coming back. You must flee!"

His eyes narrowed with concern. She must be delirious. "Ariel, stop. Whoever did this is gone. You're going to be fine, but I need to call 911."

"No time," she protested. Her eyes glazed over before returning to normal. "Go to the bottom drawer of my filing cabinet. There is a small black case. Take it. Keep it safe. You will be contacted with instructions on what to do. Please, Daniel. Do this for me."

"Who did this to you? What's going on here?" he asked, his curiosity getting the better of him.

"The princess must be kept safe!"

He froze. Princess? What the hell was she talking about? There was no royalty in central North Carolina, at least none he was familiar with. She must have read too many fantasy novels and was now imagining things. He glanced down. The blood had stopped spreading, mostly.

"Ariel, what princess? Stop talking! You're wasting your strength and I need you to be strong for me," he tried to console.

She offered a haunting smile. "I'm so sorry, Daniel. Your books…wonderful. And…true."

Ariel started to shake. Her convulsions cast her long, luxurious golden hair across the floor. It seemed an insult when the blood stained that magnificent hair, a ruining of what should never have been ruined. Froth bubbled from her mouth, and her once beautiful eyes rolled back into her head. She was dead. Suddenly confused by conflicting emotions, Daniel didn't know whether to cry or get angry again. It had been a long time since he'd had the displeasure of standing over a corpse. He found himself staring down on her body, unable to take his eyes away. He willed her to come back. To not be dead. He needed it.

Nothing for it, Daniel slowly rose and looked around the office for the first time. Stacks of papers were scattered randomly, as if someone had been searching in a hurry. A window was broken — the shattering glass he'd heard earlier. Books, once neatly ordered by size and thickness on the shelves behind her desk, were carelessly tossed around. Mementos and picture frames lay broken and destroyed. A broken coffee mug rocked gently on its side. The spilled contents pooling in the center of her desk. The mellow wood coloring of the desk was remarkably similar to the color of the coffee.

Words suddenly came back to him. Did she really say something about a princess? And a black box in the bottom of her…. Daniel looked around until he found the filing cabinet. The drawers were all pulled out and strewn around the room. *Great. How am I supposed to know which one was the bottom? More importantly, what are the odds the thing she wanted me to find is still here?*

He owed it to her to look, despite the sinking feeling that he was already too late. Daniel riffled through the files and whatnot but didn't find anything resembling a black box. The fear that her killer was waiting just on the other side of the door panicked him, making him move much too quickly.

Finally, he decided that the box wasn't worth risking his life over and turned to find the office phone.

That's when he noticed the bottom of the filing cabinet. Slightly skewed, it stuck up just enough for him to grow curious. Daniel tossed the last few pieces of paper aside and took a good look at what appeared to be a false bottom. *You sneaky woman.* He struggled a bit but finally managed to tear the bottom out. There, hidden in a small compartment built into the wall, was a shimmering black box the size of a hardcover book. He couldn't be sure, but it sounded like the box was humming.

Police sirens echoed down the corridors of streets. Why? He hadn't been able to call anyone yet. Something dark was happening, and he needed to distance himself as much as possible. The last thing he wanted was to be caught up in a murder scandal, especially after the string of emails and negative phone calls exchanged between him and victim. All of it would be damning. After all, her blood was literally on his hands. Daniel reached his hands into the false bottom.

"I wouldn't do that," a stern voice warned suddenly.

Daniel spun about and saw a tall, powerfully built man standing in the shadows, glaring at him with unnatural eyes.

FOUR

Heart pounding, Daniel tried to swallow but couldn't. His worst fear had been realized. The killer was back and seeking to finish his task. Daniel clenched his fists and dropped into what he remembered as a fighting stance from his combatives classes. His legs felt weak. His body trembled. It had been a long time since he'd been in an actual fight, and he had absolutely no advantage. He was smaller and backed into a corner.

"Who are you? What do you want?" he demanded.

The other man folded his arms across his thick chest, seeming to pause for a moment. His head cocked sharply, showing the clearly defined line of his jaw. "I should be asking you those questions, human."

Daniel froze. Human? And it was said with such clear disdain. The sirens were getting closer. "Why did you say that?"

The other stepped into the light, and it was all Daniel could do not to stare. Angelic features were chiseled into his face. It was the look of…perfection. Daniel's jaw dropped as he took in the lines and angles of his face. Golden hair, much the same as Ariel's, curved his cheeks, hanging down just past his shoulders. Stray wisps danced across his forehead. His eyes were crystalline and the brightest blue Daniel had ever seen. There wasn't a wrinkle to be found and no sign of aging. Daniel knew he was looking at a sheer impossibility.

"Your kind always seems to find a way to get under foot. Is the box still there?"

Daniel could only nod.

"Good, grab it. I will take care of Ariel."

Without waiting, the angelic man knelt beside her body, as if he knew that Daniel wasn't a threat. He gently crossed her arms over her chest and placed her legs together, head tilted back to reflect the dignity that had been stolen from her. He reached into his jacket pocket and produced a thin vial of green fluid from his inner jacket pocket.

"I'm sorry. This wasn't supposed to happen. After tonight we would have been free at long last," he whispered not soft enough to prevent Daniel from overhearing.

Daniel reluctantly dug his hands into the filing cabinet. Inexplicable electricity danced through his body from head to toe the moment he touched the box. It was exhilarating. Euphoria spread through him, threatening to steal him from the present. Daniel struggled to keep himself. It took all of his strength and will to drop the box.

"'Ware the power of that box! It will steal your soul if you're not careful."

Daniel frowned with confusion. What was the point of being told to grab the damned thing if it was harmful? "I've had enough! What's in this box? Who in the hell are you?"

The other was up and had his arms around Daniel's shoulders before he could blink. "None of this will make sense to you, nor should it. I wish I had time to explain, but I fear her killers are nearby. There is no time to waste, but my name is Xander."

"You didn't kill her?" Daniel asked, dumbfounded.

The hurt reflected back was enough to bring a tear to his eye. "Kill her? No. She was my sister."

The sounds of light feet entering the main office made him pause. His head snapped back towards the door. Golden locks of hair drifted across his face as he slapped the main light off.

"What are you doing?" Daniel asked quietly.

Xander sent him a withering glare. "Quiet! We're being hunted. Grab the box and get ready to run. We won't be able to fight our way out of this."

Part of him wanted to run, to get away from this madman, the supposed killers and poor Ariel. He didn't belong in a murder mystery. But that other part, the quiet one that made him sometimes doubt his decisions, that part wanted to find out what happened next. Unfortunately, Daniel gave in to that devious part and reached back for the box. The power was less intense but still strong enough to send the occasional jolt through him. Box secure and heart threatening to burst from his chest, Daniel turned around in time to watch Xander outline Ariel's body with the green fluid. It reminded him of the liquid from an Army issue chem light but with an almost noxious odor.

Daniel stepped back and watched in mute shock as smoke and steam bubbled up from her skin, swirling over her like so many miniature tornadoes. More, her features were changing. The soft curves of her upper ears straightened and became pointed. She looked more graceful, elegant. In fact, she was looking exactly like the man claiming to be her brother. Daniel's eyes widened, and his jaw dropped again. And then, Ariel simply vanished — lost forever in a puff of smoke and drifting flecks of ash.

Her brother whispered words in a foreign language and bowed his head before replacing the stopper in the vial and sliding it back inside his jacket pocket. He looked up at Daniel, noticing the box, and gave a nod. "Come. There is no more time."

No sooner did they file out of Ariel's office than four figures dressed in black clothes leapt from behind a few desks. The glint of silver flashed from the heavy orange glow coming from the streetlights. They spread out in a rough semi-circle, weapons drawn but hesitant to attack. Daniel could feel their ominous red eyes lingering over him before settling on the box. He swallowed hard. The box. Of course! The box must have been what this whole affair was over. He briefly contemplated handing them the damned thing and trying to run but was more than sure they'd cut him down before he ever got close to escaping. His mysterious friend didn't share that notion and produced a thin sword of his own from behind his back. The attackers snarled but held back. They were clearly not expecting to find anyone else besides Daniel.

"Give us the box," the closest attacker hissed, his speech slurred.

"You murdered my sister. The box is now mine. Do you know who I am?"

"You should not be involved. The box was never yours! Your sister was a fool to think she could stop the coming battle."

Daniel clutched the box tighter, his fingers bleached white. *Battle? What the fuck have I gotten myself into?*

"Morgen has no jurisdiction here. I claim sanctuary for this human," Xander said sternly. There was an undeniable authority in his tone, enough to make the others back down some.

It was not a long lived truce. The four attacked simultaneously. Xander ducked under a wild swing, bringing his blade up to catch a wicked slash aimed for his throat. He kicked out, catching the closest man in the kneecap. Xander threw his sword diagonally and deflected another vicious attack. Dropping low, he whirled back and threw three quick strikes at his opponent's back. Dark blood blossomed from a pair of crisscross cuts before he dropped to the ground with a shriek.

Xander came back up. Sensing the shift in offense, the remaining three attackers dropped back and fanned out, trying to draw his attention in three directions. There was precious little time left. "There is a cab waiting on the street below. Get in. The driver knows what to do. Go! Run!"

Death was reaching out, threatening to crush the life from the room. Daniel ran without a second thought. Two of the three let him go, intent on dealing with Xander. The third leapt over a desk to try and cut Daniel off from the elevators. But Daniel had one advantage: intimate knowledge of the layout and floor plan. Instead of heading straight for the exit, he ducked right and circled around before his attacker was able to react. Daniel snatched a high-backed chair as he ran past and shoved it as hard as he could. The chair tipped but still managed to tangle the legs of the attacker. Both crashed in a heap. Daniel sprinted the last few meters, slapping the elevator button repeatedly until the door opened with a loud *ding*.

The worst part was waiting for those doors to slowly close. Daniel focused on the battle rampaging through the Agency's offices. Xander was bleeding from his right bicep, and the other two had several wounds of their own. A glimmer of movement off to the right drew Daniel's attention a moment before his attacker stabbed into the elevator. The blade barely made it in. Daniel howled and instinctively put the black box between his chest and the immaculately sharpened sword tip. The explosion of power threw him against the back wall and drove his attacker back into the office. The sword disintegrated to a cloud of black particles. The elevator began to descend. Kenny G began playing.

"This can't be happening," Daniel said to his reflection in the elevator wall. "I'm going crazy."

The elevator shook as an explosion ripped through the floor above him. Debris showered him. He clutched the box tighter. An eternity passed before the elevator finally chimed open in the lobby. Daniel peered into the darkened corridor. The sun had gone down already, and the crowds were thinned. He scanned the immediate area as his Army training dictated before heading for the front door. The yellow cab was waiting outside, just like Xander had said. A nearly transparent rope of exhaust choked the air under the glare of angry red taillights.

The now-familiar chime of the elevator startled him. Xander must have failed. Seeing nothing suspicious in his immediate surroundings, Daniel dashed through the glass doors and out to the cab. His nervous fingers struggled to grip the door handle, but he finally jerked the door open and collapsed inside the cab.

"Quick, drive!" he shouted.

The cabbie looked back over his shoulder and cast a nervous look. "Sorry, buddy, this cab's taken."

"You're not listening. We need to leave now. They're coming!"

"I said the cab's taken. Get out."

Daniel glanced back, expecting to see his attackers emerging onto the street at any moment. Out of options, he said, "Xander sent me."

The cabbie's expression changed entirely. Instead of an irate little man with an apparent inferiority complex, he was concerned and focused. "Why didn't you say so? Buckle up."

Tires squealed as the cab roared off. Two figures in black crept from the shadows of the brush. Their cold, almost lifeless eyes watched the cab disappear around the corner. They exchanged a silent look and dissolved into mist on the gentle night's breeze.

FIVE

Daniel's heart raced long after the cab sped away from the Wastrel Agency. His mind reeled from overload and refused to come to terms with the basic concepts of what he had witnessed. Questions continued to plague him. Nothing made sense. The sheer absence of reason led him through twisting corridors of thought, but without any guidance, he felt lost. Ariel dead. A random stranger sneaking into the office, through a closed door at that, with instructions to take a seemingly magical item and flee. And then there was Ariel's transformation. Why did she have pointed ears?

"Where's Xander?" the cabbie asked, breaking his concentration.

Daniel closed his eyes. "Dead. He didn't make it."

Violent images assaulted him. Swords slashing. Blood dripping. Cries and groans of the wounded and that hideous rattle the moment death reached up and stole the life from the one Daniel had killed.

The cab ground to a halt, jostling Daniel into the back of the driver's seat. "What? He can't be dead! Not now. The hour has grown very late indeed."

Daniel wasn't sure what that meant and was hesitant to ask, afraid of being drawn deeper into whatever conspiracy had already claimed him. A pair of police cars, sirens howling under the kaleidoscope of lights, thundered past en route to the crime scene. The speed at which the police had arrived led Daniel to a pair of conclusions: either Xander had called them before he entered Ariel's office or there was another player involved that had yet to show himself. Given Xander's claim that he was Ariel's brother, the first seemed slightly inappropriate. The natural desire for revenge and to keep personal matters from being made public fueled Xander's actions, leaving Daniel almost, almost convinced there was more going on than he wanted to know.

Then there was the matter of the black box. Curiosity demanded he open it and find out just what was so precious men were willing to kill and die for it. He looked down on it with a frown. The box continued to hum, though gently, almost imperceptibly. Undeniable power and strength radiated from the smooth surface. From what he could tell, the box had no hinges, no rough edges despite being squared. Whoever had created it was a master craftsman. Dull black, the box depicted scenes of ancient battles that appeared straight out of one of Daniel's books. He looked closer. The images were ingrained in the paint, or so he thought until they blended and changed. In place of the initial scene was the image of a golden woman. She had tragic features filled with sorrow and confusion. She was alone and helpless. Daniel felt his heart surge. She needed to be…needed to be what? Clearly the woman was trapped, but by what? For what? He wasn't sure he was ready to find out.

"Whew! How did you get a hold of that? I haven't seen one of those in about a hundred years," the cabbie interrupted.

Daniel looked up. "What did you say?"

Realizing his mistake too late, the cabbie tried to cover. "Name's Mort."

"Daniel."

"Hey, aren't you that author guy? The one who writes about elves and such?" Mort asked in a thick, fabricated New Yorker accent.

Daniel couldn't keep from smirking. "Yeah, that's me."

"You really believe in that kind of stuff? Seems like children's stories to me. Everyone knows there's no magic in the world."

Daniel looked up, suddenly concerned. He hadn't noticed until now, but Mort had been wheeling the cab halfway across town with a clear destination in mind. Could it be part of Xander's original plan? Or was there something more nefarious in play? One thing was clear; Daniel was tired of being ignored or treated poorly. It was time to put it all to a stop.

"Where are you taking me, Mort? I didn't give you any directions," he said forcefully. Mort wasn't the kind of man with a strong backbone, if Daniel judged correctly.

"Eh, what? You said drive, so I'm driving," Mort said, panicked.

Daniel pressed his advantage. "Driving where? What is this box, and why is it so important? You know what it is. Tell me."

The cab decelerated, and Mort pulled it over. He tipped his cap back, revealing his face for the first time. The eyes were pinched close together. He had a round snub nose spotted with dark, almost black freckles. The natural curve of his face reminded Daniel of a very large toad. Of course, the greenish complexion didn't help dissuade him.

"Look, there's a lot going on that is beyond you. Hell, it's beyond me. But Xander seems to have trusted you, so that means you're all right in my book too. It's not for me to explain the box, but I have instructions to take you to the one person who can. Just sit tight, and hopefully this will be a short ride." Mort turned back around and restarted the engine. "Oh, and don't worry about the fare."

They continued at a much slower pace. Much of the earlier commotion had died down. The sirens were gone, replaced by the typical sounds of a Friday night. A different crowd stalked the streets. Club goers and sports enthusiasts wandered towards their favorite bars. Music pumped through the steel corridors from the nearby amphitheater. An occasional office window was still lit, the occupants trying to make that last dollar or finish up some report or another. No one seemed to notice the strange pair in the remarkably clean and new taxi weaving through the streets. No one, that is, except for the pair of watchers that had been following them since leaving the Wastrel building.

Daniel caught Mort passing him queer looks through the rear view mirror and saw that the man's eyes were completely black and without pupils or irises. He was about to question Mort further, that sinking suspicion that more was not right, when the cab was struck and nearly knocked over. The box tumbled free and rolled under the front seat. Daniel struggled to get it back without even realizing it. Another blow swung the cab around.

"Shit! Hold on," Mort shouted and jerked the wheel in the opposite direction before slamming his foot down on the gas.

Box finally secured, Daniel sat back up and barely managed to buckle his seatbelt when the third blow struck. Two clouds of thick, black smoke circled the cab like predators getting ready for the kill. He was able to briefly make out features that were the combination of a man and some beast. He tried to swallow, but the saliva gummed up in his mouth. *This can't be happening. Stuff like this isn't real.*

The engine roared, and the cab shot down the street much faster than any taxi Daniel had ever been in — except for the local cab drivers in Seoul, South Korea. He'd never been more afraid in a moving vehicle than he was now. Mort, on the other hand, was relatively composed and seemed to have a good handle on things. The cab moved like an eagle on the wind. A haunting sound came from the smoke, so deep and terrible it threatened to burst Daniel's heart.

"Wraiths!" Mort cried. "Where did they come from?"

Blood trickled from Daniel's nose. He didn't want to look back, didn't know if he could survive it. There was inhuman cruelty to it. Fear permeated the car, boring into his mind to awaken every old nightmare he'd ever had. Daniel screamed.

Mort went into panic mode. "C'mon man, you gotta block that noise out. Shit! Stop bleeding in my cab! This is not good. Not good at all."

Daniel couldn't tell who Mort was talking to, further infuriating him. The bleeding stopped as the wraiths banked away from the cab. He frantically searched the sky for any sign of their attackers. "What in the hell is going on?" he all but screamed.

The cab accelerated. Mort ignored him for the moment, having more important matters to attend to. Dropping the radio to a sub-channel, he keyed the mic. "Dispatch, this is Mort. I'm bringing in the box with a human. Xander didn't make it and neither did Ariel. I've got two wraiths right behind me."

"Lose the human, Mort. We will have defenses ready for you," an iron cold voice replied. There was no question of his authority, yet Mort was suddenly reluctant to follow orders.

"You know what wraiths can do, Stern. I can't just leave this guy on the side of the road. He'll be torn to pieces," he tried.

"That's not our concern. Humans are forbidden from entering the citadel. You know the rules, Mort." Stern lived up to his name.

Mort slapped one of his thick hands on the steering wheel and cursed. "Stern, I'm bringing this one in. Xander okayed him."

Stern's voice came back after a brief pause. "He's your responsibility. What is your ETA?"

"Less than five minutes. These wraiths are pissed!"

A pair of high-pitched shrieks shattered the back window. Glass fragments pelted Daniel's head, cutting him in a dozen places. He wished for a gun, anything to fight back with. Between Mort's reckless driving and the pair of immaterial monsters trying to kill him, Daniel was certain tonight was his last. The horrible scream of nails ripping through metal echoed down the street. One of the wraiths had managed to latch on to the trunk and was pulling itself towards the cabin. Its face solidified and peered into Daniel's soul. Murderous intent poured from the wraith.

"Daniel, get down!"

He ducked, burying his head beneath his arms, a moment before Mort tossed a small grey stone at the wraith. The stone exploded in a brilliant ball of light. Shock ripples traveled through the car. Paint and metal shavings flew off the cab. The wraith screamed again, a totally different sound. Daniel was sure he felt pain. He looked up, risking death. The wraith had been thrown from the cab, wounded and angered. Still, the uncertainty of whatever magic Mort had was enough to keep them back and give Mort time to floor the gas pedal.

"What the hell is going on?" Daniel shouted again.

Mort shook his head and waved him off. "This ain't the time! We're both dead if we don't make it to the citadel. Wraiths are the hardest to kill. My little trick won't keep them off us for long. Here." He pulled a small obsidian object from his jacket and handed it back. "Cover us. If one of them gets close, just point it at them."

"This is a charcoal stick!" Daniel replied sharply, taking the object just the same.

"Damned humans! You don't know a thing. It's magic, you dolt. Just point and zap," Mort snapped and turned back to the road.

Reservations noted, Daniel gripped the stick and faced rearward. He'd have preferred a machine gun with extra drums of ammo, but fortune didn't favor him. Come to think of it, fortune seemed to have abandoned and condemned him altogether. He decided to go to the nearest pawn shop and buy a gun if he survived the night. Fanciful thoughts were shattered as the wraiths grew bold again and surged forward. Daniel pointed the stick and waited. Nothing happened.

"This is bullshit, Mort! It's not working!"

"You have to will it to fire. Just think about blasting one of them," Mort shouted over the roar of the engine.

Daniel ignored the desire to use it on Mort and aimed at the closest wraith. Brilliant ruby light burst from the tip, tracing a lingering line of power across the gap to strike the wraith in the chest. Magic flared, red and black-green corrupting each other. Daniel fired again. And again. The first wraith dropped to the ground, wounded but not dead. Seeing the magic flaring from the back of the cab, the second wraith corkscrewed off to the right, re-centered on the cab and attacked.

The angle was too great for Daniel to compensate. His shots went wide, exploding in the bushes and trees. The wraith shrieked the moment before it hit the driver's side head on. Mort cursed again and struggled to keep the wheel straight. The force of the impact lifted the driver's side off of the road, nearly tipping the cab over before Daniel managed to crawl his way into position and fire twice into its face. Intense pain drove the wraith back. The cab dropped down onto all four tires and Mort was able to speed away.

Adrenalin flowing, Daniel couldn't sit still. He constantly scanned the avenues of approach for another attack. His eyes bounced back and forth rapidly. Old instincts he'd thought long gone took over. He was becoming the soldier again. It felt good, despite spending years trying to forget. Killing the wraiths was hard and, if Mort was telling the truth, next to impossible. Still, false hope was better than none.

Mort drove the cab with expert precision. Soon enough, they were out of the city and on a dark country road. Daniel couldn't help but get the impression of being kidnapped. They'd find his body in a few days, and that would be it. Unable to shake the feeling of impending death, Daniel caught the wraiths converging in front of the cab.

"Mort, they're trying to cut us off!" he shouted above the roar of the engine.

The swarthy looking cabbie merely nodded and said, "Hold on. This is going to hurt!"

The cab accelerated, speedometer pegged. Daniel gripped the back of the front seat. They were going to plow right into the wraiths. The prospect of being shredded to death by those terrible claws churned his stomach. Then Mort hit the high beams, dazzling silver lights that ripped the wraiths apart. Waves of malevolent power pulsed from the wraiths and struck the cab with more force than a howitzer firing. Daniel's head smashed into the Plexiglas divider behind Mort's seat, and the world went dark.

"Eh Bert, you see that?"

"Eh, what? Don't be wastin my time with no nonsense. I'm at the good part of this movie."

Lou clapped his younger brother, Bert, on the side of his head. "Damned fool. Ma always said you wasn't none bright."

"None bright? 'ho talks like that? Touch me agin, Bert and I'mma hurt you a good one."

Bert angrily snatched the remote to pause his movie. Satisfied, he headed to the front of their truck to see where his brother pointed.

"W'as so important I gotta stop my show?"

"Them shows ain't important, Bert." He paused and blinked, confused. "Sides, do you really think that Alf is for real?"

"Course he is! Now what you want?"

"Lookee there. That's that fella we bullied in his driveway t'day."

Bert peered closer, watching as the cab blazed away. "Nah, yer jus seein things. I'mma going back to my show."

"I'm tellin ya, Bert. It's him. What should we do?"

Bert waved him off and took up his seat. "G'head and follow if you like. Jus leave me alone."

Given enough to act on, Lou gunned the truck and headed down the road after the cab. After all, it's what the Boss would have wanted.

SIX

Daniel awoke in a small reception gallery to the right of the elaborate foyer, admiring the obviously expensive paintings interspersed between alabaster columns jutting twenty feet up to the second story. Potted plants, easily larger than anything he had ever seen, decorated the room, giving it a comfortable yet somewhat ostentatious appearance. Statues older than the discovery of the Western hemisphere were scattered liberally throughout the short hallway and two rooms he was able to see. The largest Persian rug, mixed in red, white and green with an oval pattern in the center, covered most of the marble tile floor.

He'd never been in a mansion before and certainly didn't recall hearing about any within a hundred mile radius from his home. North Carolina was a profitable state despite the relatively low cost of living compared to other places he'd lived, particularly New York and Florida. Just looking at this place made him feel small, unimportant. He swooned and sank back down onto the dark brown leather couch.

His head hurt. There was a knot on his forehead that thrummed with every heartbeat. His mouth was parched. That sick feeling you get when you haven't eaten in a while rumbled through his stomach. Bloodshot eyes ached and burned. He looked down at his watch, surprised and disappointed to find it was barely seven o'clock. Stark realization sank in. He'd been attacked and nearly killed twice in the last hour, not counting the disagreement with the two brutes in his driveway. *What the hell have I gotten myself into?*

"Ah, good, you're awake. We were beginning to worry that your injuries were more severe than first thought."

Daniel pulled his head reluctantly from his palms and found a most elegant woman standing before him. Everything about her screamed regal. High cheekbones accented her natural beauty. He couldn't help but stare at her poorly concealed curves beneath the flat grey business jacket and skirt ending just beneath the knees with matching heels. Sleek glasses reflected her amber colored eyes. But whatever illusions his mind created shattered the moment he caught the enchanting fragrance wafting from her flowing, golden locks.

"What do you people want with me?" he asked defensively, jerking back.

She held out her hands. "Please calm down. I'm not here to hurt you; in fact, we've done everything in our power to help you, Daniel."

He blinked with confusion. "You know my name too?"

The golden woman laughed; a musical sound that helped soothe his aggression. "Of course we do. Or perhaps you thought it mere coincidence that we shared an elevator earlier this evening? You've worked with Ariel long enough that everyone in this palace knows the great fantasy author Daniel Thomas. My name is Cassandra, and I have been sent to see if you are well enough to meet the man responsible for bringing you here."

The way he saw it, there wasn't any real choice. Guest or not, he was a prisoner until they decided otherwise. "I don't see that I have a choice."

"The front door is right there," Cassandra offered genuinely.

Daniel briefly considered taking her up on the offer before deciding it would only end badly. Instead, he gestured for her to continue. "I think I'll stick around and see what all the fuss is about the black box. Noticed you took it off me while I was out."

She nodded. "It is in a much safer place. You've had quite an adventure getting here. A lesser man might not have been capable enough to survive. Wraiths are very rare these days. None have been seen in a generation."

They walked down the wide hallway, passing endless family portraits of people who generally looked exactly the same. The opulence was almost insulting, but only for show, or at least he suspected. Regardless of what this place was or for what, Daniel felt himself being drawn into a much deeper mystery.

Arriving outside of two closed dark cherry doors, Cassandra bade him to wait while she went in to announce them. He clasped his hands behind his back, a throwback to his Army days, and waited as patiently as he could, which wasn't very. After two hours, he was already at the limits of control. Fortunately, she returned fast enough to keep his fuse from reigniting.

"This way, please."

Not even the gentle sway of her hips was enough to pull Daniel's attention away from the impressive collection of books, new and old, lining the walls of the circular room. Massive bookshelves ran from floor to ceiling. Each book was hardcover and etched in gold filament. The room itself smelled of a type of flower he'd never seen. Arched windows revealed an almost unnatural darkness outside kept at bay by the roar of a fireplace. A large globe of the ancient world stood on a cast iron pedestal that went up to his chest. Another Persian rug, this one more brown and circular, housed an antique desk with a small stack of papers in the middle. He couldn't help but think that this was what his dream office would look like.

Daniel took it all in with a feeling of insecurity. He'd never felt so small, so insignificant. Then he noticed the powerfully built man standing in front of the windows. Unlike everyone else, he had short, close-cropped silver hair. His suit was top line, surely costing well over two thousand dollars. Standing with his back to them, the man was evidently in no hurry to turn around. His narrowed eyes regarded Daniel's reflection in the glass.

"Some things in this world are not meant to be known to humankind, Daniel." His voice was stern, iron on a cold winter night. "It is…regrettable that you have become so deeply involved in our affairs."

"That's pretty much the way I see it too," Daniel replied tersely. "I didn't ask for any of this."

He turned around, a surprised look etched on his granite features. "No? Did you think it was mere chance your books started to decline? That you simply weren't in demand anymore because of the randomness of fortune? Every time your pen touched paper, you asked to be brought into our world. It is no accident that you are standing before me this night."

Daniel stared back at the almost crystalline eyes bearing down on him. Age lined the weathered face, a face that he had seen before. As his mind replayed past images and events, Daniel eventually put the face with a position.

"I know you. You're the police commissioner!" Daniel exclaimed suddenly.

A curt nod. "Yes, Alvin Karthis, at your service. You may leave us, Cassandra. Thank you."

She smiled and closed the doors behind her, leaving Daniel with one of the most powerful men in the county.

"Am I under arrest?" he asked, testing the waters.

Alvin found the question almost amusing. "Whatever for? Ariel's death was not your fault, nor at your hands. Regrettably, your involvement is a matter of poor timing. Ariel was killed because of the item in her possession, an item that I entrusted to her a very long time ago. She was a capable guardian. Her loss will be felt for centuries."

Centuries? Who are these people? "Nothing you just told me makes any sense. Centuries? She was barely older than me. Why is it every time I ask a question I get the run around?"

Alvin pinched the bridge of his nose and sighed. It was with a heavy heart that he had Daniel sit and listen. "Daniel, what I am about to tell you will not be easy to hear. Nor should it be. Much of the mystery in life has died, lost forever in the dust of time. Mankind is like a disease, a remarkable accomplishment considering how infantile you are." He held up a hand to silence Daniel. "Please, allow me to explain before you begin asking questions.

"My kind has walked these lands since the world was young. We are the true caretakers of the world. Our lives are dedicated to ensuring the continued life of every being, big or small. You actually know what we are, whether you choose to admit it or not. I am more than just the police commissioner, Daniel. I am the king of the High Elves."

Daniel's mouth fell so fast he drooled on himself. The sheer impossibility of what he'd just been told threatened to snap his mind. *Everyone knows that elves don't exist, right? How can anyone claim to be a mythical creature born in the mind of an author and re-imagined a thousand times over?* He expected Alvin to come over, slap him on the shoulder and claim it was all a prank. He wanted him to. But Alvin merely stood there, waiting for Daniel to digest what he'd revealed.

"That's impossible. No one believes in Elves. They're a construct of imagination," Daniel protested softly. Even as the words came out, he found doubt in them. Too much had happened to be mere coincidence.

Alvin nodded again. "Precisely the way we want to keep things. Believe me; we don't like being discovered any more than you are ready to accept the truth. Man is a petty, zealous creature. Those few times we attempted to make ourselves known and live in conjunction with one another ended badly for my kind. We were hunted, persecuted by the very same people who had extended their hand in friendship. You'll forgive me if my people are hesitant to trust you."

Daniel scratched his head as he tried to process this sudden revelation. He was a sort who had always wanted to believe in mystic creatures and ancient, nonhuman races. His stories offered a break from reality, a distancing between the stagnant and the creative. Never had he expected to stand before a man — the police commissioner, no less — claiming to be the king of the High Elves. Worse, there was no one he felt comfortable enough with to go to with the information.

Even his wife would be willing to have him take a break in an institution.

He decided to make one final attempt at rationalizing. "Why should I believe any of this? Any nut job off the street can make the same claim. I need proof before I'm ready to accept."

"Daniel, what more proof do you require? Wasn't it enough to have a pair of trolls threaten you in your own driveway? Or to see Ariel change back to her true shape when she died? Perhaps having one of my finest warriors come to your rescue from the hands of a pack of dark elf assassins? Or Mort the gnome. Or the wraiths? How much more is it going to take for you to accept our truth?"

"Truth is subjective," he protested weakly. *How does he know about the incident in my driveway? Trolls?*

"Indeed, but in can be powerful in the right or wrong hands. There are many powers in the world, Daniel. What you think you know is barely a, how do you say, drop in the ocean."

"You're telling me that I'm living in the middle of one of my books and expect me to swallow it whole. As much as I enjoy letting my imagination run wild, I'm having trouble putting this together. There has to be a reasonable explanation."

Alvin snorted. "Don't get me started on your books. Because of you and several movies in the genre, I've been forced to move some of my more visible assets deeper under cover. Hollywood is royally fucking up the way I do business. Do you have any idea how hard it is now to keep our races concealed? I'm wasting millions a day putting cleanup and suppression teams in the field."

"You kill people to keep us from finding out?"

"Of course not. Don't be a fool. We work in close conjunction with your federal government. There are…powers watching over us, helping us remain hidden if you will."

"You expect me to believe that the American government knows about you and isn't saying anything? I suppose Area 51 is your home too," Daniel snipped.

Alvin ignored the barb, refusing to play down to Daniel's anxieties.

"As I was saying, we don't kill anyone."

Daniel shook his head. "Seemed to be plenty of your people fighting and dying on my way over here."

"A regrettable experience, one we take great measures to conceal from your world. We either make those unfortunate enough to stumble upon us forget about us or we alter their futures," Alvin explained hesitantly. Daniel may have arrived with the black box, but he was far from being taken into full confidence. That day might never arrive, especially depending on if he survived the night or not.

It took Daniel a moment to connect things. "Like me. You're the reason Ariel told me she wouldn't be able to sell my latest novel."

"Partially, though there was some truth to what she told you. Traditional fantasy isn't in demand anymore. We've done our best to suppress the urge of readers. Call it selfish motive if you will. Can you imagine the reaction if it leaked out that elves, dwarves and trolls were masquerading as friends, neighbors and co-workers? The anarchy of the world wars would pale in comparison."

"Do vampires and werewolves exist?" Daniel asked. His mind was already wandering down forbidden paths. So many questions sprang up. The need to truly know what was happening around him threatened to tear the fabric of his brain, making him almost wish he'd never started writing in the first place.

Alvin shrugged. "Doubtful. Can you imagine a world where *all* of those races still exist? It would be Armageddon."

Crisp winds picked up, driving leaf-barren branches from the nearby maple tree screeching across the window. The haunting sound sent shivers across Daniel's flesh. No matter how Alvin twisted it, the man was hiding a great deal.

Daniel wanted to know more but was also wise enough not to ask beyond his bounds. The thought of having been *handled* for years stole the warmth from his bones.

A sudden thought sparked, driving him to conclusions he'd rather not think about. Ariel had told him about a princess. He'd shoved that bit aside once Xander had shown up and the fight with the dark elves had begun, but now, standing in front of the king, it reawakened and started to make sense. Still, he needed to hear Alvin say it. Anything else was too empty to make a claim.

"Why am I really here?" Daniel asked.

Alvin's face darkened, staining his rigid, handsome features. "You're here because my daughter has been kidnapped, and I need your help to get her back."

SEVEN

The silence settling over the room produced a haunting effect. One man couldn't believe what he'd just been told, the other what he'd just said. Dark times offer few choices and none of them good. Daniel studied the king harder. He appeared less regal and dominant. The stern awareness he'd had when the conversation began was replaced by a father's desperate need to know his child was safe. Daniel wondered what he would do if his own daughter ever came to harm. He doubted he'd be able to act so bravely.

"You're joking, right?" Daniel asked incredulously. "I'm no hero. People like me don't do things like that. You've got the wrong guy."

Sadness crept into the corners of Alvin's eyes. "I wish that I did."

"Ariel mentioned a princess being in danger. I thought she was just ranting before she died." He paused, considering the finite possibilities confronting him. "There's nothing I can do here. You've got an entire race with an unending supply of assets. Use them. I'm just one man. A man. What can a mortal man do against the evil you allude to?"

"I do not tell you these things lightly. Xander was my best chance of getting my daughter back safely. But, if what you say is true, he is already dead. My options are severely reduced. As for the evil, you have no idea. I told you that we were here when the world was young, but I left out a great deal. We are as ancient as the first amphibian to crawl from the oceans. The second time, of course. I don't believe there is any history of before the Great Disaster that killed most life on Earth.

"We elves came first, though no one remembers our true origins. For a time, we were a peaceful people content to tend the trees and listen to the four winds. Life was as it was meant to be. There was no want, no greed. We explored the oceans and traveled to distant continents after the great landmass split. Scholars collected the wisdom of our ages. Our cities ranged high into the trees, golden spires to challenge the sun. Those were better times."

Alvin paused to drink from a half-empty glass of water. His eyes were foggy with memories. "During our travels, we found other races. The dwarves came next, thousands of years after our discovery. We found them gruff, taciturn. Surprisingly, they haven't changed much in all this time." He chuckled.

"The more we traveled, the more we learned and the more we found that we didn't like. Trolls and ogres haunted the highest mountains. They were confrontational, and we fought many petty squabbles and battles. Occasionally, there was war, but we always managed to negotiate peace. The gnomes clung to shadows, ever underfoot and devious. It took centuries, but we finally came to a truce. They are one of our closest allies now.

"Man came much later. They were a primitive species, content with living in caves and wearing animal skins. We tried to share our knowledge, but the first primitives lacked even basic speech abilities. It was both amusing and frustrating. Eventually, we abandoned our aims and let them be. That didn't preclude them from attacking us every chance they got. One thing that hasn't changed is your willingness to make war on each other. It is a contemptible trait."

He shuffled around and slumped down in his high-backed cherry red leather chair. Alvin steepled his fingers in front of his face and continued. "Life went on for all of our races without much change. No one is really sure what happened or why, but at some point a great argument ensued, one that would consume our entire population. It's ridiculous to think that something petty is capable of destroying one of the most advanced societies to ever grace this planet, but it did.

"There was a schism among the elf clans. Many stayed with me, but a disturbing number left with Morgen. Half of our families broke from the conventional way of life. They became corrupted and turned evil. Many wars were fought. Losses on both sides were too much to bear. Our civilization shattered. The great cities were ruined. We lost the ability to communicate efficiently with other continents or clans." He paused, as if remembering a particularly gruesome event. "Dark are their deeds and desires, and the remaining high elf clans are outmatched and outnumbered. We are weak in areas we should be strong. I am not proud of that, but there is no point dwelling on it.

"The war finally ended with a truce on the shores of what you name Madagascar. The dark elves were to remain in their territories, we in ours. That truce has lasted for more than three thousand years. There have been many incidents threatening to plunge us into war, but we always managed to contain the damage and keep the peace. After all, no one truly wants to die. Not even them."

Alvin walked to the set of bay windows and stared out into the empty night.

"All of that has changed only recently. The dark elves grow more aggressive. Trolls and ogres are frequently causing havoc, threatening to reveal us all to humanity. I have scholars working around the clock to try and find some ancient prophecy or foretelling about the immediate time period. So far, there is nothing. All of our vast resources, as you think we have, have produced nothing worthwhile. I am effectively blind. Not even my human networks have been able to produce a piece of actionable intelligence.

"War is coming again, and I don't know that I'll be able to win it. My daughter is the key to it all. She is the heir to my house and the light clans. Her ascension to the throne assures strong leadership and prevents Morgen from finally conquering us. I am very old, not long for this life, but with her in my place the light clans will remain strong."

"I thought elves were immortal," Daniel suggested.

He felt his carefully constructed world shattering down around him. All the books he'd read, movies watched, none of them came close to getting any of it right, if what Alvin said was remotely true. Of course the idea that any of it was true was foolish at best. Fantasy was just that, a fictional universe in which one could lose sense of time and space. An escape from the mundane. He struggled to process it all, fearing it might never happen. Worse, he was left with the nagging question of why was all of this happening now, to him?

Simultaneously, Daniel couldn't help but wonder how no mention of the elves or other races so much as showed up in any of the human histories. The world wasn't as big as it once was and he found it highly implausible that such beings could go on for millennia without being written about. There were conspiracies surrounding Alvin and his people. Ones Daniel decided to stay as far away from as possible.

"I wish. Sadly, we die like everything else. I don't think God likes the idea of having to deal with the same people until the end of time. Someone once suggested that change is good. We are exceedingly long lived and can be killed by nearly everything you can, except your diseases."

"I could really use something to drink," Daniel said as he tried to digest the brief snippets of information he'd been entrusted with.

He wanted to go home, more than anything. Wanted to lose himself at the bottom of a bottle and forget the whole sordid affair. The violence of the past hour was almost too much. Flashbacks from his time in the desert intermingled with Ariel. He still had her blood on his clothes. The greenish fluid was similar to what Xander had used to outline her body. Ariel. As much as he wanted to break down and grieve, he knew he couldn't. Not yet. The pain was too real, the hurt too deep. Whatever else she was, she had been his friend.

At some point, deep in the recesses of his mind, Daniel abandoned the sheer impossibility of the situation and decided to dive in. Reflexes, once honed to perfection, struggled to break free. His thoughts turned back towards tactics and strategy. No great war leader, Daniel found it difficult to remember all of the minute details of being a soldier. Forget that elves shouldn't be real. Forget that he'd basically been kidnapped by a rather odd assortment of characters. All that mattered was here, now. Daniel decided to accept his fate. After all, how could he turn down the chance to become one of his own heroes?

He smiled grimly and thanked Alvin for the highball of scotch he was handed. Too many opposite thoughts collided for him to form a coherent sentence. Asking more questions was going to get him nowhere. Alvin was tight-lipped for good reason, if what he said was true. He was losing people at a rapid rate, and now his daughter had been stolen. A lesser man might have already cracked, but the police commissioner was built of sterner stuff.

Daniel thought about it for a moment. He still hadn't heard much about the princess. "You're asking me to rescue your daughter, but you're keeping me in the dark, Alvin. I'm a simple man but no fool. I did my time in a warzone and don't care to repeat that experience. People die for no good reason and are forgotten by the people who plan and win the damned things. It sounds to me like you want me to do the same thing, ruck up and head to the sound of the guns. I need more, or are you going to explain to my wife and kids how I was killed?"

Alvin spread his hands out, pleading. "What would you do to save your daughter? We are not so different, Daniel Thomas. My only concern is to have her back safely. Nothing else matters."

"I'd do the same. Who is Xander?"

Alvin hesitated. "Xander was a good friend. He was also Ariel's sister and one of my highest-ranking warriors — a general, if you will. His loss will be felt for long to come. Were times different, I would ask how he died and you managed to live, but strange things are happening all around." He gave Daniel a knowing look. "I assume you have other questions? Most, I will not answer. It was an accident that you became involved, and I sincerely apologize, but you are not entitled to our secrets."

"What about the black box?" Daniel cut to the end. He'd heard enough and was ready to move on. Alvin was a king and a politician of sorts, and they were infamous for misdirection and tangents without saying anything.

Alvin wagged a finger. "The box is the key to all of this. Morgen wants what's in the box, and I am unwillingly to let her have it. What it really is goes well beyond the reach of your imagination, but it is an item of immeasurable power. Should the dark elves get a hold of the box, they will use it to create devastation on unprecedented levels. The box must never fall into their hands."

"I'm not so sure I'm comfortable with the thought of having the one object everyone is willing to kill for in my possession. Two more questions. Why me? And who is Morgen? You're the second person I heard mention her name," Daniel replied blandly. He slammed down the rest of his drink and set the crystal on the desk.

"I am out of options. Providence has sent you to me, I believe, for two reasons. One, you have an intimate understanding of our races, though you didn't know so until now."

"Ha! I wrote stories to entertain people, not for the basis of history," Daniel laughed. "What's the second part?"

"You've demonstrated an uncanny ability to survive against creatures that should have easily killed you." Alvin regained his stature, straightening his back.

The branches scraped again, icy claws against fragile skin. Daniel rubbed the fresh stubble on his chin. The rational part said to go home and leave their troubles for their own kind. Hell, they'd gotten on for so many millennia without human involvement; another night wasn't going to hurt them. But that one part, the part that gave birth to the bizarre and fantastic adventures filling his stories, that part wanted to go on, to see what came next. No adventure really ends, but taking that first step onto one was a chance that happened only once in a lifetime.

"As to Morgen, why, she is the queen of the dark elves," Alvin said straight-faced.

Son of a bitch. "Alright, I'm in. What do I have to do?" he asked.

EIGHT

Cassandra escorted him through the confusing hallways and corridors of the palace. She hummed as she walked, much to his confusion. His earlier impression of how attractive she was had been marred by the sudden knowledge that she was an elf. Daniel shook his head ruefully. He was being guided by a figment of imagination. None of this should be possible. He should be at home right now putting the kids to bed and trying to find the inner calm to make love to his wife after a hard day's work. Instead, he was being drawn deeper into an improbable world, entrusted with not only the survival of an entire race but also returning a father's love before it was too late. *Shit.*

"How do you do it?" he asked suddenly, surprising even himself.

Cassandra gave him a knowing look and that soft smile that could melt a man's heart if he wasn't careful. "It's not as difficult as you imagine. People rarely look for things out of the ordinary. As Alvin told you, we've been among humanity since before you existed."

"His story suggested that you've been hiding for most of it," he countered.

She shrugged. "Call it what you will, but we've endured through adapting. Don't pretend to carry an air of superiority. Your kind kills more easily than we ever did, even the dark elves."

"Perhaps we've gotten off on the wrong foot," he covered quickly. The last thing he wanted or needed was to have people close to Alvin reporting back how Daniel was behaving.

"Perhaps, but it is understandable. Others have never come to terms with their sudden revelation," Cassandra chimed. "It is no easy thing to do, accepting what seems impossible, but there are a few who manage to rise above their base prejudices and tear down the walls in their minds. Those are the ones we try to recruit and cultivate. As powerful as we seem to you, we are exposed without assistance from a handful of brave humans."

"Is that how you managed to infiltrate our society?"

"There was no challenge in that. Humans are very blind. We simply walked into your camps and villages and became members of your tribes."

Daniel shook his head. "But the ears, the green blood. I don't understand."

She stopped in midstride and pointed at him. "You don't need to understand, Daniel. It's not important. What you should be focusing on is how you are going to rescue Princess Gwen and keep our world from going to war."

"Alvin was rather vague about that part," he snorted. Tired of being pushed around, Daniel struggled not to go off. The elves were giving him the run around and keeping him in the dark on purpose. He'd seen it happen before, during the war. Men had died — men who should still be alive but for the ignorance of command. He didn't want to end up in a gutter tomorrow morning.

"Do you blame him? We're still unsure where your loyalties are. You might break and run the first chance you get. Xander's death leaves us in a bind. You claimed not to be a hero, but the situation is forcing you to become one tonight, like it or not. No one can say why you were brought to us at this moment, nor do I think they should, for I have seen many mysteries over the course of my life and the true reasons are often less than desirable. I have lived many centuries, Daniel, and there is one constant I have learned. You can't fight destiny." She finished with a curt nod and marched on, the click of her expensive heels against the marble adding exclamation to her statements.

Daniel remained still for a moment longer while her words sank in. He meant what he'd told both of them. He wasn't a hero and had no aspirations to become one, either. Heroes died. That's how they became heroes. He was a parent, a father, and a coward who sat behind his keyboard inventing heroes rather than going out and trying to be one himself. Fools jumped into things without thinking. Daniel was many things; a fool was not one of them.

Still, he imagined himself in Alvin's unenviable place. His daughter stolen. His daughter dead. The pain and suffering would be tremendous, threatening to rip his heart apart. He'd want someone to step forward to help.

"I'm sorry," he finally said.

Cassandra stopped but didn't turn. "For what? Daniel, there is nothing to apologize for. You've entered a world that, from your perspective, shouldn't exist. It can't be easy. Imagine how we feel having to conceal ourselves from you. I think you are doing fine." She paused, as if changing what she was going to say next. "Here. This is it. I must warn you that our weapon smith may be a bit more than you are prepared for."

"As long as he's not Tinkerbell," Daniel grinned.

Cassandra cocked her head. "Fairies haven't existed for centuries."

Of course not. He gestured towards the door. "Lead on."

Chuckling softly, she opened the door and went in. "Goran! I've brought you a guest. Be nice to him. He's here on Alvin's orders."

"Humans aren't allowed in my workshop. You know that, Cassandra," a deep voice boomed.

Daniel froze halfway through the door. Each syllable rippled through his body, threatening to drop him to his knees. Cassandra came back to steady him. He searched the relative gloom of the cavernous room. The ceilings were well over twenty feet high. Massive desks and workbenches stood taller than his six foot frame. He immediately felt small and for good reason. The monster of a man glaring down on him was enough to make him puke his stomach up.

The giant pointed aggressively. "He must go."

"Goran, Alvin sent him here. Can you put aside your prejudice for a moment? The princess has been kidnapped, and Xander's dead. This is his…replacement."

"Xander's dead?" Much of his anger died as well.

She nodded. "And his sister. We are in trouble."

"Trouble is an understatement, Cassandra. Hope is gone," the giant suggested grimly. "Without Xander, we won't be able to withstand the dark elf assault."

"Which is why Alvin sent you Daniel here."

Goran studied Daniel, clearly unimpressed. "Bah! Never trust a human. They're dangerous, cunning and wicked. We're better off alone."

Planting her feet firmly apart, she crossed her arms just under her breasts and scolded, "This human has already survived a dark elf assassin squad and a wraith attack today. He's been exposed to our world in the worst possible way and proven he can handle it."

A thick, black eyebrow lifted curiously. "All of that eh? Maybe you're not so bad. Name's Goran."

"Daniel."

Daniel took in the giant. What he saw was a contradiction of everything else he'd witnessed thus far. The giant wore a faded Grateful Dead t-shirt (where he'd found one so large was anybody's guess) and a shell necklace. He was bald and had a heavy, sloping forehead. Goran's arm must have weighed more than Daniel's entire body. He was a monster of a man. The yellow band on his pinky finger would have been loose on Daniel's arm.

Cassandra noticed his confusion. "He comes from the Carpathian Mountains, overlooking the city of Piatra Neamt in Romania. The combination of ancient heritage and modern proclivities made him this way. It's better not to ask, but if you wish to get on his good side ask him about his new weapons systems or defense grid sometime."

"Come on now, Cass. Who doesn't like the Dead?" Goran asked with a hideous grin. Clearly, the high elf clans lacked a proper dental plan.

"I didn't say anything negative, Goran. Daniel is going to rescue the princess. We don't have the time for our usual banter," she scolded lightly.

He shrugged and looked at Daniel. "Women, right? Fine. If you're going up against Morgen's best, you're going to need some heavy-duty firepower. Follow me."

Daniel shot Cassandra a dubious glance, making her smile. "Go ahead. He's really quite sweet when you get to know him. I'll be back in a little. Alvin has me on an additional assignment."

The door closed, leaving the man and the giant alone. Daniel couldn't help but feel awkward in such an immense presence. Goran towered over him, more than twice his own height. The two stood in silence for a moment, neither comfortable with making the first move. Daniel got the feeling he was constantly being judged. In fact, this entire experience was anything but hospitable, despite the drink in his painfully empty stomach. He still hadn't decided if the elves were keeping a separate agenda hidden from him or not.

"You're the first human I've ever allowed here, but if Alvin and Xander say you're good, then you're alright with me," the giant explained between heavy strides. "What kind of experience do you have with weapons?"

"I was in the Army for six years," Daniel answered.

"Combat?"

He nodded. "Eighteen months. Six in Afghanistan and a year in Iraq. I was infantry, if that helps."

"More than you'll know, but it won't be enough. There are some real nasties out there." Goran led him past tables filled with half-finished weapons, racks of guns, and a hefty assortment of knives and swords.

Daniel didn't understand the blades. With all of the advanced weaponry in the world, why would the elder races continue to use swords and knives? Closer inspection showed him that each weapon was expertly crafted and unused. He found that odd, given that there was a war looming. In fact, nothing in the armory seemed to have been used.

"You made all of these?" he asked.

Goran nodded proudly and puffed out his massive chest. "Hell, yes. I'm the best at what I do, probably the only reason Alvin hired me on in the first place. I was happy in the mountains, you know. My clan would sit and watch the people below. I like people watching almost as much as making weapons. What I wouldn't give to be able to go to the mall and just watch."

Daniel struggled to understand what he was being told. Giants were monsters, unexplainable abominations lurking in mountain passes for stray travelers. They were supposed to eat children and scare the old. The scariest part was he could see hanging out with Goran if he was human.

"What kind of guns do you have?"

Goran rummaged through a random equipment pile. "This is too big. This won't work. Nope, this one neither. Ah! Try this. Over and under 40 mm acidic slug thrower. Magazine holds two hundred ball rounds, 3 mm. It's compact and durable with a range of close to five hundred meters. It'll knock the bad guys on their ass."

Daniel took the rifle, surprised by the weight. His old M-16 rifle had been much heavier, and that had only been around seven pounds. The rounds were equally lightweight. Goran handed him a belt of thirty acidic grenades.

"Don't get anywhere close to these when they go off, not unless you want to melt to death," the giant warned. "Nasty things, but they're great for putting down trolls or worse."

Daniel had trouble imagining anything worse than a troll, especially after his earlier encounter at home. He had written worse, but those were pure figments of imagination separating his work from the competition. Goran continued to hand down an assortment of weapons and kit. Pistols and knives. Drums of ammo and night optics. He felt like a SEAL, complete with elbow and knee pads.

"You're going to need some armor as well. The dark elves dip their arrows and spears in poison derived from the poppy."

"What's with all the medieval weapons? You'd think the dark elves would have an arsenal bigger than the U.S. Army's," Daniel said.

The giant shrugged. "Some traditions are worth keeping. Arrows and blades don't make sounds. Makes for convenient killing when you don't want to be discovered. They have their guns; don't you worry about that." Goran chuckled and continued rummaging through overstocked shelves.

"You're in luck. Fortunately, Alvin has had me working on armor for other humans. These should fit. Light and composite. It'll stop any conventional small arms ammo."

The armor reminded Daniel of dark blue long johns. They almost never kept him warm. For such thin fabric to be able to stop a bullet was almost impossible to believe. Goran sensed his skepticism and laughed a deep resounding bark.

"You'll be fine, lad. I promise."

"Only if it stops poison arrows," Daniel countered sarcastically.

Goran paused, choosing to keep his reply to himself. "Come on. There's not much time. Cassandra will be back soon, and you've got a quest to undertake. Oh, before you go, could you do me one small favor?"

"If I can."

Goran handed him a weathered, well-read copy of *Rise of the Dark Elves*. "Can you sign this? I'm a big fan."

At that, Daniel was unable to keep the first genuine smile of the evening from his face. "Does everyone know?" he asked.

"For the most part. You're famous among us, Daniel. Don't forget it."

The pair stalked back towards the entrance, passing those quick moments with idle banter and meaningless conversation. Goran wasn't willing to discuss any of the mission parameters and avoided the subject of the princess altogether, leading Daniel to conclude that Alvin was keeping secrets.

When they arrived at the door, Goran laid a finger on Daniel's shoulder, driving him down under the weight. "Mind yourself tonight. All is not as it seems. There is a traitor in our house. Your life is in danger, my friend."

Cassandra entered a moment later. Daniel couldn't be sure, but she had an uneasy look. He tried, unsuccessfully, to swallow the nervous lump growing in his throat.

NINE

The trip back through the winding high elf citadel seemed much longer than when Cassandra had taken him deep into the interior. He'd hoped to lose some of those nagging doubts and start planning for tonight's mission. That he was in Ariel's office at precisely the right moment, or wrong from his point of view, bothered him greatly. He wasn't the kind who believed in sheer coincidence, leading his mind down wandering paths fueled by thoughts of destiny or just plain bad luck. In the end, Daniel decided it had to be a little bit of both. In a fit of bemusement, he wondered how much, if any, of his imagination was going to play out tonight while on the mission to save a princess. Mission. He snorted. It had been a long time since his last military mission, long enough for him to wonder if any of it would come back. The notion was ridiculous. Of course it would. Soldiers just didn't turn off their instincts. He'd already transformed back into the reluctant soldier.

The battles with the dark elves and then the wraiths were forcing him back into a role he'd never imagined performing again. Old training principles struggled to return. The words of his drill sergeants echoed from the corners of his mind. Daniel shook off the role of husband and father as he reassumed his place with a rifle and an objective. If war was coming, as Alvin predicted, Daniel was going to be on the front line.

"You seem unusually silent," she remarked.

"Because I'm going to die?" he replied. "The giant gave me a lot to think about."

"I hope he didn't try to enlighten you with his philosophic debates. He's a good person but has his quirks."

"I would too if I was kept in the basement all day."

Cassandra waved off his concern. "He likes it down there. Besides, we haven't discovered the magic necessary to blend his race in with the rest of us. Can you imagine the panic that would spread if anyone saw him? You nearly fainted, and that was after you'd been introduced to our world."

"People always say they want change," he countered snidely.

"If you're still alive in the morning, let me know if it's everything you wanted," she replied just as smartly.

He was still trying to figure out what he'd done to piss her off when they arrived back at Alvin's private study. The king of the high elves was again by the windows, longing for his daughter's safe return. Cassandra quietly cleared her throat.

"Few things are as frustrating as waiting," Alvin said. "Isn't it remarkable that I've never learned to enjoy such a trivial thing?"

"What's the rush when you live for so long? There must always be something new to do," Daniel said.

"Fascination for the undiscovered passes quickly. I can't thank you enough for accepting the responsibility of bringing my daughter back to me, Daniel. Ask of me anything you desire and, if it is within my power, I will grant it. You deserve that much."

"I'd like to speak with my wife," Daniel said quickly.

"I don't think that is wise, considering your situation."

Daniel looked Alvin squarely in the eyes, resolved not to back down. "Considering your situation I think it is. You expect me to put it all on the line for your daughter but want to keep me from speaking to my family? That makes you a fucking hypocrite, *your highness*."

Rage distorted his perfect features only briefly before Alvin managed to calm down. "I can't remember the last time someone dared speak to me like you just did, but I do specifically recall having him executed. But as much as I may take offense, your words are true. Very well. You may use the phone in my office. My one request is that you do not speak of us."

He held his hands up in a helpless gesture. "Who'd believe me?"

Alvin dipped his head and left the room, keeping the door cracked. *To eavesdrop, of course*, Daniel thought. Time being vital, he dialed his house phone and waited. Quiet voices drifted back to him from the hall. Cassandra and Alvin. Their conspiratorial tone got his attention, but his wife's voice prevented him from understanding them.

"Hello?"

"Hi, Sara, it's Daniel."

"Daniel? What's going on? Where are you?" she asked nervously.

He instantly regretted calling. How many nights and months had she sat by the phone hoping she never got that phone call? "The Secretary of the Army regrets to inform you that…." It wasn't fair to do it to her again. He was breaking his promise to never put her through that stress. Worst, he wasn't even able to tell her the truth. "I'm at Ariel's office. I got her to agree to rep my book, but we're going to be a while. Don't stay up late. I don't know when I'll be home."

She paused. Then her tone changed. "What's really going on? Have you been drinking?"

"Don't be silly. I already told you I…."

"Are you sleeping with her? Cheating on me!" she fumed.

His eyes narrowed. "What? No. Where the hell did that come from? Listen, babe, I've got a little work to do tonight. No alcohol, and I'm not interested in another woman. You're too much for me." He winced at the double meaning laced into the words. "I have to do this, for me."

"Fine. You work late. We'll talk in the morning, mister." She hung up, clearly not believing his lies, but for different reasons.

"I love you," Daniel said into the dial tone. His heart dropped. The possibility of regret, on either side, was suddenly too real.

He almost hung up when he realized they were still whispering in the antechamber. Deciding to take a chance, he pretended to keep talking while listening to what he could.

"…if he learns the truth?"

"Then he must be dealt with. We can't afford to have this blown wide open. Not now."

A shuffle. Nervous shifting in stance. "Kill him?"

Daniel's eyes widened.

Alvin replied. "If necessary. We are too close to our goal, Cassandra, and he already knows too much."

"Xander trusted him. That must be worth…"

"Absolutely nothing. Do not cross me on this. I'll tolerate no insubordination. I think he's finished."

Long fingers curled around the golden doorknob and pushed lightly.

"Alright, dear, I love you too. See you soon," Daniel said and hung up the phone.

"Are you ready?" Alvin asked a little too formally for Daniel's liking.

He flashed a quick, false smile. "As I'll ever be. We should start before I change my mind."

Alvin appeared pleased and something else Daniel couldn't figure out. "Good. Getting to my daughter will not be easy. Morgen has her defenses alerted. They are already scouring the city in search of the box and you."

"Wouldn't the box be safer here? You make it sound like I'm going up against an entire army. It doesn't make any sense to keep it with me."

"There will come a point when you will need the box, Daniel. It is regrettable but necessary," Alvin replied.

"You're stacking the deck against me," Daniel accused. "One man against an army? This suddenly sounds like a suicide mission."

Alvin pursed his lips. "I never said you were going alone. Cassandra will escort you back to Mort where you'll be taken to see a pair of brothers. Tell them you need to see Murray. Most of the answers you seek will be revealed then."

He noticed Alvin still hadn't bothered bringing up the subject of where his daughter was and what to expect once he confronted Morgen. Overlapping shrouds of mystery pulled Daniel in deeper while leaving him disappointingly at the beginning. The only thing he knew about Morgen was that she ruled the dark elf clans, but nothing more. He tried, unsuccessfully, to put the name to anyone he might have heard of before. *I don't think I ever met a Morgen.*

"I had Cassandra put together an information packet while you were with Goran. Do take the time to read it. It has tactical displays of her fortress, troop strengths and possible locations for captives. You'll find we lack many specifics that would make your task easier. There's nothing I can do about that. Morgen is as closed to us as we are to her. It's been that way for a very long time."

"And this Murray guy will fill in the blanks?" Daniel asked.

An unexpected pause. Alvin successfully kept from smiling. "Murray knows many things. If he can't help, no one in the city can. Good luck, Daniel. I wish there was more I could do for you."

"You could change your mind and give me a platoon of your best fighters."

"You already know the answer to that. Morgen is naturally wary. She'll be prepared for a full assault, but where many will most assuredly fail, one might be able to succeed. What she won't expect is a human. You are the best weapon I have."

Daniel inspected his outfit for the first time. Pistol strapped to his left thigh. Bandolier of grenades slashed diagonally from his heart to hip. The small pack filled with ammo was heavy but more comfortable than his old Army rucksack. Goran had gone the little bit extra and made the frame out of pliable memory foam. Daniel wished the Army had done something like this a decade ago. His back might not hurt so much now. Lightweight night vision goggles hung around his neck. He felt like a badass and certainly looked like one.

"Trust Mort. He's very good at what he does and won't let you down." Alvin extended his hand. "I won't lie and tell you this is going to be easy, or even that you are the best qualified for the job. I do however, believe in destiny, to an extent. Perhaps you were meant to enter our world at precisely this moment. Perhaps it was but chance. Regardless, you are here now and in you I place my confidence. Bring my daughter home, Daniel."

A wide range of emotions jumbled his thoughts. Pushing them aside, he shook Alvin's hand. Whatever conspiracy might be unfolding behind his back, Daniel respected the fact that the man was still the police commissioner. *God only knows who Morgen will turn out to be.* He adjusted the pack, pushing it up higher. A scolding about wearing his ruck too low from one of his drill sergeants came to mind. Carrying weight was easier when it rode higher on the shoulders.

Plenty of flashy comments and witty remarks filtered through his mind, but he was too nervous and tired for clichés. As grand as they sounded in his head, he didn't trust his nerves enough right now to speak. He hadn't felt the odd combination of fear and exhilaration in nearly a decade. His stomach threatened to revolt. Daniel cursed; he'd forgotten to ask for something to eat. He hoped Mort wouldn't mind stopping somewhere on the way to Murray's. Otherwise, it was going to be along night. Adjusting the sling on his rifle, Daniel headed out the door.

Alvin waited for the door to close before turning back to Cassandra. Consternation twisted his face. The possibility of failure was all too real, and he could almost live with that. His daughter's life was the only important thing. Everyone else could die along the way, but Gwen needed to come home alive. She must.

"Follow them," Alvin ordered. "I don't want him out of your sight. Stern will be waiting for your call."

"Yes, your highness." Cassandra bowed gracefully and went to change.

The king of the High Elves stared at the door for a while longer, lost in thought. Much work needed to be done before Gwen returned, and he was running out of time. Dawn would change everything.

Once safely in her quarters, Cassandra leaned back against the wall and wept. She couldn't believe that Xander was dead. Not him. Not now. Closing her eyes, she drifted back to their last meeting. The soft breeze caressing their exposed flesh. The way his lips brushed tantalizingly across hers as he whispered to her.

"Are you certain you can do this for me?"

She swallowed hard and nodded. "Yes, Xander. I can."

His fingers traced the curve of her jaw. "Good. After my plan is finished there will never be need to worry again. Justice will be served."

Cassandra opened her eyes to the darkness of her room and, taking a moment to wipe the tears from her eyes, set about preparing for tonight. Xander might be gone, but she was going to do her part to ensure his legacy carried on.

TEN

"Back already, huh?" Mort asked cheerfully. "I knew you'd step up."

"I wasn't really given much of a choice, Mort. Alvin was pretty insistent."

The cabbie nodded. "He gets that way, especially when family's involved. You're doing a good thing."

"Am I?"

Mort put the cab back in neutral and removed his hat, revealing an obscenely bald head with too many spots, freckle or liver Daniel couldn't tell. He offered Daniel a sad look. "Things haven't been right with the clans for a long time. They won't admit it, but we need human interactions. Our kind is dying. It's not natural to hide in the shadows every single day. We've lost our sense of being, of purpose. Until you get the princess and bring her back alive I'm afraid that the clans will wallow in their failures and turn to dust. Of course you're doing a good thing." He flashed a grin, completely gruesome and better left undone. "That being said, I'm sure glad I'm not in your position."

"Thanks, Mort," Daniel shook his head, contemplating turning his weapons in and going home.

The gnome seemed satisfied and turned back to the wheel. "Where to?"

Pulling the slip of paper from his pocket, Daniel said, "We're supposed to find a pair of brothers. Schneider or something like that."

"The Schneider brothers? Shit, this is going to be a long night."

Daniel fought the urge to roll his eyes. He was getting used to being given the runaround, though it didn't help his attitude. *No wonder fantasy is dying. These elves are first-rate pricks.* His index finger tapped lightly on the trigger guard as he contemplated his best course of action for survival. Alvin wasn't in any hurry to divulge too much information. Hell, Daniel had been on worse missions with more intel back in Iraq and still barely made it back alive. Any hope he might have harbored about his chances continued to shrink.

His stomach growled, that aching pain rippling through his muscles. Base comforts would have to wait. Mort was already heading back into the city and didn't seem interested in going anywhere but to the Schneider brothers. He'd found few things in life so upsetting as not being in control of his own situation. Tonight was going to prove a monumental test of patience, among other things.

"What's the big deal about these brothers? Cassandra didn't want to talk about them, and you're starting to go all bug shit on me. Who are they?"

Mort snapped a fast laugh. "You really don't know? They're big time. Real big time. Angus is a hot-shot investment banker connected to Wall Street and most of the major banking houses in the world. His brother Fritz is smaller, but still the most respected private jeweler in central North Carolina. Come to think of it, he might be able to give you a pretty fair discount on jewelry for anniversaries or birthdays. Worth a shot, right?"

"Do you really think this is the time to think about gifts?" Daniel asked with a groan. "How can a banker and jeweler be so fierce? Most of those guys don't even have firm handshakes."

"You've never met these two. Most people run the other way when they hear the Schneider name, human and clans alike. In fact, these two have a real nasty reputation. I heard they were pit fighters at one time."

He couldn't believe what he was hearing. "Oh, come on. You don't really expect me to believe this nonsense, do you?"

Mort threw up a hand. "Don't believe me. You'll see for yourself; just don't say I didn't warn you."

"Great. I've spent the last eight years writing about this stuff only to have it all turn out to be one giant headache bordering on nightmare."

"You haven't seen nothing yet," Mort confirmed. "I bet Alvin told you to see Murray too, didn't he?"

"He did. Let me guess, Murray's a bigfoot."

"Ha! Oh, you're funny. Maybe you'll survive after all. I think I'll let you find out about Murray on your own. Wouldn't want to ruin the surprise. All you need to know is that Murray is a friend with a mean temper. Don't look him in the eye, and you should be fine. Hopefully."

Exasperated, Daniel glanced down at his ridiculously comfortable kit. He noticed he was missing one vital piece of equipment. "Mort, we need to stop at a drug store. Goran never gave me a first aid kit."

"First aid? Nah, you won't need it. Not this time. Look in one of the pockets of your pack. There should be a few tubes of a grayish material. Take one if you get wounded. I can't really say for sure what it's made of, but it does a good job of healing humans. Let's hope you don't need it, right?"

Great, more of the unknown. By now he didn't fight it anymore. His mind turned towards more essential items. Like trying to think of when he'd last eaten. Common sense said he should fill up before jumping in with both feet. Unfortunately common sense wasn't working much this night. His stomach growled again.

"Mort, I need to get something to eat."

Norman Guilt watched the cab speed away from the Citadel with mild interest. Small, colorless eyes tracked the taillights until they faded around the corner. He snorted. High elves were always so predictable. The cab was racing back to the city, carrying their perceived human savior. Humanity was weak. Guilt promised neither Mort nor the human would live to see the sun rise. Not that he had any personal interest in what was unfolding, but a job was a job. Though he did enjoy crushing gnomes. Insipid people, always sneaking about. The worst were in academia, pretending to be so much smarter than everyone else, the squishy little pricks. Guilt snarled. Brains didn't keep them from being killed like frogs.

Part of a dying race, Guilt prided himself on his prowess and ability to provide any employers with satisfaction for his particular talents. High elves or dark, dwarves or trolls, he killed them all with casual indifference. He had no love for anyone or anything in particular, no family and no friends.

Hatred went both ways. His kind had always been hunted, a favorite target for sport. Few remained. Thin muscles rippled beneath his dark turtleneck sweater. His skin was a mottled combination of grey and brown with a long, white scar ripped diagonally from his chin down. Guilt absently traced that scar now, remembering his own time being hunted by the morally superior high elves. They were murderers the same as he, only there was considerably more blood staining their hands than his.

Guilt picked up the battered cell phone and made his call. "This is Guilt. He's moving." His voice was the sound of rocks being crushed to gravel.

A woman's voice answered. "Are they coming here?"

"No. Downtown somewhere."

"Follow them, but don't get made. It's too early to kill him."

Guilt grunted and hung up. Tossing the phone down, he began to follow. The prospect of killing heated his blood with dizzying effect. It had been much too long since the last time he'd fed, and that had been but a scrawny elf without enough meat on her bones to make a proper meal. The bones didn't even taste good. A perpetual scowl engraved on his granite-like face, Guilt gunned his old Dodge Challenger to life and started the hunt. Dreams of slaughtering the entire high elf royal family entertained him while he drove.

Cassandra finished pulling on the new black leather gloves and gripped the steering wheel. A normal follower of the king with little regard for her personal safety, she found herself having difficulty accepting this new assignment. The high elf clans had been thrown into such utter disarray tonight; she felt her place was best at the Citadel. To be sent into the field, a reduction in station, was the next best thing to a slap in the face. Her pride was wounded.

Injustice from an age ago resurfaced, an old wound she had never forgotten or forgiven. The emotional scars were all that remained. Half-detailed images of the bodies lying in twisted heaps of steaming flesh, ruined from countless swords and axes. Arrows riddling the house and furniture. The hearth fire gutted and spread across the back wall, already turning the home into an inferno. Most of it was a blur, ill-defined memories that ate at her when she closed her eyes. Most of it. She'd never be able to forget the look of abject terror in her dead mother's eyes. More than anything, she wanted to know what could terrify someone so badly she died.

The physical pain was a bitter memory she'd like nothing more than to forget. Scars still peppered her hands and wrists from trying to pull her family from the fires. Healers offered to fix her, but she adamantly refused. Those scars would remain for as long as she lived. They comforted her when the memories became too much, offered her solace from her misery. They gave her purpose in the following centuries, something to look forward to.

It had taken her a lifetime to discover the ones responsible and another lifetime to meticulously plot her vengeance. Finally, tonight, her darkest fantasies were about to come to fruition. Tonight, she would have her revenge. The guilty must be punished. Atonement could only be reached through death.

ELEVEN

Stomach full, Daniel picked a piece of lettuce out of his teeth while Mort wound the cab through the frustrating maze of one-way streets en route to the Schneider brothers' house. Their reputation might be extreme among the elf clans, but he'd never heard of them before. Humans and fantasy races might be living amongst each other, but nobody really wanted to look beyond their own little bubbles.

He burped.

"Damn. Next time don't get so many onions," Mort scowled, unsuccessfully trying to wave off the stench.

"Sorry. So how do I approach these brothers?" Daniel changed subjects. He'd already been threatened, attacked and then drawn into a mystery the size of a grand quest in one of his books and decided it better to be prepared for the next obstacle rather than meet it blindly.

"Don't ask so many questions. They don't like it," Mort replied, nose still crinkled. "They're good people," he chuckled, "but have a tendency to go off on short notice. What can you expect from dwarves, though, right?"

"Somehow I can't imagine dwarves as bankers and wealthy investors. Aren't they supposed to live underground and dig holes?"

Mort shook his head sadly. "You damned fiction writers, always think you got it worked out. Fact is you don't know a thing about us. Sure, you write and write until your fingers are sore from hitting the keys, but you look out a window and make up whatever nonsensical romantic figure you think will sell. How many times have you cast the elf in the hero role? Gone off on some epic quest to save the kingdom and rescue the girl? Trolls and goblins are always the bad guys. And dwarves are just pissed off at the world, right? One of my best friends is a goblin. He works third shift at a fire station, and he's saved more people than any elf I ever knew."

Daniel thought about it. Humankind was loaded with stereotypes, some close to true with others off the mark; why would the fantasy races be any different? The concept that the two species might have more in common than he supposed was starting to gain ground. Much of it made sense; after all, they'd been living amongst each other since the dawn of time. It was entirely plausible they'd been learning from one another and adapting all that time.

"What do your books say about gnomes?" Mort asked quietly.

"The annoying ones with red hats that hang out in gardens or the shady, nefarious characters willing to sell anyone out for the right amount of coin?" Daniel joked.

Mort laughed, getting the joke. "All depends on how much money you got."

They shared a laugh that died much too quickly. Nervous tension refilled the space between them. Daniel felt shadows encroaching despite the nullifying orange glow of the streetlights. He felt tired, lethargic. Maybe he shouldn't have eaten so much. The onions and mustard were rolling around his stomach with the definite intent of coming back up — which was a shame considering his muscles were already in near revolt. He'd been out of the fight for so long, it wasn't natural anymore. Muscle memory returned easily enough, and any fool could hold a weapon. Using it effectively when the enemy was charging into your position was something else.

"Oh, don't take the guns in with you. The Schneiders are notorious for taking offense to weapons their family didn't make," Mort suggested. "One of them isn't quite right in the head. Can't recall which one, though. Sorry, Daniel."

Instead of commenting, Daniel decided to think. Mort really was trying to be helpful, more than likely figuring his life was on the line as well. People tended to act differently when their lives were in jeopardy. *I guess these guys feel the same*. He closed his eyes and tried to refocus on his task. *One thing at a time. First, get the brothers, and then, find Murray*. Getting too far ahead of himself would only lead to an early demise and a cold wooden box.

Daniel tried to figure out where he was. None of the buildings or landmarks were familiar, meaning he was in a part of town he'd never been in. Which wasn't saying much. There were plenty of places he hadn't bothered to explore since returning to North Carolina. Most of his time was spent in front of a computer screen or sitting at a local coffee shop or bookstore trying to flesh out a plot or storyline. What was left was divided between cleaning the house, taking care of their kids and walking his dogs. That seclusion hampered him now.

They passed countless fast food joints and gas stations, strip malls and shopping centers. None of them was familiar. Neither were the street names. He was lost. *Great.* He grinned. *Yet another chip in the deck stacked against me*. The invasion of Iraq was certainly a worse situation, but at least he'd been expecting that. Tonight's events had come on with such speed and intensity he was left shaken, unconfident.

Blacking out during the wraith attack was the worst possible moment. The Citadel was unfamiliar, though it probably shouldn't have been. There weren't too many mansions in the North Carolinian countryside, certainly not enough for that particular one to go unnoticed. It was possible the elves used their magic to conceal the Citadel's true nature. He'd written about glamour spells and the like enough to think they might be real after all. Daniel was about to ask Mort when the cab turned suddenly down a one-lane side street.

"Act cool. We're being followed," the cabbie said.

It took a surprising amount of self-control to keep from looking behind them. Daniel double-checked to ensure his rifle was locked and loaded and adjusted his vest. "Wraiths?" he asked.

"No. There's a dark purple Challenger about a block back. It's been on us since we left the Citadel."

"One of Morgen's, then. Why haven't they made a move? They've been on me since I left my house," Daniel said.

"What? The trolls? I wouldn't worry about them. Lou and Bert are part-time thugs, not much of a real threat. They get paid to do odd jobs for both sides. Last I heard, they worked at one of the local gas companies, driving trucks or something. Besides, you don't think they'd both be able to fit in a Dodge do you?" Mort snickered at the ridiculous notion of trolls driving a small car.

Daniel failed to find the levity in the situation. "Who is it, then?"

Mort shrugged. "Can't tell. There's a lot of strangeness going on this night. Could be anyone."

"Mort, level with me. What's so special about tonight? I'm having trouble thinking the kidnapping and Ariel's murder happened all on chance."

A long, almost mournful sigh briefly fogged the windshield, telling Daniel he'd come close to the truth. Mort remained silent for a while longer, unsure of how much he should and shouldn't tell. In the end, the idea of staying alive was more appealing than avoiding the ire of the king of the high elves.

"None of this gets back to Alvin, all right?"

Daniel gave a curt nod. "You have my word."

"Tonight is the anniversary of the splitting of the clans. Sure, it happened over a thousand years ago, but both sides are still pretty sore about it. Those of us who choose to remain neutral — relatively, of course — don't really care so much. We get a lot of work during this time, though. The elves are insistent on either going to war or rejoining into one big happy family. Personally, I don't see how that is going to happen. It's been way too long. Grudges have turned to hatred.

"Anyways, tonight was supposed to be the wedding of Princess Gwen and Xander. Their union would have secured Alvin's bloodline as the rightful rulers of the high elves and given him the advantage over Morgen. I guess the old lady didn't care for that so she had Gwen kidnapped."

"And Xander killed."

"And Xander killed," Mort agreed. "It's really just bad luck on your part. You should have taken no for an answer and stayed home. Hey, where'd he go?"

Daniel turned. The Challenger was gone. A tingling sensation crept up his back, cold and menacing. Daniel struggled with the helplessness of his situation. His fingers gripped the cold metal of his rifle as he switched on the laser optics. The tiny red beam reminded him of a campy science fiction movie.

"Mort, how does everybody know who I am? It can't be because of my books," he said as soon as the thought entered his mind.

"Some of us know you through your books. I kind of enjoyed them, but I like comedy anyway. The higher-ups have known you from the moment you started firing query letters off for your first book. You were a potential threat to our existence, after all. Don't go thinking you're special. They do it to all of the would-be authors and such. It's a security measure you see. It was no accident your contract got bought out after the success of *Dark Elves*. The clans, light and dark, wanted to keep a closer eye on you. We've been watching you for a long time." The hesitancy in his voice alarmed Daniel.

"What aren't you telling me?"

"Look, you're not supposed to know this, but your emails with Ariel were hacked by Morgen's people. They knew you were coming," Mort replied sadly.

Daniel's thoughts exploded. "My wife and kids! I need to get home now!"

"Relax, buddy. Alvin dispatched guards to keep them safe. Morgen won't mess with them. She's avoided getting into a shooting war for this long and won't risk that happening now. I think she's just having a bit of fun to pass the time."

"Mort, I swear I'll bring Alvin's entire world down around him if my family is harmed. I'll fucking kill him myself," Daniel threatened.

The gnome didn't reply. He couldn't. Thoughts of his own wife and seven kids being threatened scared him to the bone, but how could he admit that to a complete stranger, and a human? The cab pulled into a parking garage. Mort snatched the ticket and found a shadowed corner with clear avenues of approach. There wasn't a car for ten spaces, preventing anyone from sneaking up on them.

"This is it. The Schneider brothers live on the third floor," he announced.

Daniel stared at the back of Mort's head. Three quick breaths helped calm him, but it wasn't enough. Years had passed since he'd been this jittery. Daniel and Mort eased out of the cab and headed towards the elevator. Then all hell broke loose.

TWELVE

The snap-thrum of arrows being fired made him duck reflexively. Glass shattered. A tire exploded. Bolts struck impossibly in the concrete around him. Dazed, Daniel shoved Mort to the ground and started to pull his hands over his head before realizing he could fight back. Flashes spat from the end of his rifle as he laid down enough suppressing fire to break contact. He and Mort shuffled to the front of the cab where he tried to assess the situation.

"What the fuck!" Mort exclaimed. "My cab!"

"Forget the cab, Mort. Help me figure out where this fire is coming from or we're both going to be in the morgue," he snapped, automatically falling back into Army mode.

Another pair of arrows plunged into the wall over the roof of the cab. Daniel fished into his pocket and came up with one of Goran's specials. The giant had seemed more than pleased with himself as he described his homemade concussion grenades. Daniel didn't see what the big deal was, having used flash-bangs to clear buildings before, but he let the giant have it. Now he was grateful Goran had been so insistent. Daniel pulled the pin and heaved the spherical grenade.

"Plug your ears," he warned and did the same.

The blast shattered car windows. He thought he heard, briefly, a set of screams. Daniel grinned savagely and popped up on one knee. The laser beam sliced into the gloom. His eyes naturally followed. Four figures lay sprawled, writhing and holding their heads. Daniel didn't waste time. Taking aim, he fired a three round burst into the body of the nearest one. Blood sprayed. The dark elf jerked once and was still.

His body started to dissolve even before Daniel rose up and started firing on the move. The remaining dark elves scrambled. Daniel took a second in the rib cage, dropping him instantly. The elf dissolved without a scream. Daniel's nerves calmed as he began clearing the parking garage. This time of night, there were hardly any cars, giving him long fields of fire and limited avenues of enemy approach. He shot the third elf in the back of the head, brains and gore splattering the nearby Toyota.

The fourth elf turned and drew a wicked-looking blade. He charged. Daniel didn't slow down. He stitched three rounds across the elf's chest and a fourth in his head for good measure. When it was over, he was standing alone, only the quickly fading blood stains evidence that a firefight had taken place. His heart was pounding. Tiny beads of sweat dripped down his face. Then he realized where he was. *Shit. What was I thinking? Sara will kill me if she finds out what I just did.*

"It's clear, Mort," he called after verifying the vicinity was empty of more bad guys. He still couldn't believe he'd been foolish enough to charge into an unknown situation with little regard for his personal safety.

The gnome poked his head out from the ruined cab, shock and horror twisting his normally bland features. His lower lip quivered in a strange combination of trying to speak and struggling to contain his fear. Clearly, he hadn't been expecting to get involved in any actual fighting.

Daniel dropped his empty magazine and reloaded. The sharp *snap-click* echoed through the now quiet garage. He jogged back to Mort and slapped the gnome on the shoulder. "Third floor, right?"

Mort nodded.

"Let's go. This was probably just a scouting party." Daniel headed for the elevator without waiting for confirmation. Any doubt was gone, replaced by years of training and the predatory instinct of a professional soldier. All it took was a near-death environment to put him back in the proper frame of mind.

The elevator chimed suddenly. Daniel froze. Half a dozen dark elves, all dressed in black combat fatigues and carrying what looked like strange combinations of crossbows and snub-barrel rifles emerged, automatically fanning into a crude semi-circle. They shouted curses in their native tongue; Daniel didn't understand the words, but the intent was clear.

"Mort, stairs!"

He fired off a quick burst and fell back at a run. Mort was already ahead of him, having seen the mass of elves coming in from the street. They were surrounded and cut off. Their only chance was to make it to the Schneiders. More arrows zipped past them — short, gun-blackened bolts dipped in poison. Daniel felt one bounce off his pack. The impact thrust him forward, saving his life in the process. A stream of bullets tore through the space he'd just occupied, blasting huge chunks of concrete from the wall ahead. More bullets sped towards them as all six dark elves started firing.

Mort cried out, reaching for his right leg. Daniel cursed when he saw blood running down the trousers. Mort had been hit, and, depending on if the round had severed the artery or not, might die long before they made it to the stairs. Daniel dug into an ammo pouch and tossed a fragmentation grenade behind them. The elves were wise to the trick and hung back far enough to avoid being caught by shrapnel. The distraction gave Daniel enough time to throw an arm under Mort's shoulders and carry/drag him to the stairs.

They rounded the corner moments before rounds hit both sides of the entrance. Daniel let Mort slump down on the steps. The bleeding was slowed but still coming out at a steady drip. Deciding the wound wasn't life threatening, Daniel turned back to the approaching dark elves. Rounds struck everywhere the instant he poked his head out. Chips of concrete slashed across his cheeks. Dust choked him. He ducked back, poked his barrel around the corner and fired blindly.

"Can you move?"

Mort nodded. The color was drained from his face. "It hurts like a bitch."

"Start moving. When you get to the next flight call down, I'll cover you on the way up. Got it?"

Mort nodded.

"Good. Now move."

Daniel watched the gnome start hobbling his way up and fired another burst. It seemed almost too long before Mort called down for him. Firing again, Daniel rushed up the first flight and took up a hasty firing position at the joint in the stairs. The view gave him a clear line to the door, the only access point for the dark elves. He'd be more than able to kill anyone coming through the door, provided his assumption that the elves didn't know modern military tactics was accurate. The small, round object bouncing into the stairwell showed him his error.

Daniel ducked right before the grenade exploded. Echoes of the blast ripped into his eardrums. He barely heard Mort's cry. So much for having a tactical advantage. The bottom of the stairs suddenly went dark. The elves had shot out the lights in order to conceal their approach. Without seeing any shadows or hints of movement, Daniel would be just as blind as his enemy.

"I'm up!" Mort shouted much louder than he should have. The grenade must have temporarily deafened him.

Daniel backed his way out of any line of fire as the first elf crept into the opening and sent a wild stream of bullets in his general direction. There wasn't much chance of being hit by more than a ricochet, but Daniel had had enough. He was going to run out of ammo long before he ever got close to rescuing the princess. That was a problem for later. Right now, he needed to keep them alive long enough to get to the Schneider's. He pulled the pin on another grenade and dropped it down the hole. It bounced down, exploding at chest level. Daniel grinned. He hadn't planned it like that, but the effect was probably the best he could have hoped for. Dark green blood sprayed through the stairwell, evaporating into mist before a single drop touched anything.

"Son of a bitch," he cursed.

Another elf jumped in, firing as he came. Daniel's rounds drove in under the collarbone and wormed through his stomach before he died. Instinct urged him to stand fast and wait for the remaining elves to come at him and, for a moment, he did. Then it dawned on him that the elves weren't stupid and had access to the elevator. They could already be moving to cut him off. Time was against him now as well.

"Mort, you have to move! We're going to be flanked."

The prospect of dying trapped on the stairs so close to his objective was sobering. Daniel rushed the final flight, abandoning tactics and covering fire. He had to reach the third floor before the dark elves or it was all for nothing. Mort was struggling but seemed to have figured out how best to move without aggravating the wound more.

They gained the third floor together, and Daniel wasted no time easing the door open and slipping into the long hallway. The carpets were dark red, so at least no one would see his blood after they moved his body away. His hopes dashed when he realized the stairs were in the middle of the building as opposed to one of the ends. Unless the Schneiders lived in the apartment directly across from him, he and Mort weren't going to make it.

"Which way?" he asked, desperation creeping into his voice.

Mort winced. "Right. Apartment 321."

The elevator chimed. Raised voices echoed up from the parking garage. They were too late. Trapped between two forces of unknown size, Daniel decided to charge the elevator. He reasoned there could only be so many dark elves stuffed in there. Who knew how many more were flooding up the stairs. The smoke grenade billowing through the hallway made him drop, dragging Mort down with him again.

Bullets spit from a dozen rifles in both directions. Daniel held his fire, deciding to keep his location hidden for as long as possible. His mind grasped at tactics and discarded them just as quickly. There wasn't a scenario he imagined that didn't end with him being shot to death. Nothing to lose, Daniel began firing. He clipped one in the ankle, dropping him. A pair of rounds punched out the back of the elf's head the moment it hit the ground.

The commotion coming from the stairwell rose, confirming his worst fears. He didn't have enough bullets to take care of this problem, and Mort was next to useless. An arrow whizzed past his head. The elves now had a target to shoot at it. Daniel fired blindly, hoping to hit anything before that one shot took him out. Rounds traced arcs through the dark smoke. The elves on the stairs started firing. Fortunately, the angle was too severe for them to hit him. For now.

Two massive figures suddenly emerged down the hallway. Both were dressed in kevlar body armor and carried an array of heavy weapons. Death flashed from their guns as they advanced on the dark elves. Taken off guard, the elves desperately tried to retreat back into the elevator. Reactive bullets tore huge chunks of flesh out of them, killing each of those struck instantly. Acrid haze clung to the figures, wreathing them like ancient gods.

The elves in the hall broke, unable to withstand the fury of the assault. All exits were cut off. One repeatedly hit the elevator button. Panic and fear marred his face. Three more dashed towards the stairwell. All three were cut down as they jumped over Daniel. He buried his head in his arms, whispering prayers. Mort cried out.

Abruptly, the madness stopped. All of the dark elves were dead or severely wounded. The smoke started to clear, giving Daniel his first true glimpse of the pair of avengers stalking towards him. Powerfully built, stocky and wearing the nastiest looks he'd ever seen, the Schneider brothers barely regarded them. They were hunting. One stepped past Daniel without a glance and entered the stairwell. Gunfire shook the building.

The other, possibly the meaner, gave him a disapproving sneer. "Get inside, human. We'll handle this."

And then, he, too, entered the stairwell. The screams were cut off when the door closed.

THIRTEEN

"You'll live," Angus Schneider growled as he finished inspecting Mort's wound. "It's just a flesh wound. Might hurt to walk for a few days, but I wouldn't worry."

He shook his head, curly black hair washing his neck. His jaw was the strongest Daniel had ever seen, thick and ominous looking. Bushy eyebrows concealed some of his face, giving him a shadowed look. A salt-and-pepper beard was kept at a few days' length. Daniel barely made out the top lines of a tattoo poking from the top of his body armor. Scratches and dents riddled the armor. He was, without a doubt, the most menacing financial advisor in North Carolina.

Fritz was just the opposite. He lacked muscle mass and was wiry instead. There was a cagey look in his eyes that set Daniel on edge, almost as if he got off on the violence. Wild and unpredictable. Those types of people scared him. Fritz had close-cropped hair and harsh grey eyes. His nasty disposition looked to be engraved on his face.

"What are you doing caught up in all of this, Mort? I thought you knew better," Fritz asked angrily.

The gnome shook his head. "Wasn't my idea. Alvin has me taking Daniel around for the rest of the night. Big things are happening."

"This is all about the princess?" Angus asked suddenly.

"Yes. Xander was killed a few hours ago. He gave Daniel the black box."

Their eyes widened. "A human has the box? Is Alvin mad?"

Angus shrugged, "At least that explains why the dark elves are trying so hard to kill him."

"Wouldn't you do the same if your daughter had been kidnapped?"

The brothers stopped and looked at Daniel, clearly disbelieving a human could be responsible for their continued existence. Neither seemed pleased.

Daniel met their glares with one of his own. "How did those dark elves know I was here?" he asked accusingly.

Angus bristled with insult. Fritz balled a fist, drawing back to strike. Mort dropped his head into his hands, wincing in anticipation of the coming blow.

"Mind your tongue, boy!" Angus snarled. "I don't often agree with my brother, but I'm inclined to let him knock your teeth down your throat. Mort, didn't you tell this prick we don't like questions?"

"I told him," the gnome replied weakly.

Angus grunted. "Typical human." He extended a hand. "I'm Angus; this is my brother Fritz. He's always angry because of ingrown toenails. If Alvin trusts you, I guess I do as well."

Daniel struggled not to wince when the power of the dwarf's grip threatened to break his hand. "Daniel. I don't want to do this anymore than you want me involved in your business, if that makes you feel better."

The dwarf grunted. "Losing Xander is tough. He was the best of us. You seem to know your way around a gun. Prior service?"

"I was in the army. Airborne infantry out of Fort Bragg."

Angus was impressed. "You're going to need every bit of training you got tonight. Alvin doesn't send business our way unless he's sure no one else can handle it."

"You avoided my question," Daniel interjected softly. The prospect of getting his face smashed in didn't sit well. "How did they know I was here?"

Crimson flashed his cheeks, but Angus managed to calm down enough to answer. "You're either being watched or there's a spy in Alvin's house. Either way, we weren't notified you were coming."

Daniel heard the annoying theme music from Wii Sports Resort coming from the living room. A pair of controllers lay where they'd been dropped abruptly. Beer bottles, some empty and others full, half-filled the glass coffee table. An empty pizza box sat on the corner, only crumbs and random bits of crust left. Nothing to suggest Angus was lying.

"We had a tail, but he disappeared around Ninth Street and Sawyer Avenue," Mort said.

"Mort, you had an entire company of dark elf commandoes trying to kill you. There's no possible way a tail could've assembled that much firepower in a limited time," Angus replied. "There must be a spy in the Citadel. It's been a while but Morgen has her hands in just about everything."

"Or it could be the human," Fritz snapped. Thick, blue veins popped out of his neck and forehead.

"That's probably the dumbest thing I've heard tonight," Daniel fired back. "Up until a few hours ago, I didn't know you people existed. What possible reason do I have to spy on you? Those bastards were trying to kill me!"

"Calm down, Daniel," Angus said as he stepped between them. It wouldn't be the first fight in his apartment, but he didn't want to go through the hassle of cleaning up after. "Like Mort said, big things are happening tonight. Like I said before, they don't want you. They need that box."

Daniel, finding the argument suddenly pointless, pointed towards the worn copy of *Rise of the Dark Elves* half buried on the bookshelf by the television. "You like to read?"

"Again with the questions," Mort sighed.

"A little. Why?" Angus asked back.

"That book by your TV. I wrote it."

Angus turned to see what he was talking about. "You mean the *Dark Elves*? Get out of here! I must have read that about ten times now. Makes me laugh every time. Mort, you didn't tell us this guy was a comedian."

"Why does everyone keep saying that?" Daniel asked. "My point is I'm an author, not a spy."

"An author with a mission," Mort chimed in. "We should be going. The dark elves will get suspicious when their commandoes don't report in."

"The gnome's got a point," Fritz agreed. "If we're going to be stuck with this human, we should get on with it. Where did Alvin tell you to go next?"

"You're supposed to take me to see some guy named Murray," Daniel replied tersely.

Fritz actually laughed. "Murray, huh? Okay, we can do that." He passed his brother a private look. "We haven't been down to see the big guy in a while."

Angus rolled his eyes. "I didn't plan on seeing him for a good long while either. His temper is worse than ours."

"I'll go get the gear," Fritz offered.

Daniel grew suspicious. He hadn't seen any reason for the sudden change of composure in the dwarf, and that made him nervous. Fritz was a loose cannon. The mission was getting increasingly dangerous, and Daniel wasn't sure if any of his companions had his back. The dark elves were intent on stopping him and regaining possession of the black box by any means at their disposal. How many lives had already been lost? And it was barely eight o'clock.

"I'm going to need more ammo. I wasn't expecting to get into it so quickly," Daniel told Angus.

The dwarf grunted, suggesting he should have known better. "We have a few thousand rounds of caseless lying around. You should probably bang out some of those dents in your pack too. Goran's a goddamn genius when it comes to designing weapons and kit, but he hasn't had any field time in almost a millennium."

"Do you have anything stronger? These guys aren't holding much back."

Angus rubbed his chin thoughtfully. "I don't think so, but we know where to go. You're going to find out the dark elves aren't exactly tactical geniuses, but they have numbers. Last I heard, they outnumbered us more than five to one."

"Why hasn't Morgen launched an offensive and wiped you out yet?" Daniel asked. Five-to-one odds were better than all of the firefights he'd been in during the war. An army that size would be able to crush its enemy in a single night. For the second time, he got the suspicion he was being left out on critical information.

"She can't. Despite her numbers, she lacks the black box. That's why Xander was at his sister's office, I'm guessing. He was sent to retrieve it for Alvin. The only way to ensure its safety is to keep it locked away in the Citadel."

Daniel frowned. "He didn't even bring the subject up. We talked a little about it, but I still have it. An object that powerful shouldn't be on the streets."

"That certainly explains why the dark is trying so hard to kill you. And it brings up another foul point," Angus concluded. "They know you have the box. That means Morgen will pull every string she has to stop you. I'm talking hit men, mercs, killers, you name it. Hell, the unaligneds will more than likely make a move for you tonight too. Right now, you're the most popular man in the city."

"You're full of good news," Daniel said. *At least I see why dwarves are always portrayed as so grumpy.*

"Let me go get that ammo for you. Tonight is going to be a long night. We should be about it quickly before we lose any advantage."

"My cab is ruined. The dark elves destroyed it trying to kill us," Mort told them.

Angus nodded. "We've got transportation. You should probably stay here, though. They won't come back once we're gone. I doubt they'll come back before we leave, either. Only the foolish mess with the Schneider brothers in their own home. With that wound, you'll only slow us down, and I don't want your wife coming down on me for letting you get killed."

The gnome waved off their concern. "I'm not arguing. Just let me call back to Stern. He's probably trying not to kill someone right now."

Angus smirked. "That's the truth. He's always been wound too tight. I'll be right back."

Daniel leaned back in the wicker chair and wiped his face. He gave Mort a brief smile. Their time together had been short, but he was starting to like the gnome.

"There's not much to say," Mort cut him off before he could speak. "We're both doing a job. I'm not cut out to be a warrior."

"I'd feel better if you came with us," Daniel admitted. "You're a good man, Mort. Thank you for keeping me alive."

Mort snorted a light laugh. "The trick is to stay that way, right? I wish I could help more, but…you know. Alvin picked right, Daniel. You stay safe. Get the princess back and go on with your life. Stay safe," he repeated.

Daniel stared down at the wounded gnome. Far from being friends, he took an odd liking to Mort and wished him well. The dwarves returned before he could say anything to that effect. Fritz frowned at him but held his tongue. The dwarf had already made up his mind to kill Daniel if he showed the slightest hint of betrayal. Angus, however, looked like he'd been invited to the prom by the prettiest girl in school. He tossed a duffle bag full of ammo, grenades and other nasty surprises at Daniel, whistling as he came.

"Mort, it's been a pleasure. You'll be safe here. Help yourself to food and drinks until your wife comes to pick you up. We've got it from here," he said cheerfully.

The gnome smiled despite the annoying feeling of abandoning Daniel. "Sorry about the mess."

"Nah. Nothing maintenance can't fix," the dwarf said as they shook hands. Angus turned to Daniel. "Ready, chief?"

Chief? What the hell? "I guess so. Let's go see Murray."

Fritz shouldered his way past and went outside, leaving Daniel glowering. "Don't mind him. Humans have a way of screwing him over. Especially you fools in love. Can you imagine how many engagement diamonds he's had returned?"

"It's been my experience men like that quickly turn into liabilities," Daniel countered as he hefted the duffle on his right shoulder.

Angus's eyes narrowed threateningly. "Don't you worry about my brother. He's more than enough for what needs doing tonight. I'd look to yourself before questioning one of us."

Doubts still plagued him, a side effect of working with strangers. Back in the Army, it was easier. You lived and trained with the men you went to war with for months and years before deployment. Tonight, he was an outsider. Daniel knew nothing more about the Schneiders' tactics aside from them charging headfirst into the fight. His chances of surviving continued to drop. Nothing for it, he shrugged and followed Fritz.

Angus slapped a meaty backhand across Daniel's chest. "Are we going to have a problem?"

"No. No problem. You watch my back, and I'll watch yours."

Satisfied, the dwarf nodded and gestured towards the door.

"Hey, Daniel!" Mort called. "Try not to let Murray eat you!"

The door clicked shut before Daniel could ask.

FOURTEEN

Almost expecting another ambush, Daniel couldn't stop looking over his shoulder. The night promised delightful tortures, half-realized nightmares that only a runaway mind could produce. Still, he was impressed with the tactical prowess of the dwarves. Fritz walked on point. His eyes never stopped moving, roving back and forth. He'd learned the hard way what level of deception and trickery the dark elves were capable of and had no intention of being caught like a rookie on his first operation. The heavy machine gun in his hands looked sterner than Army issue and was most certainly heavier.

Angus directed them down the bullet-riddled staircase. Once in the basement, Fritz stalked through the empty corridor. The machine gun waivered only slightly as he adjusted his line of sight. Daniel hung back, relegated to pulling up the rear. It wasn't the most comfortable position, given how sneaky the enemy was. Goran's engineering aside, he wasn't ready to place his trust in the pack that had already saved his life once. He moved as quickly as he could, however, struggling to keep up. The dwarves were in a hurry, but he didn't know why.

Mort's parting warning kept him stewing. *Try not to get eaten. Why would Murray eat me? Unless he's a cannibal, and even then, why would the Brothers Grimm here let him do that?* Mulling over the pointless got him nowhere but angry and confused, so Daniel focused on his surroundings. The basement was in stark contrast to the near immaculate hallways and living floors of the apartment building. Broken lights pockmarked the long corridor, giving it an eerie presence. An old mop leaned against the right wall. Boxes and a ruined mattress lay cluttered together in the alcove leading into the boiler room. Something in the machine shop hummed a low, rhythmic growl.

A cold draft blew in from ground-level vents. Despite that, the basement was warm, humid. Daniel wasn't sure, but it felt like it sloped downward. *Straight to the pits of hell, no doubt.* Fritz led them unerringly, stopping in front of a seemingly empty janitor office. Daniel was about to say something when the younger Schneider hit a secret button that opened a door in the back wall. Trails of cobwebs drifted lazily like forgotten lovers. Fritz gestured with his head and went inside.

The tunnel was exceptionally dark, almost unnaturally so. It had an earthy smell. Roots and stone jutted from the rough walls. Spiders and other insects scurried off at the sudden commotion. Large creatures Daniel couldn't see ambled off out of the light. The refinement and sophistication of the building never made it this far down. And it was just the way the brothers liked it.

"This tunnel leads to a cavern close to the main reservoir. We've got an armored Suburban fueled and ready to go. It's one of those emergency-use-only types of vehicles," Angus explained after he closed the entrance.

"I can't see a thing," Daniel told them. He ignored the snort echoing back.

Angus slapped his back. "I keep forgetting humans can't see in the dark. Didn't Goran give you night vision?"

"He did, but I don't know how to use it."

He held them out for Angus to inspect. The dwarf looked them over quickly and handed them back. "This is amazing. The technology is built into the lenses. All you have to do is wear them like sunglasses. Incredible. Hey, Fritz, we need to make it a point to go see Goran. He's got new toys."

"I like the ones I already have," Fritz replied and kept walking.

Angus shrugged at Daniel. "You really can't please everyone, can you?"

The trio pushed on. Daniel felt like he was on patrol again, only instead of the hairy streets of Mosul and Tal Afar, he was being sucked deeper underground. Claustrophobia had never been an issue for him. Then again, this was the first time he'd been in a tunnel with two angry dwarves.

They couldn't have been more different. Daniel was quiet, trying to be as stealthy as possible in the event the enemy was ahead. Fritz and Angus stormed through the tunnel like bulls, careless of any noise they made. He hoped they didn't have to sneak up on anyone soon.

The tunnel gradually widened until it dumped them into a large cave. Fritz turned on the overhead low-intensity lights, blinding Daniel in the process. Angus chuckled but said nothing else. When he could see again, Daniel stared up at the lights. Long banks ran the length of the football field-sized cave. He wasn't sure, but it looked like fire dancing in the hexagonal bulbs. They gave off a chilling glow and immense heat.

"Fire?" he asked.

Angus nodded. "Wizard fire. We installed them a couple hundred years ago. A wizard owed us a favor. They set the right mood for what happens here."

"Was he anyone I know?" Daniel asked, starting to get used to the notion of being surrounded by all of the characters from his novels.

Angus gave him an odd look and shook his head. "I like you, Daniel. You make me laugh."

"Thanks, that's just what I was going for," he replied drably. "What do you two do down here?"

"None of your business, human," Fritz said menacingly.

"What did I do to piss you off?" Daniel asked suddenly, surprising even himself. "All I'm doing is what was asked of me, and you're treating me like a leper."

Fritz wheeled, barely remembering to lower his barrel. "What did you do? You came to us! Your kind strides across this planet like conquerors. Not once do you stop and see the damage you've caused. Not once do you care about reparations for past injustices. You come and rape the lands in the name of expanding humanity. What does it really mean? You've destroyed more lives, more races than you'll ever know. I find the very smell of you offensive."

"I didn't do any of those things!" he protested, weakly. "I joined the Army to help people, not kill or rape them. You can't judge an entire race because of the actions of a few!"

"No? How many novels have you written? How many times have you exploited our races, our societies for personal gain? You may not have done it physically, but you've raped us in your own way." Fritz stalked off in a circle before leveling a finger at Daniel. "Alvin may have charged you with this mission, and us, but that doesn't mean I have to like or accept it. You stay out of my way, and I'll stay out of yours."

"Fine by me," Daniel snapped back. *I'm tired of your better-than-thou bullshit anyway.* "Angus, how long is it going to take to get to Murray?"

"Not long at all. Have you ever seen the city's underground generators?"

"I don't think so."

He flashed a tricky grin. "That's because there aren't any. Murray takes care of it. If you think we're obstinate, wait until you meet him."

Daniel could only shake his head ruefully. Asking further questions was pointless. Neither brother seemed inclined to give more than the most basic answer. Taciturn, dwarves were made to be alone. And they were fine that way.

They led Daniel to the Suburban with the personalized license plate of BADASS! He wasn't surprised. Everything about these two suggested unparalleled arrogance and bravado. Those traits might prove problematic when it came time to rescue the princess. He tossed the duffle in the back and, without bothering to wait to be told, climbed in after. Angus took the wheel. The front of the truck dipped considerably once both dwarves were strapped in. It drove more slowly than an armored HMMWV and roared like a tank. Maybe he imagined that last part, given the dimensions of the cave. The only things missing were spikes jutting out of the side paneling and a machine gun turret built into the roof. Daniel looked up quickly. *Nope, scratch that last improvement. Looks like they already thought about that.*

The drive went by quickly, much to his approval. He didn't like being underground or with two extremely disgruntled dwarves. The first yawn came as a surprise. Up until now, he hadn't realized just how tired he was. The four miles split between both dogs and the sudden crash of his adrenaline rush hit harder than he'd expected. Darkness crept in. His head produced a fleshy thump as it hit the side window. Only his snoring was louder.

FIFTEEN

Daniel immediately noticed the drastic change in temperature. The tunnel and cave were humid but manageable. Here, hundreds of meters underground and beneath the main power grid, it was stifling. He had trouble breathing. Sweat coated his body the instant he stepped out of the truck. Angus and Fritz suffered likewise but were better adjusted to it. They'd clearly been down here often enough that it didn't bother them. Daniel reached for the bottle of water he found lying next to him in the back seat.

"Don't drink all of it now," Angus warned. "It gets worse the deeper we go."

Daniel's heart sank. "Deeper?"

"You didn't think this was it, did you? Murray is nestled nice and deep under the city and for good reason."

Fritz suggested, "Let him find out for himself."

Angus could only grin. "Oh, I think his first glimpse of our friend will have him pissing down a leg. You know, I think Daniel is the first human Murray's seen in over a thousand years."

"Can't question good taste. Come on. Alvin will be calling soon."

The earth was darker here, a rich, black color, healthy and pungent. The bottom layers were comprised of clay and rock. Where the floor of the tunnel leading out of the apartment building was well worn and smooth, the surface here was coarse, wild. Various types of fungus grew out of the walls. A thin veil of mist clung to the air. Daniel caught familiar odors sprinkled amongst something far worse. He nearly gagged.

"What is that?"

Angus shrugged. "Brimstone, maybe. Definitely has an acidic quality. Reminds me of old batteries."

Daniel couldn't find a reason to reflect the dwarf's smile and wondered if they were under an old landfill. His stomach threatened to revolt. Bile rose in his throat. Then he noticed the half gnawed on bones brushed against the walls. Deciding some questions just shouldn't be asked, he tried to ignore them. Besides, neither brother seemed affected. *Not that their reaction is any indicator of good judgment. These two outright scare the hell out of me.*

Fritz gestured with his blockish head, and the trio entered the tunnel. They stopped abruptly when Angus answered his phone. The theme to the *A Team* echoed down the tunnel. Daniel buckled suddenly as the ground lurched and a deep rumble shook the world. Combat reflexes kicked in. He dropped into a fighting stance, knees bent slightly, weapon unslung and raised in search of a target. The visual distortion of the night vision turned his world a mottled green-black. Shadows deepened, concealing potential threats. It never dawned on him that what happened was natural or that he shouldn't be concerned. Neither of the Schneiders reacted.

The shrill bells of a cell phone ringing broke the silence.

"Angus Schneider. Hey, Tom! Yeah, I can talk. Hold on let me pull it up."

Daniel and Fritz shared unbelieving looks. Angus scowled and waved them off.

"Alright. I can put the trade in, but it won't go through until tomorrow morning. Also, I'd think about taking your investment out of big pharma and dropping it back into tech. Apple, Samsung and Google are jumping right now. Might be worth it. Let me pull up the details when I get in the office, and I'll call you back around lunchtime. Okay, talk to you later, my friend."

He hung up and slipped the phone back in his pocket.

"Finished?" Fritz asked snidely.

Angus balled a fist. "What? The markets overseas are open. I have a day job, you know. What kind of investment banker would I be if my clients can't get in touch with me?"

There are times when a man needs to hold his tongue and keep his opinions to himself. Daniel rightfully decided this was one of those times. The night continued to get worse. His belief system steadily crumbled under each new assault to his senses. Elves and dwarves. Murder and kidnapping. Logically, none of this should be happening. The base desire to go home to his wife and kids grew stronger with each new experience in the mythical world coexisting with his own. Sheer improbability collided with reality, punching holes in everything he'd once thought to be true.

Trying to reason through it was near pointless. Elves and dwarves did exist. Otherwise, this was the biggest, most intricate prank anyone had ever pulled. Daniel might still have been inclined to disbelieve it all if not for how Ariel had magically transformed after her death or how the dark elves had simply disappeared once they were killed in the parking garage. Truth can often be skewed by individual perception.

A deadly combination of acceptance and want took root deep inside him. This was the world he'd always dreamed about, ever since he was a young boy playing in the backyard with his brother. They'd gone to see the animated version of the *Lord of the Rings* when they were still little. The movie had sent him on an unavoidable path. His natural gift for writing and the fond memories of defending the castle from orcs and goblins with sticks for swords gave him the foundations for creating his own worlds filled with fantastic and mythic creatures.

The sudden discovery that his imagination wasn't so farfetched was like the opening of unexpected gifts on Christmas morning. Any feeling of joy or triumph was surprisingly absent, however. The races he'd once delighted in sending on epic quests were almost too real, too humanized. Elves weren't the heroic, mysterious beings of illumination he wrote. These dwarves, while naturally grumpy, were more interested in making money than war.

His perceptions had been turned on end, leaving him in near total blindness to what was really happening.

Daniel was savvy enough to recognize subterfuge. He'd played too many games during his stint in the Army to remain ignorant when others tried to pull a fast one. Alvin, as police commissioner and quite possibly the most powerful man in the city, was purposefully avoiding telling Daniel a great many truths. Too much of tonight's events were far too convenient, leading him to question whether the high elf king was being disingenuous for other reasons.

Certainly, there was an immeasurable level of being too distraught to explain his secretive actions. Combined with their unwillingness to let humanity know they existed, that gave Alvin every reason to maintain his hesitancy in trusting Daniel with that information. What it didn't explain was the suspicious glances and unspoken innuendos passed between the king and Cassandra. Only Mort seemed willing to give him the truth, or at least as much as he thought he could get away with.

Regardless of who said or didn't say what, Daniel hated it. Then he remembered the earthquake and suddenly grew furious that neither brother seemed disturbed by it.

"What made the ground shake? That roar wasn't natural," Daniel hissed back at the brothers.

"Oh, it was natural, just not in your world," Angus chuckled. "That, my friend, was Murray. He knows we're here."

Daniel tightened his grip on the rifle. "I get the feeling you're not telling me everything."

"Because we're not, dumbass," Fritz said. "You're going to have to trust us."

"Like you trust me? It goes both ways. I have a job to do, and you two are part of my backup. So either help or get out of the way." Daniel pushed past and headed down the tunnel. It was time to find out what Murray was.

Angus grabbed Fritz by the shoulder. "You're being too harsh on him. Alvin sent him. We should trust him."

Fritz flashed a smile. "I'm actually starting to like him. He's got spunk."

He followed after Daniel, leaving Angus confused. The tunnel wasn't nearly so long as the previous one. Daniel quickly found himself standing at the edge of a great opening, the entrance to the most massive cavern he'd ever seen. Fires burned brightly, scattered around carelessly. Puddles of a dark boiling liquid steamed. Noxious odors produced a dizzying effect. Daniel coughed. Bile polluted his mouth, and he spit it out.

Stalagmites and stalactites reminded him of so many wicked teeth. Mold and dying moss clung to the lower parts in their decay. The ground was hard, baked and cracked in a million places. Scrub brush dotted the surrounding area, giving the cavern an odd look. The smell of death clung to the air in a miserable pall. Daniel halted, his rifle raised at the low ready. Night vision failed to show any viable targets. Another roar made the ground tremble. Fresh gouts of flame blasted the ceiling, spreading across the cavern in a destructive blanket.

Massive fireballs dripped down, nearly hitting Daniel. He moved without a clear objective. Not that it mattered; one drop of fire would incinerate him. He ducked under the overhang of a large group of boulders moments before flames splashed onto the spot where he'd just been. It sizzled and hissed angrily, melting the ground. Daniel clicked his weapon off safe and pushed forward to confront whatever foul creature had caused such destruction.

The dwarfs stayed back, deciding to let him discover the truth on his own. They'd been the only two people down here for so long it was enjoyable seeing another's reaction. Daniel kept going, bounding between boulders in three- to five-second rushes. Always his weapon stayed trained on the immediate area. Any enemy popping out to surprise him would catch a salvo in the chest. He hoped.

Daniel paused when he spied a semi-circular wall of tri-colored rocks standing three times as tall as he. Another blast of flames spouted upwards. Whatever it was, the creature was inside the stone ring. His breath coming in ragged bursts, Daniel tried to keep calm. Waiting served no purpose so he rushed to the giant opening and rounded the final corner. And froze.

Murray, in all of his thirty-five ton glory, was a dragon.

SIXTEEN

Very few sights were powerful enough to make Daniel stop in awe. He'd seen the famous ziggurat of Ur, flown over the pyramids of Egypt, stood in the Khyber Pass, walked the tunnels under the Demilitarized Zone separating North and South Korea, but never in his wildest imaginations did he ever think to see a living, breathing dragon. The beast was one hundred and fifty feet long. Barbed spikes reminiscent of a stegosaurus formed the clubbed end of the tail. Man-sized claws tapped impatiently on the glassed-over ground while Daniel could only stare.

His armor was a resplendent red-orange, so bright it rivaled the sun. Murray watched him with eyes the color of the brightest sapphires. Unparalleled intelligence hid behind the sparkling gems. The dragon looked down on Daniel over his long snout, clearly as surprised as Daniel was. His teeth were long and wickedly curved and three rows deep. Long, leathery wings were swept back over his hind legs. His wingspan was an unmatched two hundred feet. When he spoke, his voice trembled like thunder in the heavens.

"What does a human want down here?"

Daniel swallowed his apprehension. His knees shook, throwing a nervous tick into his voice. "A...Alvin sent me."

Murray snorted. "Alvin. What does that prick want?"

Daniel's mouth opened and closed. The question, laced with disdain and contempt, forced him to change his method of approach. "His daughter's been kidnapped, and I'm the one chosen to bring her back."

"The king of the high elves has entrusted a human to save his daughter? I find that highly unlikely. Where is Xander? I would like to speak to him."

"Dead. He got killed trying to recover a box from his sister's office. She was my agent," Daniel explained. He hoped to only throw just enough information out to entice Murray.

"The box of Carthantos? He gave it to you?" It was Murray's turn to be shocked.

Daniel nodded. *Whatever that is.*

"Impressive, isn't he?" Fritz asked once he stood beside Daniel. "Murray's not like most of his kind. It took a while, but we were finally able to convince the dragons that survived the great purge that they stood to benefit more from an alliance with us than trying to eat us. I suppose I could thank you. Humans are the reason we get along now."

The dragon shifted focus. "Fritz? I should have known. No one else would dare bring a human down to see me. Where's Angus?"

"Went back to feed the meter. Did Daniel tell you about the box?"

The dragon nodded. "I find it difficult to believe Alvin entrusted the box to a human. Is Xander truly dead?"

"That's the rumor. He got ambushed trying to recover the box from his sister. That's where Daniel comes in."

Murray shifted. Rocks and loose dirt tumbled from the ceiling. "Times are dire indeed if the paladin is dead. Human, do you have any idea what is inside that box? Perhaps you might not be so eager to aid us if you did."

"I haven't gotten a straight answer from anyone yet. I understand the secrets and trying not to let an outsider know too much, but sending me into the middle of a war blind will only get the wrong people hurt."

Murray blinked twice. "I tried to keep a pet once. A dog. He was a good dog, but I never quite got the notion of caring for him. Of course, that grand experiment ended abruptly when I accidentally sat on him."

"I don't understand," Daniel replied.

"My point is that we sometimes get into matters over our heads without thinking first. My dog and now you tonight." He shook his mighty head. "Life seldom cares about our opinions. Do you know why I am down here? Trapped so far beneath the sun I can no longer recall what it looks like or the feel of those delicious rays of heat? The high elves rule only because they tricked and manipulated their way into positions of power. They got humans to do their bidding. Not all of your wars were of your making. Elves have little regard for any but their own kind.

"Once, back in the beginning, my kind ruled all we could see. The skies, land and water all fell under our domain. It remained that way until the great desolation changed the planet. Elves crawled out of their holes and assumed control. What few of us remained were hunted for sport. Only a handful lived when we made our truce. The elves pushed us underground, forgotten creatures best left to memory. I am nothing more than a relic. Alvin wants to keep me that way."

Daniel nearly suggested that Murray just break free and fly away. The idea was foolish. He'd be shot down by the Air Force without second thought. People tended to overreact to the things their minds couldn't rationalize. A dragon soaring through U.S. airspace would throw the known world into disorder. There would be war, a great purge against all things unnatural or unholy. No, Murray was trapped in his cavern until the ending of the world.

"How long have you been down here?" he asked instead.

Murray's head drooped as if his pride surrendered to reality. "Too long. I am nearly six thousand years old, and I haven't seen the sun in over four thousand years. The elf king wants to get rid of me, but Morgen won't allow it. I'm too valuable, and he knows it. Put me in range, and I'll swallow that bastard whole. Probably why he sends others to do his dirty work."

"Like me," Daniel concluded.

Murray nodded. "Like you."

Angus strolled up, casually stretching as he entered the dragon's inner sanctum. He stopped abruptly, seemingly surprised Murray hadn't eaten Daniel yet.

"Angus! What rock have you been hiding under?" the dragon bellowed joyfully.

Pointing up, the dwarf replied, "You're the one underground, my friend. How have you been?"

"Like a mushroom. Kept in the dark and fed shit."

His laughter was the most hideous and amusing sound Daniel had ever heard. Vibrations threatened to burst his eardrums, so loud and deep his very bones nearly rattled out of his skin. The dwarves, sharing the joke, weren't affected. Both races enjoyed a bond that nearly made him jealous. He hadn't found anything so tight since his Army days. He left them to their amusements and took in Murray's sanctum.

A huge movie screen covered most of a wall. Daniel found it hard to believe anyone would want to watch old 80's television on such a large scale. They didn't even play reruns on television anymore. But there was the red Ferrari and that horribly painted helicopter. Daniel started to think the entire mythic race was stuck a good thirty years behind current events. Between Goran being into the Grateful Dead and Murray watching old DVDs of *Magnum P.I.*, it was no wonder Alvin lacked any command and control.

An extraordinary amount of mattresses and pillows was piled up along the far wall, too many for Daniel to count. *I guess even dragons need to be comfortable. It must have taken years to get this many down here. And that smell! Like old people and wet dog. A lot of wet dogs.* A gilded mirror the size of the front of his house hung against the back, though for what was anyone's guess. He briefly thought about asking before more important issues took over.

Murray must have read his mind, for the dragon finished chuckling and fixed Daniel with a stern glare. "The box of Carthantos is very ancient, young Daniel. It was forged from a meteorite by the wizard Ulthal before the continents broke apart. Nothing on this earth is capable of breaking this box. Terrible magic powers it. Ulthal poured his life's essence into it at his moment of death."

"What is it for? What could possibly need to be contained in an artifact so strange and powerful?" Daniel asked. He idly reached down to feel the box. The vibrations were subsiding, though addictively powerful.

"Many items have been stored within, though none so powerful as right now. This box contains the heart of the dark elf queen."

Fritz and Angus exchanged dubious looks. Neither had been expecting such a bombshell when Daniel first arrived at their apartment building. Of all the powerful totems in their long histories, the queen's heart held the most potential to bring ruin down on them all. Their initial reaction was to turn and leave. Daniel and his box were nothing but trouble.

"Her heart?" Daniel was in disbelief. "I've read a lot of fantasy and horror stories. Some of them had to do with mysterious hearts still alive after being torn from their owners, but this is too much. Without a heart, the body dies. Nothing can survive that."

"Stop thinking like a human," Murray scolded. "Haven't you seen enough to make you believe in more than just your limited experiences? Elves are the closest beings to immortal left, next to the Angels, of course. The magic imbued in the box keeps her heart beating. Morgen lives so long as the box remains shut."

"So all we need to do is open the box, stab the heart, and all of this ends tonight."

Murray shook his head. "So simplistic in your approaches. Don't you think that hasn't been tried already? It is no small accident that Alvin gave it to Xander and Ariel for safekeeping. The box can only be opened with magic comparable to what sealed it in the first place. Normally, Alvin uses it as a bargaining chip to ensure the dark clans don't rise up. We wouldn't want your books coming true, now, would we?"

Another fucking comedian. I might need to find a new line of work. "All jokes aside, where are we going to find the magic necessary to open the box? And what does Alvin expect me to do about it when I get to the dark elves stronghold?"

"Do you have the box now?" Murray asked.

"Yes," Daniel said.

"Place the box on the obsidian dais and step back. Oh, and don't look at it when I begin. You'll go blind."

Daniel took a spot alongside the Schneider brothers and waited nervously as the dragon rose up and marched over to the ancient black stone. Another gift bestowed by the late wizard Ulthal, the dais channeled the eldritch energies from the earth's core and deep space. Such a combination might pose a threat to civilization if it ever fell into the wrong hands. Fortunately, only a handful knew about it, and Murray was the most formidable guardian alive.

The dragon reared back and blew a concentrated beam of golden flames onto the box of Carthantos. Invisible magic redirected the flames, forcing the trio to duck. Murray frowned and blew a stronger stream. Again, the box repulsed his efforts. Angered by the unexpected complications, Murray closed his mouth and studied the box. He hadn't seen it for so long, since Alvin had first pried Morgen's heart away, that much of his knowledge was lost. The dragon wasn't accustomed to defeat and wasn't about to give up.

Murray reared back, spreading his wings out behind him, and launched the most powerful gout of flame he was capable of. The ground trembled. Rock and stone melted in volcanic fury. Heatwaves blasted through the cavern, dropping Daniel and the dwarves to the ground. Fritz screamed, but it went unheard. A puddle of molten rock exploded. The world brightened to the point of blinding. And finally, the box began to give in. Murray's assault eventually made the box change color, from dark black to pulsating purple. At last, the dragon relaxed.

The cavern fell strangely silent. Echoes of tremendous power died quickly, replaced by the gentle call of nothingness. Murray dropped back to the ground, head hung low. His chest rose and fell rapidly. Steam poured from his nostrils. Leathery wings encircled his barrel shaped body. Exhaustion burned his lungs, and his muscles ached. The massive exertion had taken him nearly to the point of collapse.

"That…was not fun," he gasped.

Angus pulled Daniel up and brushed himself off. "Murray, are you alright?"

"Look at the box!" Daniel exclaimed with a strained whisper.

One by one, they looked down at the box of Carthantos. It was beating. Like a heart.

SEVENTEEN

Mort winced when he moved his leg. Most of the pain was gone, but enough remained to irritate him more than he preferred. The gnome wasn't accustomed to pain, at least not from being shot. He'd been a spy, for lack of a better term, for the OSS during World War II and made it through the entire war without a scratch. Korea had been harder for him to fit in, Vietnam worse. By the late 1960s, he'd lost the desire to go into harm's way with the promise of little reward. Any obligations to duty and country were more than satisfied.

He eventually settled down and married. They'd produced twenty-three children over the course of the next nine years (a healthy byproduct of having young by the litter), and life was good. At least until tonight. Mort had known bad things were on the horizon the moment Xander had shown up with orders from Alvin. Nothing good ever happened when the paladin of the king's house was involved. Matters had progressed downhill rapidly once Daniel had come out where Xander had gone in. Two hours later, Mort was wounded and out of the game.

Mort finished the glass of scotch and water he'd helped himself to after the Schneiders left and looked at the clock. It was a quarter past eight. Time to get home. He collected his hat and jacket and made for the front door before remembering his cab was all but destroyed during the dark elf attack. *How ironic. A cabbie needing to call a cab. Ah, life remains funny, I guess.* He snorted a quick laugh and started to look for the house phone.

A knock on the door was unexpected but no real cause for alarm. No one dared confront the Schneider brothers in their own home. "Hold on! I'm coming."

Mort hobbled over and peered through the small looking glass. He smiled and opened the door. "What are you doing here? I didn't know Alvin had anyone else out working tonight."

Two gunshots barked out. Mort was killed instantly. His body dissolved to ashes before it hit the ground.

"The box is alive?" Daniel asked incredulously.

"As much as anything. I don't pretend to understand the mechanical principles behind it, but Ulthal spent the better part of two decades designing it. This is his grandest achievement." Murray shuffled over and collapsed on the pile of mattresses. Much of the vibrancy of his scales was dimmed.

Daniel, surprising himself, moved closer to the dais, now resembling just another ordinary black stone. "Can I touch it?"

The dragon considered him briefly. No human had ever seen the box of Carthantos before in so much as Murray recalled. Without that base interaction, it was impossible to tell what side effects, if any, might stem from close contact. Unfortunately for all of them, there was no time for study. He cocked his head.

"Theoretically, you should be fine. I can't remember any instance of magic working on your species. You have a nullifying effect, a random gene that has frustrated wizards and elven scholars for as long as they have recorded their history. You can be a most dangerous species, Daniel."

"At least that partially explains the open hatred," Daniel said.

"Partially," Murray replied dismissively. *If you only knew the horrific experiments conducted on your ancestors in the name of progressivism and science. You'd never have agreed to help us.*

The unspoken threat in the dragon's voice raised Daniel's guard. He was already on edge enough to want to ask more. Reaching out with a shaking hand, Daniel tenderly placed his fingertips on the beating box. *It's alive*! The rhythmic *thump-thump* of a beating heart was just audible enough for him to hear. Most, if not all, of the electrifying energy he'd initially experienced was gone or perhaps it had just subsided enough that he was used to it already. Regardless, Daniel didn't feel the tension pulsing through him.

Instead, there was something darker within. He felt hatred, raw and unmitigated but directionless. The abandonment of hope. The box sang a song of eternal damnation for any foolish to dare opening it. The box of Carthantos felt evil. Daniel jerked back, his eyes tortured with anguish. "This box is evil."

"No, not the box. It is Morgen's heart that beats within. The evil you feel is coming from all the malevolence she had stored up when Alvin finally made her bend a knee and accept defeat."

"I can feel it. It is almost sad, in a way. No person should have to live with the knowledge that her soul is irredeemable in the eyes of God," Daniel whispered, though he wasn't sure where that thought had come from. Did the elder races believe in a god?

"Morgen was not always evil. Once she was noble and pure. She was the fairest lady in all the lands. It was a golden time. Those days are all but gone now. Fallen into rot and shadow. There is no glory left in the world of elves."

"You make it sound sad," Daniel said.

"Isn't it? I have no love for the pointy-eared fools, but they were once almost majestic. They let their greed turn to complacency. The brilliance of their cities faded into obscurity. It is a self-inflicted wound they've never been able to overcome."

Memories, both calm and haunting, pulled the dragon into silence. His hatred over past injustices was boundless, but his life hadn't always been a torment. There was a time, so far past the memory was mostly faded, when he had been happy. Murray sighed. Dwelling in an unchangeable past was pointless. He was a prisoner, a willing subject to the whims of a king more distracted than majestic.

"Too long have I been trapped in this tomb. I long to feel the winds on my scales, the freedom of roosting atop the tallest mountain without care or concern. One day, I will be free again."

Daniel didn't know why he said what he did, other than that his heart compelled him. "If I can help, I will. Once this night is over, I'll return and see what I can do."

"That would be…most kind. Few bother to show me kindness."

"Fair enough. What do I need to do with the box? Can we open it and use it to kill Morgen?" he asked.

"Ha! You still expect things to have easy solutions," Murray laughed. "The only way to open the box is to be in Morgen's presence. Her essence is the one thing strong enough to unlock the magic. You must get close to her if you wish to kill her."

Daniel felt deflated. He had no intentions of getting anywhere near the queen of the dark elves. She'd already devoted so many resources to stopping him, it wasn't inconceivable she was willing to do more. His position grew increasingly more dangerous the further the night progressed, and he lacked a strong support system. A quick look back confirmed the Schneider brothers were distracted with another petty argument, leaving Daniel on his own. He had enough weapons and the brains to get out of unpleasant situations but was missing the necessary knowledge to defeat the dark elves. Alvin had set him up. But for what purpose?

That part he couldn't figure out. His first thought was that the elf's mistrust in humanity made Daniel an unpleasant reminder of their fallibility. There had to be more. Up until this evening, he'd been just another man living in a world where elves were but processed figments of imagination torn from frayed pages of old novels. He was trapped in a puzzle with pieces missing.

"Murray, what's the connection between Alvin and Morgen?" he asked suddenly.

The dragon raised his weary head. His eyes conveyed sadness. "Theirs is a story of lost love and wasted lives. Alvin and Morgen were once married. She was the queen of the high elves before the schism."

Daniel felt his jaw drop. He knew the revelations shouldn't have surprised him. After all, he was a fantasy author, and that sort of plot twist was a well-played favorite amongst his peers. It made perfect sense that the heads of the two clans were former lovers turned bitter enemies. The dichotomy between good and evil was so complex, so intricate, that the two were nearly inseparable during the best of times. When darkness settled in, drowning out the sun, the lines of morality blurred, and good suffered.

He couldn't shake the feeling he was being duped into taking care of someone else's dirty laundry. The elves were playing him for the fool, and now he was trapped until he found either the princess or the sharp end of a blade. Alvin's neglect at sharing information was nothing short of a betrayal of confidence, making Daniel's life infinitely more miserable and challenging.

"The son of a bitch," he hissed.

Murray nodded, his massive head bobbing casually in agreement. "Elves are not to be trusted, Daniel. You should study mythology more. The Vikings held them in little regard. They can be cruel and wicked. That's partially the reason behind the schism. Morgen refused to stand in mankind's shadow any longer. She wanted the glory, to be in command of a world that worshipped her for the golden goddess she so desired to become. It was all a lie. Alvin tried to tuck her away, convince her the two worlds wouldn't mix. She rebelled, took half of the families with her, and plunged our world into an unending war. Alvin is using you, though to what end I know not."

Daniel had half a mind to turn around and walk out. Police commissioner or not, Alvin needed a strong punch in the mouth, a reminder that his kind was pointless in the modern world. But since he wasn't a naturally violent man, Daniel just stood there and ground his teeth angrily. The numbers weren't adding up. Two of the most powerful beings on earth, and they couldn't find an exit from their grievances? Alvin. Morgen. *What am I missing*?

Too many inconsistencies plagued him. Daniel needed to find the link between king and queen. The obvious conclusion was that princess Gwen was their child and they were in the middle of a custody dispute. One thing he'd learned long ago was not to get involved in family affairs. They never turned out the way you intended. Unfortunately, he didn't see any way around it. High and dark elves were determined to slaughter as many of their kind as possible, and he was at a loss.

"Why tonight? What's the significance?" he asked suddenly.

The dragon yawned. Hot breath and rotted meat soured the air. "What's tonight? I've been down here so long I don't know what year it is, much less the day."

"October 30th," Daniel answered.

The dragon's head dropped slightly, some of the gleam faded from his eyes as if painful memories had returned to haunt him. "Today…is the anniversary of the schism. As well as the princess' wedding night."

Daniel's heart sunk. Anniversaries held the potential to be good or bad. If Morgen was making her move now, that meant she must be ready to reopen the war and launch an offensive designed to cripple the high elves for good. The reconciliation might do the clans good, but under the helm of the dark queen who presumably still held a grudge against humanity and her estranged husband, the world wouldn't stand much of a chance. Assuming the clans were as widespread and powerful as both Murray and Cassandra hinted at. Daniel wished Mort were with him. The gnome had a way of easing his fears. The Schneider brothers were boisterous but relatively harmless. Not the company he needed at the moment.

"I need to find the princess and get her home before either Morgen or Alvin can execute their plans," Daniel told the dragon. "Do you know where she is?"

"Locked away in Morgen's stronghold, no doubt, but I can't help you find it. She likes to move around, stay fluid. It keeps Alvin constantly guessing, frustrating him to great ends. What about it, Schneiders? Where's Morgen hiding these days?"

Fritz rolled his eyes and headed back to the Suburban. Angus threw a quick jab, catching him in the shoulder as he passed. "Last I heard, she was holed up under the convention center downtown. Getting to her won't be easy, though. She's got enough defenses in place to beat back an army."

"An army of three is all we've got. She's anticipating a full-blown war, not a three-man team creeping through the back door," Daniel replied.

Bristling at the term *men*, Angus folded his thick arms across his chest. "Possible, but still dangerous."

"Stay home if you're scared. I want to get this over with."

Murray barked a rolling laugh. Stone and brick showered down around them. "I like this one, Angus. He's got the kind of fire that makes you want to believe."

"Yeah, I believe alright. Believe we're going to get greased tonight," the taciturn dwarf replied and gestured with his head. "Let's go then. The night won't last forever."

Daniel headed out, chest swelling and trepidation in check. "Thanks Murray. Don't forget what I said. If I can, I'll get you out of here."

"Good luck, Daniel. You're about to enter a dark world," the dragon said.

"I'm already in it, trying to get out."

EIGHTEEN

They drove in silence. The long, winding tunnel was especially dark, as if the mysterious powers controlling the world held a secret. Not even Goran's night-vision glasses eased Daniel's discomfort. His skin crawled, that nervous feeling right before something bad happens. Icy fingernails scrolling across an old window locked in winter's deep. He absently gripped and released the pistol grip on his short barrel rifle, mind racing through as many eventualities as he could imagine.

There was nothing to suggest the coming fight was going to be easy or pleasant. Dark elves died quite well but were mean little bastards with a mind for murder. He'd already come close to quitting several times tonight. Death was too real. Would anyone ever find his body, he wondered. Probably not. Their reluctance to accept him was proof enough that he wouldn't even be a memory. Reaching into his pocket, he fished out an old, weathered wallet and stared longingly at the faded picture of his wife. *I love you.*

The thought was too much. His heart swelled, threatening to burst with useless emotion. Daniel needed a clear head if he was going to make his back to her. Any sentiment now was nothing more than weakness, a timid distraction capable of leaving his corpse in cold, forgotten places. Tears clouded the corners of his eyes. He wiped them away with a cuff and sniffed once. Angus glanced briefly in the rearview mirror.

"Morgen's not entirely bad, you know."

Daniel cleared his throat and shoved the wallet away. "I don't see what that has to do with anything. We've got to cut through her army first."

"Hired guns at best. Don't make the mistake of thinking those thugs want to die tonight. Dark elves are nasty pricks, but they do enjoy life. Watch how fast they break once we kill enough. Even the bravest tend to break and run once the bodies start piling up," Fritz added unexpectedly.

Both offered amused looks.

He shrugged. "What?"

"Angus, it doesn't matter if they break or not. We can't afford to go barreling in through the front door like John Wayne up Mount Suribachi. This mission calls for some sort of secrecy." A feat Daniel highly doubted either dwarf was capable of.

"Our grandfather fought on Iwo Jima," Angus replied proudly. "Fritz and I were still too young but loved his stories when he came home."

"Why don't I doubt that?"

Fritz rolled his eyes in disapproval. "Do you really think our races can just sit and hide while the world goes to shit around us? We fight. There's not much choice in it. Either we sit by and watch you destroy the world, our world, or we pitch in and try to shift the outcome. Angus and I were in the Gulf War with the 3rd Infantry Division."

Confidence bloomed suddenly. A bond formed. Camaraderie between fellow warriors. The Schneiders had done time in Iraq, albeit ten years before Daniel, but they had each chewed some of the same sand. A smile genuinely warmed his face. "I was with the 101st in OIF I. We skirted up the desert, around Baghdad and occupied Mosul."

"Bah! This new war is nothing. We kicked Saddam's ass between his shoulder blades in four days," Fritz laughed. "How long did it take you? Three, four weeks?"

"We had a different objective. You vacationed in the Saudi desert for six months. I got there and conquered the country. Different wars."

An uncertain silence settled through the truck. Angus broke it with a soft chuckle. "101st huh? Airborne pussies. Armor was where it's at."

Even Daniel laughed.

The Suburban emerged into a paved access way. Motion-activated lights marked their passing, forcing Daniel to curse as he hastily removed the night vision goggles. The tunnel wound in tight circles until it emptied in a small parking garage under the Observer Times building. It only took a few moments for Daniel to get his bearings. Finally, he recognized where he was. The park directly across the street was a favorite of his wife's, for reasons beyond his comprehension. The central fountain was nice, carved with majestic lions and an angel looking down. Red-orange trees half-emptied of leaves wreathed the park. A trashcan sat in front of them, abandoned and empty. All but one of the streets lights were out. Daniel gripped his rifle.

"The park is never like this," he whispered. *Why am I whispering? It's not like the dark elves are inside the truck with us.*

Fritz dropped his window and poked the barrel of his heavy machine gun out. The simple move eased Daniel's fears, if briefly, and helped him focus.

"Guns up, my friends. I think we have company," Angus said as he made a right turn.

Daniel noticed a purple Challenger sitting dark and quiet behind the far row of holly bushes. His bad feeling worsened. Blue-white flames exploded in front of them. Paint peeled away in a cloud. Both front tires melted to the rim. Angus hit the brakes hard, slamming Daniel's head into the back of the driver's seat. A series of thuds struck the side of the Suburban.

"Get out!" Fritz bellowed and let loose a stream of rounds.

The machine gun's bark was like thunder. Daniel kicked his door open and rolled to the ground an instant ahead of Angus. Arrows prickled the truck above their heads. Rolling right, Daniel decided to fire. Tracers stretched across the night. He didn't have any targets but was taking enough incoming fire to be able to return it in a general direction. The Suburban exploded without warning. Pieces of metal and hard plastic shredded the air, followed closely by another wave of blue-white flames.

"Fritz!" Angus roared.

Daniel dropped the empty mag and fumbled in an ammo pouch for another. "We need to get out of the fucking street!"

"My brother is still in there!" Angus protested and started crawling back to the wreckage.

A trio of armored dark elves popped up from behind the low stone wall lining the street in front of Daniel. He caught one of them in the chest with a three-round burst. The dark elf grunted and flew backwards, wounded but not dead. His partners kept coming. Daniel exhaled slowly and fired again. And again. He was rewarded by the second elf disintegrating and the third combat rolling for cover. There wasn't any. Daniel killed him with prejudice and turned his rifle back on the wounded one.

"Clear!" he shouted back over his shoulder.

No response. He turned and was amazed to see Angus dragging his brother into the park. Arrows clattered off the street. A pair of spears struck the trashcan, piercing both sides. Angus cocked sideways and fired from the hip. Rounds struck the building. He grunted and finished dragging his brother to cover. Daniel, crouching, hustled over to their position. Tiny beads of sweat lined his forehead.

"They've got us cut off," he said needlessly. "Is he going to be alright?"

Fritz growled, an angry, gravelly sound reminiscent of nails scratching down a blackboard. "Just some shrapnel. Don't worry about me, Airborne. There are plenty of dark elves closing in from behind."

Daniel frowned but knew better than to argue. Besides, there was no time. He could feel the circle tightening. "We've been set up, Angus. There's no way anyone could know we went down to see Murray or where we'd come out and when. Alvin has a spy in his ranks."

The dwarf nodded. "Any idea who?"

He didn't. "There's a purple Challenger tucked back down the street. It looks like the same one that followed Mort and me to the Citadel."

Angus's flint-like eyes hardened briefly, almost too fast for Daniel to catch. "Time to split up. Fritz and I will handle the main body. See if you can swing around the flank and come up behind them."

"Got it."

Daniel slapped Angus on the shoulder and stalked across the park, carefully ducking under the natural cover the bushes provided. The enemy rate of fire seemed concentrated on the dwarves, leaving Daniel free to move quickly. Small, round objects crashed through the bushes. Grenades. He dove. Blue-white flames exploded, blinding him temporarily. He shook his head, desperate to get the echoing ringing out of his ears. Whatever magic the dark elves used was potent enough to beat a human down without killing him.

The bark of Fritz's heavy machine gun thundered down the street with unabated fury. White-hot flames spit from the barrel. Daniel resisted the urge to look back, knowing his problems lay before him, not behind. A thought struck, and he fished out of his night vision. The world lit up in hues of red, orange and yellow. Daniel smiled. Goran's little toy wasn't only night vision; it had thermal capabilities as well. He easily spotted his targets.

Instead of firing, Daniel used the thermal glasses to avoid the dark elves. He stood a better chance of flanking them without being seen, provided elves couldn't see in the dark either. It was a necessary risk if he hoped to have the element of surprise. Otherwise….

New sounds drifted over the battlefield. Metal crunching bone. Steel striking steel. A group of dark elves managed to close on the Schneider brothers and engage in hand-to-hand combat. He snarled, knowing the dwarves would make quick work of their enemy. Cut-off screams rose into the night sky. Hot plumes of breath clouded before the combatants. Ropes of blood, so green it reminded Daniel of spring, flew in lazy patterns. Bodies crumpled and broke apart in clouds of ash in the kind of combat humanity hadn't experienced in hundreds of years. Daniel felt sickened by such reckless slaughter.

Whatever else they were, the Schneiders were expert warriors. They approached their work with song and verse, recalling times of old when great armies of dwarves and goblins had clashed on nameless fields. Dwarves were bred for the battlefield, and knife work was what they did best. Angus and Fritz attacked, slashed, parried and stabbed with the cold precision that only comes from a lifetime of training. Daniel almost felt sorry for the dark elves. Almost.

Still crouching, he gained the far wall of bushes and tried to calm his breathing. Nerves and adrenaline were his biggest obstacles tonight. Human bodies didn't dissolve upon death. Daniel thought back to a night in Iraq. He'd lost two men that night, one to a sniper, the other a roadside bomb. Daniel's eyes automatically scanned for suspicious piles of trash or broken street curbs. Enough grenades were being thrown to make him believe the enemy wasn't above acts of terrorism.

Weapon at the ready, eyes sighted through the scope, Daniel edged closer to the corner and poked the cold barrel through. The back end of the Challenger was in view, partially blocking his line of sight. A pair of old bread trucks was parked just beyond. He guessed they'd been used to transport the dark elf commandos here. So where was the driver of the Challenger? Daniel's fingers curled around the pistol grip under the barrel of the grenade launcher. That uneasy feeling increased, leaving him feeling more worried than secure.

A handful of heat signatures ran by, heading towards the sound of the guns. He let them pass. Judging from the raw carnage being dealt on the far side of the park, the dwarves would make short work of them. He didn't know why, but the Challenger drew him closer. He needed to know the driver's identity, to discover the mole and blow this madness wide open. The car and driver became his top priority.

Tinted windows stared back at him, menacing in the orange-tainted night. Thermal vision didn't show much. He figured the car was warded by another sort of magic. A few hours ago, the thought would have been a silly childhood fantasy inked on paper and distributed around the world for the enjoyment of all. Now, he didn't give it a second thought. The box of Carthantos, elves dissolving upon death, magic grenades were proof that the world was a more dangerous and terrible place than he'd ever imagined.

Daniel edged up to the back end of the car, easing up to peer inside. Empty. No driver. No spy. He cursed, trying to figure out what his next move should be. The dwarves were surrounded and in need of assistance. Whatever else they may be, they were fellow soldiers, and Daniel was too professional to abandon his comrades when the shit hit the fan. Tightening his grip, he raised the rifle and moved.

"I wouldn't do that," a menacing voice growled in his right ear.

NINETEEN

Daniel froze. The cold metal pressed harshly against his head threatened to end his life should he make one false move. He tried to swallow, but his mouth was too dry. The idea of rolling right and turning on his attacker briefly passed before he remembered death moved faster than he did. There was no chance of outrunning a bullet, magical or not. Reluctantly, he lowered his rifle to the ground and raised his hands.

"Wise. A lesser man would already be dead."

"What do you want?" Daniel asked defiantly.

A hard shuffle. The barrel pressed harder for a moment. "Morgen wants to see you. Now."

Morgen. All of this had been staged to ensure Daniel had an audience with the dark elf queen. So many lives sacrificed, for what? He failed to understand the inconsiderate whims of petty dictators or royalty. Good men died for nothing more than an opinion. A passing fancy. Latent anger returned. His muscles bristled beneath the form-fitting armor.

"She could have called," he snarled. "No one needed to die tonight."

He sensed the shrug. "Her business is her own. I do not interfere. Get up, slowly."

Daniel obeyed. A dark taint in the voice compelled cooperation. No fool, Daniel recognized the reaching fingers of death.

"Get in the back seat."

Norman Guilt shoved him in and closed the door before getting in the driver's side. Daniel briefly gave thought to jumping out and making a break back to the dwarves. Instinct told him he wouldn't get very far before his captor either caught him or shot him dead in the street. Instead, he buckled his seat belt and waited.

He saw his captor for the first time. A brute of a man with stern, granite-like features, his jaw was made for punching, squared and harsh. His brow was so prominent it made the steel-colored eyes appear small, almost nonexistent. Leather gloves sheathed massive hands. Daniel got the impression he had a barrel stuffed down his jacket, he was so large. But there wasn't an ounce of fat on him. He was all muscle and as dangerous as any other creature Daniel had met this night.

"You didn't show up on my thermal vision," Daniel said.

Guilt said nothing, turning the engine over and driving away. He'd thought there was only one emotion left to him: hatred. Too many of his kind, friends and loves, had been murdered for sport to leave him with anything else. Every elf and dwarf was a wicked creature with a black heart and ill intent.

Early humans were just as bad, taking up hunting the gargoyles for sport and recognition amongst peers. Guilt blinked. He failed to understand how any race could justify the wholesale slaughter of another. Humankind was equally vengeful, but for reasons he failed to comprehend. Their minds were closed, too narrow and inexperienced to truly enjoy the wonders life offered. Now he was stuck minding one who inspired…curiosity.

"Don't speak much, do you?" Daniel pressed. He'd just about had enough.

Guilt passed a menacing glare but kept quiet. He wasn't paid to deliver rousing conversation. He was an assassin, the very best.

"Why all the killing? What does Morgen stand to get out of it? She's wasted so many lives tonight, and it's only nine. Goddamn it, say something. Anything. I don't care what."

Guilt looked at him, deadpan. "You should learn to keep your lips together. They will get you killed."

Daniel snorted. Plenty of things had threatened to kill him in the past, and he always beat the odds. Not much for believing in luck, he focused on the elements within his control, a rapidly shrinking pool of possibilities. He studied his captor more closely. Too solid for an elf. Too emotionless, calculating for a dwarf. Not big enough to be a troll and much too cunning to be a goblin. He ran through the list in his mind. Gnome, dragon, giant. None of them seemed likely. No, this man was something else. Something worse.

He decided to prod a little more. "You're no elf. You don't look like a dwarf."

"Stop talking."

Daniel sneered. "Make me."

Guilt lashed out so fast Daniel barely registered the movement. An iron fist slammed into his temple so hard he blacked out immediately. The Challenger drove on.

The axe blade bit deep, nearly severing the dead elf in half. Angus lowered the mighty weapon. His chest heaved from exertion. It had been far too long since the last time he had been forced to battle so hard. The dark elves died easily, but sheer numbers offered a great fight. The dwarf scanned his surroundings for signs of more.

"I think we got them all," he growled.

Fritz slumped down, blood pouring down his right side. A nasty cut ripped across his left cheek. The black shaft of an arrow pierced a thigh. Burn marks and heavy bruising covered most of his body, aftereffects of the wizard fire that had destroyed their Suburban. His breathing was shallow. Eyes fluttered rapidly.

"That's nice," he managed between gasps.

"Fritz!" Angus rushed to his brother's side. Dismay dug into the grooves and wrinkles of his face as he began looking over the wounds.

His brother pushed weakly against him. "Stop pawing me. You're worse than mother was."

"Mother would crack your fucking head if she saw you like this, you big dummy." Angus shook his head angrily despite being pleased at his brother's defiance. Defiance was a good thing. It meant Fritz still had fight left and that, though his wounds were deep and potentially life threatening, he wasn't about to die. Not yet, at any rate.

"I'm fine. What happened to Daniel?" Fritz asked. "And why does my face hurt so damned much?"

Daniel! Angus grimaced suddenly. He'd forgotten all about the man during the fight. "I don't know. Last I saw him, he was circling around behind the elves. Stay here and don't fall asleep. I'll be right back."

"What about my face?"

Angus charged through the park with the stealth of a rhino marching down a flight of stairs. Grace and guile were pointless at this stage. Battle axe in one hand, short-barreled machine gun in the other, the dwarf covered the park in a matter of moments. There was no sign of Daniel ever having been there. No blood. No shell casings. Not even a turned blade of grass. Worry set in. He'd seen Daniel in action and had no doubts about the human's martial prowess. But none of that seemed to matter since he had entirely disappeared.

Circling out to the street, he hooked right and doubled back to Fritz. The purple Challenger was missing, presumably taking Daniel with it. Angus scowled. Failure mocked him. He wondered what he was going to tell Alvin when the king demanded a progress report. Losing the chosen one minutes after figuring out just what they were supposed to do was an irrevocable black stain on their reputations. The Schneider brothers would be reduced to laughingstocks.

"He's gone. Shit!" Angus said as he crouched down beside Fritz.

"Relax, man. It's not like we don't know where he went."

"What do you mean?"

Fritz chuckled. "Think about it. He went to see Morgen. There's only two players in the game tonight,

Angus. Alvin and Morgen. The rest of us are just in the way. Mom didn't teach you anything, did she? 'Course, that doesn't take into account the obvious spy in Alvin's house."

"We can worry about spies after we find Daniel," Angus said. "You realize there's almost no chance of getting into Morgen's lair now?"

Fritz nodded and groaned. The pain was intensifying. Darkness crowded in around the corners of his vision. "Was never much chance to begin with. Go check the truck and get whatever's salvageable."

"Right."

Angus powered over to the wreckage. Most of the Suburban was slagged down to streams of molten silver metal. There were no wizards registered in North America, so where had the dark elves come up with wizard fire? And in quantity. Other discrepancies bothered him. Dark elves certainly had the numbers, they always had, but they fought worse than goblins most of the time and with piss poor equipment.

The commandos sent to stop him had been armed with the best and had at least a modicum of tactical knowledge. Someone was funding and training the dark elves, but who? Why? It didn't make sense, and that meant he was missing the vital clue to solving the riddle. Something very big was happening right in front of them, and he was blind.

The entire upper half of the vehicle was gone. Angus peered down into what was left. Half of the duffel bag was a burnt husk. Bullets and random goodies lay scattered across the floor. Most of it was unsalvageable. He tossed the bag aside. Ruined weapons clattered uselessly about. But there was more. Hidden beneath the clutter, glowing with power unimaginable, was the box of Carthantos.

His breath quickened as he reached down to snatch it. Things had just become a whole lot more serious for the Schneider brothers.

"Yes?" Alvin said after answering the phone.

"Morgen has captured the human. The dwarves are ambushed. One is wounded, though not badly, but knocking them both out of commission. They shouldn't be a problem for the rest of the night."

"The box?" he asked.

"Unknown. The firefight was fierce. Many dark elves were killed before Guilt managed to complete his task."

Alvin sucked his cheeks in. "The box is the key. Morgen cannot be allowed to get control of it. Not yet."

"I understand."

Hanging up abruptly, the king of the high elves clasped his hands behind his back and began pacing the room. All his carefully wrought plans hinged on possession of the box. Without it, all he'd striven for would end fruitlessly. Alvin lacked the faith necessary to let his agents in the field continue without additional help. He decided to call in a very special favor.

TWENTY

So high up, the annoying orange glow of countless streetlights wasn't so bad. Daniel could actually see stars clearly, brightly. He hadn't seen a clear sky since his time in northern Afghanistan. Disappointing, when he stopped to think of it. Of course, it was no great accomplishment. Anywhere in the world without consistent electricity held the same results. A few towers and high-rises jutted up into the night sky like so many broken teeth, reminding him of a foul mouth eager to devour all it saw. Strange, how everything appeared more sinister since the early revelation.

A quick glance around the room confirmed he'd never been here before. Cases of books, hard bound and gilded with gold filigree, ran from the ceiling to the floor. Marble tile flooring checkered the room. Oak paneling, aged and stained dark, accented the room, giving him the feeling of an old castle. Leather chairs and a chaise were sprinkled about seemingly at random. For the briefest moment, he thought he was back in Alvin's private study, but the view was too spectacular.

Daniel stretched and groaned. His head hurt. The thump had turned into a bump, throbbing and pulsating angrily. He felt like he'd been hit with a sack of quarters. His fingertips gently probed the cheek, jerking away almost immediately. The bruise was huge. He fished his tongue around the inside of his mouth to ensure all of his teeth were still in place. That small consolation didn't do much to assuage his wounded pride.

"My apologies, Daniel. Mr. Guilt has a tendency to strike first, if you take my meaning," a golden female voice soothed from across the room.

"Who in the hell is Mr. Guilt?" he asked.

"Norman Guilt. Perhaps the best special acquisition talent in the western hemisphere. I use him for various odds jobs."

She stepped out of the shadows and stole his breath. Daniel loved his wife, but the woman standing before him was one of the most beautiful he had ever seen. Stark raven hair hung halfway down her back. Her slender shoulders were feminine and fit. The slope of her breasts was enticing, accented by the plunging v of her silk, dark purple blouse. Her cheeks were soft and inviting, lips just plump enough for kissing. He followed the lines of her body down over her hips and to those incredibly toned legs. The grey business skirt was hemmed an inch above her knees. Daniel was awed by the sight, but it was the eyes that piqued his interest. Her eyes were hard, piercing. They'd seen too many bad moments with a decided lack of good. They were cruel and filled with malice.

"Like kidnapping?" he asked.

She smiled, at once warm and malevolent. "A necessary act. Tonight is very important, and I can't afford to take unwarranted chances. Perhaps a drink will cure your aching head?"

It would, but now wasn't the time. "What is he, some kind of hell-bent dwarf who hates his mother?"

She laughed again, the song golden. "He's a gargoyle, one of the few remaining. Worth every dollar I spend on him."

A gargoyle? Try as he might, Daniel couldn't grasp the concept that he'd just been kidnapped and beaten up by a creature that should be carved atop a gothic cathedral. Sensory overload throbbed behind his eyes. Maybe that drink wasn't a bad idea after all.

"You must be Morgen," he stated.

She bowed as graceful as any queen. "Indeed. Morgen Halpern, at your service."

"I've seen you before," he added much too quickly and winced. He sounded like a lovesick high school boy meeting the object of his affection for the first impossible time.

Her grin was infectious. "Of course you have. I've been on more than two hundred magazine covers and numerous fashion campaigns. Don't let the fact that I am the dread queen of the dark elves fool you. There's not much work for a queen these days. You damned humans have seen to that."

"I was coming to see you anyway; why bother kidnapping me?" he asked.

The smile melted into abstract bitterness. "You were coming to kill me. There's a big difference. Mr. Guilt was one insurance policy, nothing more."

"I think I'll have that drink now."

Morgen snapped her fingers, and a wraith materialized from the corner shadows. Cold red eyes glared at Daniel as if remembering. Legless, the immaterial creature floated to the bar overlooking downtown and returned with Daniel's drink.

Daniel accepted it, reluctant to touch such a monster, and wondered if it was one of the pair that had attacked him earlier. Finished, the wraith returned to the shadows and disappeared. Queen and author stared at one another, each trying to determine the best approach.

"I've always enjoyed being here, though membership dues can be a little much. The view is marvelous, especially in late fall at dusk. The combination of colors in the leaves reminds me of…better times, when the world was young. I would stride among the trees for hours, sometimes days without seeing another being. Oh, how I would sing. The trees enjoyed it."

He shifted, suddenly uncomfortable. "What made you change? A life like that doesn't sound so bad. Beats the hustle of the world we live in now."

"War happened. Our race may have grand traditions of society and elevated civilizations, but we are prone to the same wasting diseases as humans. I've become thoroughly convinced that armed conflict is what we were all truly bred for. Why else would so many be led to slaughter in the name of so little?"

He paused. Most of humanity's wars were sparked by petty jealousies or religion. None of the mythic races so much as hinted at believing in a god. That made them more human than his own kind in his eyes. Any sense of moral superiority fizzled. Daniel smirked like a child entrusted with a powerful secret.

Morgen caught the look but maintained her composure. "You think we're no better than you for succumbing to our wants and desires? At times, I might agree, especially concerning my estranged husband. He is as cold-hearted as they come. What did he tell you about me?"

The gentle crackle of an honest wood-burning fireplace played tricks with his mind, making him hear things that weren't true. Daniel took a sip, winced. He hadn't taken a drink straight in a very long time. The scotch burned down his throat, nearly forcing a curse from his lips. Whatever Morgen was, she had good taste in liquor at least.

"He said you were the evil one," he lied.

She laughed dismissively. "Did he? That must make sense to a man of little colors. Very little in the world is as black and white as you would like. No doubt Alvin explained that this was all my doing and that I forced his hand?"

"The conversation might have come up." The last thing he wanted or needed was Morgen knowing exactly what had happened at the Citadel. He still held at least a small measure of power. Every little bit surrendered shoved him closer to being pointless. "I don't understand why you've decided to turn the city upside down because of a lover's spat, though. Seems to me like a little counseling might do you good."

"Counseling? Don't be naïve. I was the most powerful female in the history of the world, at least until humans came along and rewrote history with the story of Eve spreading her sinning legs at creation's dawn."

"Not a big fan of the Bible, I take it?" he pushed.

"God has his uses for each of us. Useless stories don't," she retorted. "I can waste the night trading pointless witticisms, but to what end? You're a single human. There is nothing you can do to stop me from achieving my goal."

"A few hours ago, I was under the impression dark elves were figments of my imagination. Look at me now," he fired back. "Nothing you say makes any difference."

He was rewarded by the flash of crimson in her cheeks. She shifted uncomfortably from one leg to the other and folded her arms across her chest. "A few hours ago, you were irrelevant. You overestimate your importance, Mr. Thomas." Morgen sat in the high back chair opposite him. "I've come too far, lived too long in abject ignorance to be foiled at the last moment by the likes of a failing writer. Give me what I want, and I will consider letting you go home to your wife and lovely children. They really are the future, you know. Humans procreate like insects. It's the only real reason you now dominate the earth."

"Save the scientific diatribe, lady, and leave my family out of this. What do you want from me?" He didn't take kindly to having his family threatened.

She gave him a most disbelieving stare. "Why, my heart."

So that's it. Morgen wanted the box of Carthantos. With it, Alvin would be powerless — or so Daniel had been led to think. Finishing his drink, he said, "You could have taken it at any point since your thug knocked me out."

"I could have, but you don't have it on you," she said calmly. "Where did you leave the box, Daniel?"

"Ask Guilt. Who's to say you're his only employer?"

"You've obviously never heard of the loyalty of gargoyles. He informed me that you did not have the box when he insisted you join us."

Daniel shook his head. "Doesn't mean Alvin's not paying him more. He could be en route to the Citadel right now."

The statue at the base of the winding staircase suddenly came to life, transforming from an armored warrior into Norman Guilt as he should have been. The gargoyle was fearsome to look upon. His skin was steel grey and scaled. Muscles rippled everywhere. His eyes were hollow, empty sockets driving deep into his brain cavity. Long claws stuck out from his elbows. His leathery wings were pinned back lazily. A row of horns curled up over his head. Guilt crouched, akin to classic images of his kind. Daniel had never seen a more terrifying sight, and it showed.

Morgen, satisfied with her carefully engineered display, rose smoothly and said, "Come now, Mr. Guilt. Let us not frighten our guest. His fragile human mind isn't quite adjusted to see you in all of your glorious form."

Guilt growled, low and menacing. "As you wish."

His body began to quiver. Eldritch energies pulsed off his body in sheets of rippling green and blue. A few short seconds later, Norman Guilt was in human guise again. "I do not enjoy being called dishonorable."

"Daniel was merely trying to stall by putting together any feeble scenario he could. I'm sure he meant no harm in it," she smiled. "Did you, Daniel?"

The defiance was gone. He was forced to accept he was in over his head. Nothing made sense, no matter what he tried to rationalize. Gargoyles and dragons. Kings and bitter queens seeking revenge. He was living one of his novels. And in his novels, the good guy wasn't guaranteed to live. In fact, more times than not, one of the main characters died right before the end. Daniel felt his life expectancy start to drop.

"No," he replied. "It's like she said."

Guilt grunted and stalked off to the large bay of windows overlooking the heart of Raleigh, that old longing tugging at what was left of his heart. Morgen let him go. He'd done his part for the moment, though their next move remained to be seen. "My heart, Mr. Thomas. I would like it back."

"I don't have it," he said, realizing he must have either dropped it in the park or left it in the Suburban.

Her eyes hardened. "Of course not. Why would you? Earlier, I mentioned that Mr. Guilt was one of my insurance measures. I didn't want it to come to this, but your stubbornness leaves me little choice."

His head lifted slightly, chin tilted up. Fresh concern assaulted his eyes.

Morgen snapped her fingers, and the flat screen television above the fireplace turned on. Soundless, he was forced to watch as the dark slowly broke to reveal his wife in a very dark room with a handful of candles for light. She was tied at the wrists and ankles. A white rag gagged her, but the look in her eyes said enough. Fresh streams of tears ruined the mask of grime on her cheeks. Her wrists were red, raw from struggling.

"Sara," he whispered and strode towards the television.

Morgen stayed quiet, carefully measuring the man before her. She deliberated telling him the truth, all the while knowing he'd never believe her. *That's the trouble with being labeled the bad guy. No one cares if you speak the truth or not.*

"Let her go now," he demanded weakly.

Typical. "Why would I do that?"

"Damn it, let her go! She's not part of this," he protested. "I can get you the box. Just let her go. Please."

Her head cocked slightly. "I truly think you're a good man, Daniel Thomas, even if you do have a tendency towards writing bullshit. I take no pleasure in any of this sad affair. That being said, you are a cleverly placed obstacle that needs to be removed. I don't want any more blood on my hands than necessary, but I won't hesitate to slit her throat if I think it will get me what I want."

He struggled to keep the wave of tears from bursting loose. "I need time."

"Time is not your ally, I'm afraid. The box must be in my possession before dawn. You have less than ten hours to deliver my heart," she said sternly.

"I need to get back to the park and find the dwarves."

"I should have known Alvin would involve the Schneider brothers," she snorted. "My estranged husband is ever predictable. Mr. Guilt will escort you back to those damnable dwarves and retrieve the box. After that, I will have your wife sent home to you."

He blinked rapidly. "No."

"Pardon me?" she asked, taken back.

"You can have the fucking heart, but you're not calling all of the shots tonight. I've nearly been killed more times tonight than in my entire life. I've seen things that *do not* exist, and, now that I have, I don't think they deserve to. You and your kind are a stain on the world. An unnecessary strain unworthy of the oxygen you steal from us. You want the box? I'll bring it to you, but only after I get Sara back."

She stewed with thoughts of having Guilt rip him to shreds and devour what remained. *The obstinate fool has no idea of the game he's playing at. Perhaps I should just kill the whole family. There'd be fewer questions or chances for complications.* But the queen of the dark elves was not a cold-blooded murderer — liar, cheat, extortionist perhaps, but definitely not a killer. Worse, the more she thought about it, the more she realized that she was in practically a mirrored position.

"Very well," she finally said. "Go get the box and meet Guilt at the Dorton arena on the state fairgrounds campus. You have one hour."

"My wife will be there? Unharmed."

"That depends on whether you succeed or not," Morgen replied.

Daniel exhaled for the first time since seeing the image of his wife being held captive. "Deal. One hour."

"Mr. Guilt will see you out," she said and turned her back on him.

He was getting tired of that. Guilt scuffed closer, wordlessly forcing him towards the door. Daniel stopped, a sudden thought popping up. "What about the princess? Alvin sent me to get her back."

Morgen's shoulders stiffened. "Leave my daughter to me, Mr. Thomas. She is not your concern, no matter what Alvin suggests."

TWENTY-ONE

A light sprinkle started shortly after Daniel arrived at the state fairgrounds. Nothing hard, but enough to irritate him. He didn't mind being wet. That was all part of Army life, but he despised the process of *getting* wet. That slow, or remarkably fast, process where his clothes were soaked and a bone-numbing chill set in was one of the most miserable he could imagine. And that was saying a lot given his past.

He watched the tiny drops bead on the windshield with passive interest. Events continued to develop at a breathtaking pace, forcing him to stop and reconsider his actions. The intrigue of both sides threatened to draw him in too deeply. He got the feeling that this was about more than just a failed relationship and control of the daughter. Dozens of lives lost, kidnappings and threats. Daniel knew he was missing that vital piece to connect it all together.

And now they had his wife. It had taken a great deal of restraint to keep from lashing out at Morgen while she showed him the video. That and a rather nasty gargoyle ready to snap him apart. Elves, high and dark, clearly had no qualms about operating without any moral restraint. The insult of it came from him not wanting the involvement. Ill luck and bad timing had left him at the bottom of a deepening hole with no foreseeable way out.

He'd never questioned what drew him to fantasy. It was a gift. Daniel's natural ability to put words on paper blossomed with barely a spark of imagination. Now those words were turning back on him, forcing him into someone he didn't want to ever be again. Choices. It always came down to choices. Seldom were they worth making, though. Daniel was becoming increasingly aware that his choices were all sour. He still had one advantage. Morgen and Alvin had no idea who he had been, only what he was: a fading fantasy author. They didn't know about his military past or his combat experience. He planned on turning that back on them at some point and showing just how disciplined and trained a U.S. Army combat veteran could be in the face of extreme adversity.

His fingers tapped a random song on the steering wheel. Too many thoughts were colliding in his mind for him to stay in tune. Distracted, he kept looking at the roads, desperate to see headlights coming towards him. Nothing. Night mocked him with its casual indifference. Shadows coalesced into faces, laughing and mocking. They watched him in silent judgment.

One thought in particular disturbed him the most. Xander. The man was certainly exotic and charismatic but if he was as important to their mythology as they all claimed why did he get killed so easily? Something just didn't add up. The dramatic entrance coupled with a heroic last stand left Daniel suspicious. He'd written enough books to know when a character wasn't as simplistic as he seemed. But with Xander out of the picture, save for the favored memories of those he'd encountered this evening, Daniel had no way of knowing for sure. He made a mental note of asking the Schneider's the next time he ran into them.

Daniel replayed the final few moments with Morgen. She was as calculating as they came, devious and starkly transparent. At least from his initial read. That made her dangerous. He decided it was best not to cross her. So when she'd offered him her phone and dialed Angus Schneider's number, there had been no hesitation. Complicating matters was how easily Angus had answered and accepted his tale. The dwarf had agreed to meet him at the fairgrounds with the box of Carthantos. Morgen had insisted on having Guilt travel along, just in case. Daniel wasn't too keen on that part, but his wife was the prize. There was nothing he wouldn't risk for her safety.

The haunting pale glow of headlights turning into the main parking lot quickened his heart. "Finally."

Daniel adjusted the jacket Morgen had insisted he take, claiming it wouldn't suit her needs if he caught a cold in the coming drizzle, and passed Guilt a questioning look. The gargoyle yawned.

"Do I get out or what?" Daniel asked.

Guilt craned his neck. The bones creaked, sounding like breaking rocks grinding together. "Out."

He slammed the door behind him, pulled the collar up around his neck and went to meet the Schneiders. The old bread truck was a poor combination of faded white paint and rust. Thick, black smoke belched from the exhaust, and the air wreathed around it smelled of burnt tires. Clearly, this wasn't the Schneiders. The click of a door opening and shutting drew his attention. He turned to find Guilt standing beside him.

"Your wife is here," the gargoyle stated with too much indifference.

Daniel thought about firing off some witty retort but realized it would fall on deaf ears. Norman Guilt was not a creature prone to being impressed with bravado, false or true. Daniel held his tongue, knowing that sometimes it was what went unsaid that meant the most. He wondered if gargoyles were capable of humor.

Guilt grabbed him tightly by the bicep. "Do not think to pull any tricks. Morgen is more forgiving than I."

"I just want my wife back. You can have the fucking box."

The answer satisfied Guilt. He let go and folded his hands over his waist as the bread truck rumbled to a halt. It backfired once and almost groaned. The vehicle lurched as two massive figures spilled out. Daniel immediately became aggressive. These were Bert and Lou, the same trolls that had assaulted him in his own driveway. And they had Sara.

"You again, eh?" Bert snickered with a deep rumble.

Daniel shrugged in a weak attempt at nonchalance. "We're like reality television. Just can't get rid of us."

Lou cracked his knuckles. The loud snapping echoed across the parking lot. "You need a good poundin'. Boss don't like smart mouths."

"Probably how you got hired," Daniel snapped. "Where's my wife?"

"Where's the box?" Bert growled.

"It's coming."

"No box, no woman."

Daniel felt desperate. "Show me my wife. I want to know she's not harmed."

The trolls exchanged confused looks. Neither was keen on thinking for themselves. Clearly, they hadn't been expecting any difficulties, especially from a man they'd already tried to intimidate. They blinked, scratched their heads and stood with open mouths as they tried to think of something witty to say. Daniel could have sworn he heard Guilt chuckle softly, but the gargoyle remained outwardly stoic.

It started to rain harder. Heavy drops pelted the four men, leaving wet stains on their jackets. The wind picked up just enough to make it miserable, at least for Daniel. None of the others seemed affected. Daniel pulled the jacket tighter yet. He didn't like being cold or wet, and the night only promised to worsen. Perfect weather for foul deeds. The trolls grunted something in their own language, getting heated to the point of arguing. Finally, they turned back to Daniel.

Bert said, "Fine. You can see, but no touch."

"That's good enough for now, but I want her sent over as soon as the Schneider brothers arrive."

Bert and Lou paused at the mention of the dwarves. Neither had been told that bit of information. Their air of superiority melted away under the prospect of facing ancient foes.

"Maybe this ain't such a good idea," Lou hissed much louder than he thought he did.

Bert waved him off. "Quiet, you! We can handle a pair o' dwarves."

"But it's the Schneiders!"

Bert cuffed him on the side of his head. "Get the woman. I heard enough."

The smaller, not that it really mattered, of the trolls ambled to the back of the truck, muttering curses under his breath and rubbing his head.

"Problems?" Daniel asked lightly.

Bert's fisted clenched. "Just keep them dwarves away from us. We don't like dwarves."

"The two are old enemies," Guilt supplied out of sheer boredom. "Sworn to kill each other until there is but one remaining. Best not to interfere."

Daniel said nothing. His mind was already racing through how best to use the information to his advantage when the time came. All it would take was a single spark. The wrath that ensued promised to allow him and Sara an easy, so much as possible, escape into the night and the opportunity to think things through. It might not be enough, but he'd certainly elevate his position between the warring clans.

The burlap sack over her head prevented him from positively identifying her, but he recognized the Tweety Bird t-shirt and her favorite exercise pants. Locks of hair tumbled out from under the sack, lost amidst her muffled cries. Her hands were tied with old bailing twine, and her left sneaker was untied. Daniel felt his throat and cheeks start to burn. No words could have properly expressed his sudden anger. He'd been fighting it since leaving the downtown club, but now, seeing Sara being handled so, he grew furious. *Too bad the fucking gargoyle stripped me of my weapons.*

He lurched forward, barely making it a step before Guilt gripped his shoulder powerfully. "Sara!"

Muffled cries. She struggled, or at least tried to, but Lou was too strong.

"Happy?" Bert sneered.

Daniel struggled with containing his rage. He was outgunned and outmatched for now. Hopefully, the Schneiders were bringing the cavalry. Hopefully. "Relax, Sara. Everything is going to fine. Just trust me."

He'd heard the same too many times in the past, and it always went in one ear and out the other. Did anyone truly believe it was going to be alright when absolutely everything was stacked against them? He highly doubted it, but people still said those calming, magic words. In the movies, that phrase was usually followed by a gunshot to the head or worse. Neither troll seemed to be armed, though at their size they didn't need to be. One of them could have crushed her head like a plum before he had the chance to shout.

Guilt cocked his head. "You are a foolishly optimistic species."

Daniel frowned. "It gives us something to look forward to. How do I know you're not going to double-cross me?"

The gargoyle flashed a quick smile. "You do not. Nor should you. However, Morgen is not one to go back on promises. She gave you her word. That should be good enough, for a human."

"See, there you go with that word again. I'm getting the feeling you are biased, Mr. Guilt," he replied.

"Perhaps."

Another set of headlights blared into the parking lot on high, leaving Daniel with no doubt as to who was driving. The Suburban was remarkably similar to the one the dark elves had slagged earlier, though this one was black. It jerked to a stop a few meters away. Small clouds of dust rolled out from under the tires. Angus jumped out with his perpetual frown. He seemed darker, moodier since the ambush. Daniel immediately noticed the .45 strapped to his left thigh and the angry looking AK-47 on his shoulder.

"What the fuck is going on here?" he demanded and spit.

Guilt released Daniel. "There is no need for ignorance, dwarf."

"We should have finished killing your kind a long time ago, gargoyle. Shouldn't you be shitting on an abandoned rooftop?"

Guilt ignored him, or so it appeared. Daniel found it frustratingly difficult to read the gargoyle accurately. The passenger door opened, and Fritz slipped out. Half of his face was bandaged, and there were painful looking burn marks running down his right arm. The wounds merely served as a catalyst to bring him into the old berserk battle rage. The cold look in his eye suggested terrible things for any caught in the glare.

"Glad to see you made it," Daniel offered.

Angus brushed him off. "Would have been nice to know what happened to you. Instead, you left us hanging out to dry."

"Stones over here didn't think you needed help. He insisted."

Fritz pointed angrily. "Bullshit! You turned your back on us in the middle of the fight. Just like a human."

For once, Daniel had no reply. He could have stayed with them and gotten bogged down with no way out. Instead, he'd seen a chance and taken it. War is a fickle mistress prone to changing whim like the direction of the wind. He'd seen similar scenarios play out in Iraq and was left feeling helpless. There was no rhyme or reason as to who died or how. Bullets went in straight lines. People went off chance. He held no regrets about the current change of events that had brought them all to the state fairgrounds, though they might have turned out much better.

"Did you bring the box?" Guilt asked.

The dwarves were insulted. "Of course we did. Dwarven honor."

"That means nothing to me. Bring out the box."

Rising tension filled the air with dangerous electricity. All it would take was a single spark to set the whole thing ablaze. Angus dug into his jacket pocket and withdrew the box of Carthantos. The trolls leaned back. Daniel sucked in his breath. Only Guilt remained unaffected. Fists clenching and unclenching rapidly, Daniel stepped forward. The box. Sara. Morgen and Alvin. Everything was coming to a head, and only now did he find himself drastically underprepared for it.

The explosion was sudden, unexpected. Bright lights flashed, and everyone went blind.

TWENTY-TWO

Fully armored figures in combat gear rushed in, scores of them looking identical. Midnight black armor covered their bodies from neck to heel. The only spot of color was an oddly placed red band around their right arms. Mirrored visors on their helmets reflected the stunned looks of Daniel and the others. Wicked looking weapons were locked and loaded and aimed at each of them. The *click-click* of marching boots suggested even more troops coming.

Daniel blinked rapidly, trying to get rid of the spots flashing in his eyes. He still couldn't see, and his ears were filled with an intense ringing. The assault was akin to being caught by his first IED. That explosion had left him rattled, robbing his confidence in the process. It had taken a while before he was ready to get back into the fight.

"Everyone on the ground! Hands behind your heads!" an authoritative voice commanded. The sound was muffled by the helmet's speakers. "You as well, gargoyle. We have what we need to handle you."

Daniel obeyed. He thought he could hear the others follow suit. None of that mattered. His one and only concern was getting Sara to safety. The rest could go to hell for all the trouble they'd caused him. The soldiers closed in, wary to remain just far enough away to avoid getting caught by the pair of vengeful dwarves. Whatever else they might be, they were far more experienced and disciplined than the dark elf war parties had been. Daniel became truly worried for the first time tonight.

"So long as no one does anything stupid, we can conclude this affair without any violence," a vaguely familiar voice announced. "There's been enough killing to last all of us for a while. Don't you agree, Daniel?"

He froze, still unable to place the voice. "Who are you? How do you know my name?"

"That is perhaps the dumbest question I've heard in a while, my human friend," the voice replied. "Hasn't it dawned on you that practically everyone in the clans knows your name? I'll let that pass for now. We met earlier tonight, and you did me a great service."

Daniel struggled to think. So much had happened. Then it hit him. It could only be one person. "Xander?"

Emerging through the ranks, he bowed. "None other."

"Xander!" Angus blurted out.

"But you're dead?" Fritz said, confused and irritated.

"No one actually witnessed my death, friends. So I thought it best to play it up, for the time being. Tonight's events are spiraling out of control, and I needed time to think. The war we have all dreaded for so long is about to erupt unless I can get to Princess Gwen in time. Daniel, I would greatly appreciate your continued help."

"My help has nearly gotten me killed too many times," he replied.

"Pussy," Fritz called.

He ignored it. "I just want my wife back. You can have the rest."

Xander glanced at the bound and blindfolded Sara. "Ah, yes. A most regrettable turn of events. All Morgen's doing, you understand? Bert, Lou, how about you be good trolls and let the lady go?"

"Aw, we wasn't going to hurt no one, Xander, honest." Bert wrung his hands nervously. Sweat pooled under his thick chin.

Lou jumped in. "Yeah! We was just supposed to scare 'em a little! Boss's orders."

"Gentlemen, you are no longer employed by your Boss. You work for me now. Problems?"

The trolls looked at each before simultaneously nodding. "Nope. Not so long as we get paid."

"You'll be paid handsomely at sunup," Xander said.

It was enough for the trolls. They released Sara and ambled off to stand behind their newest employer. Work was work, after all. Daniel didn't wait for approval before rushing over to her and embracing her tightly. Tears welled, and she sniffled. Her arms wrapped around his waist. She wasn't so hard as to keep from crying.

"I am so sorry, baby. So sorry. You never should have been brought into this mess," he apologized repeatedly.

Sara pulled away to look up into his eyes. "Daniel, what in the hell is going on? These bastards came barging into the house and demanded I come with them or they'd kill the kids. What choice did I have?"

He hadn't hated anyone in years, but now he found the idea of eradicating all of these races more and more appealing. Elves and dwarves were little different as far as he was concerned. Their ambiguous approach to morality was proof enough of that. Mankind didn't believe in them anyway; what harm could come from wiping them out?

"It's alright now. I'm taking you home. This is over," he replied.

Xander cleared his throat. "Sadly, it's not. You still have work to do tonight, Daniel. The Princess is…"

"Not my problem," Daniel said. "I've done what you asked. I'm sorry about your sister. Ariel was a good woman, but I've had enough. You can play your games without me. Besides, you're all so keen on frowning down on us humans, you don't need me."

"That's where you're wrong. Ariel's death is…hard to swallow, but she understood you for what you truly are."

Daniel shook his head ruefully. "Yeah, what's that?"

"A savior."

Even the dwarves looked surprised.

"Wrong guy. I'm just a struggling author who got involved in the wrong world. All I want to save is right here before me. We're going home, and I'm going to try and forget this whole sad affair."

Xander eased closer, motioning for his guards to lower their weapons, slightly. "Do you really believe Morgen is just going to let you walk away? She's the most powerful woman in our world. People like you can't make clean exits, especially now that you have been shown our deepest secrets."

"I hardly think Alvin and Morgen have been so foolish. Besides, I got the impression neither really cared for me," Daniel replied. "Who are all these soldiers?"

"Acquaintances. They're here to ensure no one overreacts. Mr. Guilt, I think it's about time you winged away."

The gargoyle visibly stiffened, foul eyes blazing in the dark. Rain sizzled as it struck his face and neck. "Morgen was specific. I am to stay with the human."

"And I say your task is complete. Daniel is safe with me now."

"The box?" Guilt asked.

Xander frowned. "The box is not your concern. Morgen's heart belongs to me again, just as it always has."

The gargoyle remained statue still. No emotion registered on his granite-like face. "The box does not belong to you. You have no rightful claim."

Unable to stand it any longer, Sara shouted, "What in the holy fuck is going on here? Princesses? Hearts in a box? Elves? This doesn't make any sense!"

Xander deadpanned her and placed a finger to his lips for silence before resuming his conversation.

"I am engaged to the princess of the high elf clans, gargoyle. I have every authority. Don't make the mistake of thinking me weak, not here. Not now. When the war comes, I wonder whose side you'll be on."

Guilt shrugged, an obnoxious grating sound. "Whichever pays the most. I do not suffer from the moral complexities of your kind."

"All the more reason to bring you to extinction." Xander ignored the assassin, instead looking back at the dwarves. "Angus, Fritz, bring me the heart. We've got much to do before the sun rises and none of it here in this damnable parking lot."

Angus made it a step before Fritz laid a halting hand across his chest. "This doesn't feel right, brother."

"It's Xander. He's never done wrong by us," Angus whispered back.

"Then why the soldiers? Who are they? Not house guards and not part of the army," Fritz spoke low, in his native tongue.

Angus studied the soldiers closely. Their kit and uniforms were unlike any he was aware of in the clans. "Perhaps Alvin's created some new type of commando unit to fight Morgen? The king doesn't take many into confidence."

"Is there a problem?" Xander asked, patience worn thin. "I would like to get my bride back before Morgen kills her. She and I have…unfinished business to attend to this night."

Daniel pulled away from Sara just enough. "Why would she kill her own daughter? That doesn't make any sense."

"Morgen's heart may beat within the box of Carthantos, but she is cruel beyond measure. No blacker soul has lived. Murdering her own flesh and blood would not only keep her in power but also break the deadlock between the clans. Her armies would sweep through Alvin's house in days. Every last one of us would be hunted down, one by one, you included, Daniel. There would be no safety, not in the worlds of men or elves, from her vengeance. Morgen will stop at nothing to gain ultimate control and reunite the clans under her banner."

"Sounds to me like the clans need reconciliation. How much difference would it make who was in charge?" Daniel countered. There was a dangerous element in Xander's voice that left him on edge. He'd heard it many times before, some in his head as his fingers danced across the keyboard and occasionally by men he'd reported to. Every time had ended badly.

"It would make all of the difference in the world, though I wouldn't expect a human to understand. Our kind is nothing like your own."

"Who made it that way? You had enough chances throughout time to live together, in the open and unafraid of potential disparity. Instead, Alvin took you deeper underground, isolating your races from humanity like each was a murderous disease. That's not the kind of leadership I'd follow."

The heir to the high elf throne bristled. "How dare you! The ignorance of your species shines through your words. Regardless, I still have need of you. The danger is far from passed. Only when Morgen is stopped and her heart crushed will you be safe to return to your home and your quaint life daydreaming about us."

He couldn't keep the sneer from lacing his final words. There was clear disdain between human and elf, and for good reason. Daniel was only touching the tip of the problem, and what he saw disturbed him to no end. The elves were hell-bent on gaining revenge for past wrongs. Thankfully, aside from him, they were content with keeping to themselves.

"They say fantasy is dead. Guess I was wrong," Daniel said.

"About what?"

"The notion that elves were heroic figures. That dwarves stayed underground, filthy and drunk, and that dragons burned everything for a little gold. Things are never what they appear, eh, Xander?"

The elf prince glared, clicking his tongue on the roof of his mouth. He had half a mind to plunge his sword into Daniel's heart and be done with it, but that didn't suit his purpose. He needed the human if his plan had any chance of success. War seldom made room for individual choice.

"No, I suppose they aren't. I make no apologies for my kind, as I'm sure you won't for yours. We are what we were intended to be. And what I am is pressed for time. The box can only be opened by a human, as ridiculous as that sounds. That's why I need you, Daniel. Without you, Gwen will die, and the high elf clans will be subsumed by evil."

He should have expected a ploy like that and was slightly embarrassed that he hadn't. How many times had he thrown a similar twist in one of his stories, just to mess things up? Enough that he shouldn't have been fooled. Daniel frowned. He was going to be seriously pissed if he woke up tomorrow and all of this was just a silly dream.

"What's he talking about, Daniel? Who are all of these people?" Sara asked from his shoulder. "I want to go home. The children…"

"Are safe. I have my people watching them to ensure no harm befalls them whilst you are gone," Xander supplied.

Did he just say whilst? "Leave my family out of this, Xander. If you need me, you get only me."

The elf cracked the faintest hint of a smile. "It was never my intent to get them involved in the first place. Purely a cautionary move by Morgen to ensure you behaved. My apologies, Sara; you need not remain her any longer. I will have my driver escort you back to your home."

"I'm not leaving my husband to you madmen," Sara snarled, showing her teeth for the first time.

Daniel smiled.

Xander was taken aback. "But your children? Surely you must…."

"If my children are as safe as you made them out to be, I want to stay with my husband. They might be safe, but I have no doubt that one of you is going to plunge a knife in his back the instant you don't need him anymore."

"Are you sure about this?" Daniel whispered.

Her eyes glimmered fiercely in the headlights. "Absolutely. Don't trust any of these bastards."

Sighing, Daniel gave a curt nod and asked, "Where is she being held?"

Xander returned the nod, that dark twinkle still lurking just behind his eyes. "Morgen is no fool. She will not have Gwen anywhere within the city limits. Isn't that correct, Mr. Guilt?"

The gargoyle shifted uncomfortably. He paused before answering. "You know I will not answer you."

"And you know I have no issue with blowing you into chunks of gravel. Your kind can be helpful as well as deviant. Which side of history do you wish to be remembered on?"

Guilt remained still. He blinked once, shimmered into his true form for a split second. Few bothered to test his loyalties, so few he wasn't sure how to react. The vast majority of the clans frowned upon his species. For one so high ranking to offer him terms was unheard of. Norman Guilt swept his gaze meticulously over each of the major players arrayed around him.

The dwarves bristled with hostility, an emotion they labeled as passion. Violent, but not much of a realistic threat. The giants were already in Xander's pockets but weren't fighters. In fact, neither of them had ever hurt anyone before, a fact they carefully kept quiet to ensure future employment. It was Daniel and his wife that gave Guilt the most trouble. He was a rogue, a wild card capable of bringing both houses down without much trying. But he was much more. Guilt tried to recall if there was any relevant prophesy pertaining to the humans. That left Xander and his soldiers. He got the immediate impression the soldiers were unquestioningly loyal to the elf prince and more than eager to hear their guns bark. He snorted. Xander was as crude a statesman as any politician. The shining star of the clans, light and dark. Whatever he offered would be backed up by Alvin.

Guilt finally nodded. "The princess is not in the city."

Xander smiled at his personal triumph.

Daniel groaned again. Home was becoming a foreign concept. "Where in the hell is she? No one said she'd be in another part of the state."

"Relax, Daniel. Morgen knows what she's doing. Keeping Gwen close by would only invite the wrong kind of attention. My guess is she shipped her off to a secure location the moment she captured her." Xander looked back at Guilt. "Where did Morgen take her, Mr. Guilt?"

Unreadable, the gargoyle gave in. "She is being held at the state zoo."

"Morgen took her all the way to Asheboro? You've got to be kidding me. It'll take two hours to get there!" Daniel protested.

"Sir, we've got incoming," one of soldiers called.

Xander spun. "Details."

"Sixty to seventy on foot. Heavy weapons and closing in from three sides."

Heavy infantry. More of Morgen's killers. Xander gave Guilt a withering look. "What else does Morgen have planned?"

The gargoyle shrugged. "I'm not in her confidence, Xander. I get paid for my services, nothing more."

The elf grimaced, "Captain, deploy your squads accordingly. I don't want any of them getting through the perimeter. Not until I can get the box and Daniel away."

"Hey, what about us, Boss?" Bert grumbled angrily. "We got things to do."

Lou nodded rapidly. "Yeah. We ain't never hurt nobody! You know that. We're just used for muscle. Neither Bert nor I came here to die tonight."

Rolling his eyes, Xander said, "Yes, yes. I meant all of us. Now go take cover. This is about to get nasty."

Fritz pulled one of the largest handheld guns Daniel had ever seen out of the truck and smiled. "Good. It's about time."

TWENTY-THREE

Daniel looked back at Sara for the hundredth time. She was clearly nervous and out of her element but refused to admit it. All the more reason to love her. They'd met shortly after his last tour of duty in Iraq. Not the sort of relationship his parents approved of, but they'd made it work. Loving her was one of the easiest things he'd ever done. That love shone like a beacon now as he looked at her.

Her initial defiance had wilted some under the threat of being caught in the middle of a battle. Plenty of civilians talked a good game about guns and fights, but very few had the stones to back it up. More often than not, the ones who talked the loudest were the first to break and run. He'd had his own doubts at first. Taking the box from Xander had been the hardest thing he'd done thus far. After making the commitment, it had only been a matter of time before old instincts resurfaced and he found himself back in Army mode.

Up until now he really hadn't had anything worth fighting for other than staying alive. He didn't care about the self-induced problems the elves struggled with, didn't care about the box or Morgen's heart. He'd kept going just to get home again. But now, with Sara only a few feet away, he was willing to kill everyone thrown his way. He chuckled quietly. *And there won't even be a body as evidence.*

"Are you sure about this?" he asked again.

She tried to smile. "We don't seem to have much of a choice now, Dan."

"No, we don't. Whatever happens, just stay behind me and keep your head down. Plug your ears if you can, because it's going to get loud once the firing starts."

She nodded. "I will."

"I love you."

Smiling, Daniel adjusted his grip and slipped Goran's night vision on. The dark elves' thermal images immediately registered. He blew out a long, slow breath. There was a lot more than sixty. Luckily, the main body was still far enough out to give him time to think. Not much, but hopefully enough so he didn't get them both killed. The Schneider brothers were closest, entrenched behind a set of concrete barriers. Fritz's machine gun poked out menacingly. The smaller dwarf looked ready to murder an entire division and quite probably could. Daniel didn't know much, but he hadn't seen a more fearsome fighter since becoming embroiled in this nightmare.

Angus yawned and stretched, bored. Extra belts of ammunition lay cluttered at his feet, ready to be fed to his brother. Daniel almost thought he was seeing things when Angus pulled a cigar out of his blouse pocket and shoved it in his mouth. The dwarf, sensing he was being watched, turned and gave Daniel a wink and lit up.

"Here they come," Daniel whispered to Sara.

She nodded, eyes shocked with fear, and plugged her ears as best as she could. He shifted his grip slightly and took aim. The dark elves were almost at the perimeter, and still Xander held the order to fire. His breathing slowed. Daniel took that as a bad sign. He was getting used to being back in the fight. The last time, it had taken him years to let go of that pent up aggression and feeling of godliness. Repercussions were going to have to wait. The enemy was almost on top of them. He exhaled and drew a bead on the nearest target.

Xander rose from cover so suddenly it shocked most of his own troops. He pointed a gleaming sword at the dark elves and bellowed, "Fire!"

The perimeter erupted in a stream of brilliant flashes as each soldier fired simultaneously. Daniel was briefly awed by the precision and timing. Dark elves burst apart in sickening clouds of ash and smoke. So many lives ruined like sand slipping between fingers. Initial shock fading, he pulled the trigger and took aim again. He was rewarded by a puff of smoke and an empty place where the heat signature cooled to nothing. The killing was made easier simply because the bodies vanished. Otherwise, he would already have been heaving his guts behind a dumpster.

Fully half of the first wave was gone, but the dark elves were intent on breaking the lines. Incoming fire started to rake through the defenders. Chunks of concrete blew out of walls. That unwelcome zip-hiss of rounds flashing past his head forced Daniel lower. His rifle cycled on empty, and he dropped the mag. "I'm black!"

Fritz, the devil's own grimace etched into his face, rose and unleashed his own brand of hell. Shell casings tinkled on the ground in a steady stream of tarnished gold. Gunpowder residue clung to air, a haze forming around the brothers. Angus continued puffing on his cigar, the smell almost obnoxious in the midst of the firefight.

"Grenade!" someone shouted.

Men dove for cover.

Blue wizard fire erupted in a knot of Xander's soldiers. Daniel watched, horrified, as three men were incinerated to oblivion. The flash blinded him. Not even Goran's special glasses were strong enough to protect him from a wizard's fury. He couldn't help but feel that the bad guys always got the better weapons. It sounded cliché, especially given the fact that his allies included a rather large, disgruntled dragon.

More explosions rippled through the defense. More men died screaming. Nothing for it, Daniel turned back to the incoming enemy and started looking for the one responsible for the wizard fire. The thermal glasses flickered and went dark without warning. He cursed, throwing them down. Clicking on the red laser sight attached to his rifle, he swept over the enemy. Each time he fired, another died.

It was a horrible waste of life. Seldom had men committed such atrocity without any thought of retribution. Elves and dwarves slaughtered each other with ruthless passion. Daniel felt sickened. Even the worst man deserved better. He fired again. Another dark elf died. A line of rounds stitched across the barrier protecting him. White powder choked his nose, making him cough.

"Daniel!" Sara shrieked.

He spun, automatically worried. What he saw made that worse. Enormous figures were emerging from the shadows on their flank. He'd seen images of such beasts, artist's renderings in the worst possible way. Ogres. Each was heavily armed and armored. Mere bullets wouldn't be able to penetrate their armor. Their steel grey skin was the color of poorly boiled meat left out to spoil. Fangs the size of his fist protruded from their jaws, hot drool clinging to their chins. What they lacked in intelligence, they more than made up for in sheer brutality. Easily ten feet tall, the ogres reminded him of massive boulders rumbling down a mountainside in an avalanche. All muscle, they were pure death.

"Shit," he breathed. "Xander! We've got a problem!"

The elf lord dashed to his side, gleaming sword now useless at his side. Not even elf weapons could cut into those thick hides. His expression sank. Clearly, he hadn't expected Morgen to pull off her gloves this early. "We can't stand that."

"All this time, and you don't have anything capable of dropping them?" Daniel demanded. "You can kill a gargoyle!"

Xander snatched his collar. "These are ogres. They don't transform into human guise. They are next to impossible to kill without significant numbers."

"What are our options?" He fired at a dark elf that popped up uncomfortably close and watched with satisfaction as he dissolved.

"Flee," Xander said flatly. He keyed his headset. "All units, disperse into fire teams and fall back. Meet at the rendezvous point in one hour. Disengage! I repeat, disengage!"

A pair of grenades exploded. More men screamed.

Daniel made the mistake of looking down at Sara. The abject terror in her eyes was nearly too much. He never should have gotten involved. But it was too late for regret. He needed to find the quickest exit and get her to safety. Nothing else mattered. He could live with dying, as odd as that sounded in his head, but would never be able to forgive himself is anything ever happened to her.

"Where's the rendezvous point?" he asked over the roar of increased gunfire.

A line of ten soldiers had come to Xander's side and were pouring as much fire into the ogres as they had. One of the brutes actually grunted and fell but quickly got back up. His chest plate smoldered, and Daniel could just make out the smallest dent with the impact grenade undetonated in it.

"Jordan Lake. The boat docks on the west ramps," Xander shouted. "Get your wife and get out of here now!"

Pulling Sara up, he started to run. A great roar erupted behind them. The ogres had met the defensive line. Bodies and parts flew, trailed by ugly ropes of blood and flesh. The screams were higher than the barking guns. Ogres roared and kept coming, barely slowed by the defenders. Daniel turned, against his better judgment, in time to see an ogre grab the nearest soldier and crush his head to pulp. Brain matter and bone spilled between his fingers before he shook the corpse away and searched for another.

Fresh bile rose and he couldn't keep it down. He vomited on the run. They'd barely made it a quarter of the way back to the cars, and the ogres were closing fast. Daniel knew there was no way they were going to make it in time. Still, he gripped Sara's hand tighter and pushed them both faster. Their breath came in heated plumes of fading vapor. Their muscles ached. Chests rose and fell too rapidly. Death, ever a fell companion, was uncomfortably close.

Norman Guilt appeared suddenly in his gargoyle guise. More beast than mortal, he spread his mighty wings and dropped into a fighting stance. Red eyes blazing, he gave the briefest look to the humans. "Get behind me."

Sara choked down a scream, never having seen anything so gruesome. The idea of being devoured by such a creature was horrifying, and it was all she could do to stay on her feet. The sounds of chaos intensified, steadily marching closer.

"Guilt, we need to leave, now!" Daniel barked.

The gargoyle shook his head stiffly. "The ogres will not stop until you are both dead. I can slow their progress, for a time. Stay behind me and, no matter what, do not go back."

The sonic impact from Guilt taking flight nearly knocked them to the pavement. Sara was drawn towards the battle, a vicious sight that went far beyond her meager imagination. Half of Xander's mysterious soldiers were down, and the ogres kept coming. Most of the dark elves were gone. The Schneider brothers fired off the last of their linked ammunition and displaced back to the vehicles. Even the stubbornness of dwarves knew when to quit. She saw the two trolls, Bert and Lou, cowering behind a rusted green dumpster and found it ridiculous that two people so large were hiding.

Questions suddenly jumped into her mind, leaving her exhausted from the sheer levels of improbability. Daniel saw the pain and confusion clashing behind her light green irises and felt his pride swell. She was a fighter — a fact neither of them had had any reason to know until now. *Funny how life-threatening situations show you who you really are.* He looked back up in time to watch Guilt slam into the nearest ogre. Bone and rock cracked and split.

His wings beat against the formidable ogre, slashing and cutting through the armor. Bone fragments were ripped through muscle and tissue. The ogre growled in pain. Hot blood flooded down his chest. Guilt continued his assault, furiously striking the ogre. He knew, as did the ogre, that surprise was the only way he stood a chance. Razor sharp claws as hard as iron dug and ripped. Needle-like teeth bit chunks of diseased flesh. He moved faster than Daniel's eyes could follow, faster than the beleaguered ogre could stop. In the end, the battle was decidedly uneven. Norman Guilt was fighting for his life and for the lives of others.

Halfway through the battle, Daniel noticed something peculiar. Bodies from dozens of soldiers lay scattered at broken angles. Mangled heaps of flesh in mockery of what once had been. Pools of blood cooled rapidly in the autumn chill. Bodies. Blood. *The soldiers aren't elves! They're human!* He looked around, eager to tell his revelation before realizing how foolish that was. Everyone was trying to either escape with their lives or die like heroes.

"Come on, we're heading to the vehicles," he bent down and told his wife.

Sara, to her credit, merely nodded and followed his lead. They sprinted the rest of the way back to the parking lots around the long, one-story building used for trade and dog shows. Most of the gunfire was subdued, drowned out by the building mass. A handful of cars lay just ahead: their potential freedom. Daniel felt hope for the first time since fleeing Ariel's office. The RV on the far side of the parking lot exploded in a shower of metal, wood and plastic. A rapidly deflating tire bounced twice as high as a man and rolled on past Daniel and Sara. The ogre breaking free of the wreckage hardly slowed down.

Hope died.

TWENTY-FOUR

Shoving Sara behind him, Daniel dropped to a knee and took aim. He figured his only shot was at the face. Iron hide or no, nothing wanted to catch a storm of lead to the face. Flashes burst from the muzzle as he fired on full automatic. The ogre threw up an arm to keep more rounds from striking. The first two, purely incidentally, took him in the right eye. The organ exploded outward in a shower of black blood. Howling in pain, the ogre staggered, nearly dropping before rage took control.

His one good eye focused on Daniel. Knowing he was dead, Daniel emptied his magazine into the stunned ogre's face. The ogre charged. Thundering footsteps shook the ground. A pair of crows, come to investigate the commotion, burst into flight from nearby power lines. Daniel fumbled for another magazine, but his pouches were empty. Nothing left, he tossed the weapon to the ground and drew the boot knife Angus had tossed him right before the dark elves had attacked.

A dark blur sped across the parking lot and crashed into the advancing ogre. Guilt. The gargoyle struck at the neck, hacking, clawing and biting until he split the inch-thick outer skin and proceeded to sever the spinal column. The ogre gave a dumbfounded gurgle before falling to his knees. His remaining eye rolled back in his head. Paralyzed and dying, the ogre collapsed in a mountain of useless flesh. Guilt didn't stop until he managed to tear the head free and fling it away.

Sara threw up violently.

"Hey, everyone else is leaving!" Angus shouted to his brother.

Fritz did his best to ignore him. Desires burning too hotly to quench compelled him to continue fighting. He wanted — no, needed — revenge for his wounds sustained earlier in the Suburban. No amount of dark elf deaths was enough to satisfy the loosed berserker in him. He laughed merrily as he continued to gun down enemy elves. Angus briefly considered slamming the metal pipe at his feet into the back of his brother's head but abandoned it just as quickly. *Probably only crack the pipe, the daft bastard.*

"Fritz! We gotta move before those damned ogres close in!" he bellowed.

Stunned, Fritz swung his machine gun towards the melee slowly dying on the right flank. Very few of Xander's elite soldiers were still on their feet, compared to all of the ogres. Several suffered from various minor injuries, but only one had fallen. This battle was already over. All that remained were the dying. Morgen's forces controlled the field, and ogres were notorious for not taking prisoners. Not even the berserker in him was ready to face those sorts of odds. He squeezed off a few more bursts, shredding clumps of dark elves, and was rewarded by their disappearance.

Very few dark elves remained, and most of those were cowering or heading back towards the tree line on the far side of chain-link fence. He'd done his part. Facing a squad of ogres wasn't in his best interests. Reluctantly, he nodded and looped the sling over his free shoulder. "Let's go. I don't want to get into that scrape."

The dwarves picked up and headed back towards their vehicle. Angus swept his gaze over the battlefield one final time. What had seemed like a fairly simple exchange had quickly degenerated into a senseless scrum where only the meanest were going to survive. The scene reminded him of ancient battles now lost to the dust-covered pages of history, fond memories of standing triumphant on his own battlefield when the sun set. Angus sighed and decided this was one battlefield he didn't mind abandoning.

"Hey! Them dwarves are leaving, Bert!" Lou said in a panic-laced strain.

Bert stared after them, amused and amazed to watch them tuck their tails and run like whipped dogs. Older by a few years and more than a little experienced, he was expected to take care of his brother. Even promised their Ma on her deathbed he'd do right. Bert looked at the unleashed hell and knew he'd failed. "This ain't what I promised Mama, Lou. Real sorry 'bout this."

Lou eyed him queerly. "What do you mean? Ma's been dead for a long time."

Bert slapped him on the side of his head. "Ya dumb bastard! I'm tryin' to make a point!"

"Best get on with it. Looks like them ogres is coming all mean and ready to kill," Lou said, swallowing hard.

"What should we do?"

He shrugged. "Dunno. What do you think?"

"I wanna run, but Xander ain't said nothing about splitting," Bert growled. Real fear choked him. He didn't like violence, and this was about as close to it as he could imagine.

"Xander don't give a hoot if we live or die. I say we run like them dwarves."

Bert agreed. Running was their best and perhaps only shot at surviving. Trolls and ogres being distant cousins, neither relished doing battle with the other. These ogres had a particular advantage. They were armed and ready for murder. Xander might be employing the trolls, but he sure wasn't setting them up for success. "Let's run. Get back to the van and home."

The trolls burst out from behind their protective dumpsters and ran as fast as they could, which wasn't very. Brute strength and unending endurance were their skills, not speed or agility. Not bothering to look behind, Lou and Bert concentrated on their bread truck, nothing else.

Lou grunted suddenly and pitched forward. Blood fountained from his chest, followed closely by the folded metal spear point. Bert skidded to a halt and stared down at his wounded brother. Lips already turning blue, the smaller troll rolled to a side. His mouth was slack. His eyes glazed, unfocused. Kneeling, Bert clutched his brother tightly to his chest, cradling him gently. The feeling of utter helplessness paralyzed him. Blood continued to pump out much too rapidly. Lou's features took on a pale cast.

"S'rry, Bert," he said, and then he died.

Lou's body dissolved to ash in his hands, leaving the older troll weeping uncontrollably. Angered, Bert clenched his fists. The last remnants of his brother slipped between his fingers. He bared his teeth and bellowed a nightmarish howl. Old hatreds and forgotten feelings of immense power resurfaced, and he felt strong again. He rose slowly, picking up the very same spear that had murdered his brother.

Bert saw the killer leering down at them. The ogre was obviously pleased with the ease with which he had killed the troll. Hot breath steamed from his mouth and nostrils. He flexed his massive upper body. The muscles of his broad chest rippled, bulging the form-fitting armor. Prepared for a true challenge, the ogre dropped down into a fighting stance and beckoned Bert on.

Ogre and troll collided in a terrific thunderclap. Bert immediately began hammering his opponent, his brother's murderer. Fists pounded into the granite-like flesh. Each blow was capable of crushing a normal man. Bert attacked like a madman. He watched his brother die a thousand times. The ogre, slightly taken off guard by the intensity of the assault, reeled back.

"You killed my brother!" Bert roared, and centuries of suppressed anger suddenly released.

Grunting from heavy blows to his stomach, the ogre managed to block the next swing and countered with an uppercut. Bert's head snapped back, bits of teeth and blood spewing out. The ogre lurched forward and tackled him to the ground, never stopping his attack. He delivered just as much punishment as he took, but neither could continue at such a pace. Even ogres had limitations.

Bert managed to bring his knee up between them and kick out, forcing enough space to hammer the ogre in the sternum. A rush of air woofed out, and the ogre buckled. Bert's right fist struck him in the temple, bursting the eardrum. Howling in a pathetic combination of pain and fury, the ogre rocked back on his knees and clutched at his ruptured ear. Bert kicked, catching him in the groin. Finally able to get free, the troll slowly pulled himself back to his feet and attacked.

Every blow that struck brought a trickle of blood from the ogre's battered face. The normally grey skin was already turning purple and black from bruises. Bert hit harder. Teeth chipped and shattered. The nose exploded with a violent spray of mucus and blood. Cartilage burst into thousands of shards. Realizing he had lost, the ogre scrambled to get away, but Bert was too fast — too spiteful.

A giant foot crushed ribs as he kicked the ogre in the middle of the chest. He leapt up, as high as a man is tall, and thundered down on top of the beleaguered ogre. A loud snap echoed above the sound of withering gunfire. Bert shattered the collarbone and punched hard in the throat three times, pulverizing the trachea. The ogre shoved Bert away and wrapped both hands around his own neck, desperate for oxygen.

Suddenly ashamed, Bert stumbled back a handful of steps and watched in horror as his brother's killer slowly asphyxiated. Tears reluctantly swelled. His eyes felt raw, irritated. The ogre fell back and died with a strangled rattle. The body burst apart in ashes. Bert had won, but at a cost he wasn't sure he wanted to live with.

"Lou," he whispered.

"Get back to the trucks!"

Bert sank to his knees amidst what remained of his brother. His battle was finished.

Xander picked himself up, the freshly broken rib digging painfully into his side. Blood trickled from his mouth and nose. The battle was quickly deteriorating in Morgen's favor. Most of his soldiers were dead or wounded enough to be combat ineffective. Daniel and the gargoyle had already fled. The dwarves, while excellent fighters, were by no means heroes and had displaced. Bert and Lou were his only reliable backups, and even that was iffy. He had no love for trolls but felt his heart ache as Lou crumbled to dust in his brother's hands.

Drawing his sword, Xander rose to meet the remaining ogres. The blade glinted sharply in the rain-choked night. Mists stretched out from distant corners, clinging to his ankles. He snarled and brought the sword to the high guard. Made from metals not of this earth, the sword had been a family heirloom for centuries. Its history was as great as many of the forgotten elven heroes. And now Xander was the wielder.

The blade felt light despite his waning strength. Sweat and no small amount of blood stained his black clothes. A nasty cut under his right eye promised infection. His muscles ached. His body was sore. Too many decades had passed since last he'd picked up the sword and hove through enemy ranks like a blind instrument of justice. Snarling, he scanned from left to right.

Only a handful of ogres remained, but those were more than enough to rip him to pieces before death's merciful embrace smothered him. For all their strength, ogres had one exploitable weakness. Their eyesight was next to blind. Xander charged, ducking under a stunned ogre and swiping his blade across the thin skin of the throat. Blood fountained in a visceral display, wetting his hands and face. The ogre screamed and knew it was dead. Its hand swept down in vain attempt at swatting the pesky elf away. Xander was already gone.

Other ogres jerked up at the sound of their comrade dying. The biggest bull roared, a deep, resonating sound that shattered windows a mile away. As one, they charged. Xander danced among them, swinging and dipping beneath furious swipes. His heart pounded. Adrenalin and stress formed a lethal combination, pushing him harder, faster. He was the champion of the high elves. Very few on earth could match his ferocity and skill in battle. The ogres quickly realized this and fell back, if slightly, to regain the tactical advantage.

For all the fervor surrounding his status as champion, Xander knew he was at the limits of his strength. It was time to go. Slipping between a pair of generators, he ran as quick and silent as only an elf could. The ogres milled aimlessly for a moment. Their target had disappeared, leaving them with only the ghosts of what remained of the human soldiers trying to flee. Not a one of the ogres bothered with pursuit. Humans weren't the targets. Well, leastwise not these humans. Morgen specifically wanted Daniel and Sara. Everyone else was left to their discretion.

Xander clung to the shadows, only bothering to sheath his sword after realizing the ogres weren't chasing. Circling around, he made it back to where Bert sat weeping. Large piles of ash, once his brother, lay scattered around the troll. His great shoulders jerked with uncontrollable sobs. His life had changed in the span of a moment, for that was all it had taken for the ogre to murder Lou.

"Bert, it's time to go," Xander whispered, suddenly reluctant to intervene. He, too, had known the pain of ultimate loss, and it continued to gnaw upon his heart relentlessly.

Bert looked up. Tears streaked down his face, and his eyes were red and sore. "I ain't leaving him. Ma wouldn't be proud."

Curse him and his loyalties. Can't he see his brother isn't coming back? "Listen to me. There are about ten ogres searching the grounds for us. Not even my skill and your rage combined are enough to win against those odds. We need to leave, to link up with Daniel and the others at Jordan Lake."

Bert shook his boulder-shaped head. "You go. I ain't leaving."

"Goddamn it, Bert. This isn't the time. Your brother is gone. Nothing you do is going to bring him back, and sitting here will only get you killed. Come with me, and I promise you the opportunity for revenge. Dying now would be pointless."

He wiped his nose on a torn sleeve. "You sayin' I can kill these bastards for what they done to Lou?"

"Yes."

That single word was all it took to get the seven-foot tall troll up and moving. He was decidedly quiet as he crept away from the battlefield, a feat Xander was both amazed and concerned over. Trolls were formidable enough, but knowing they had the ability to sneak up on you made them all the more dangerous.

Together, the pair managed to make it to Bert's bread truck. Xander winced, but it was the only vehicle capable of carrying the troll. He gestured for Bert to get in and start the engine before jumping in the passenger seat. A foul, intense smell immediately slapped Xander in the nose, producing a harsh gag. He looked over the random piles of garbage, mostly old Hardees wrappers and Miller Lite cans. The back of the van, however, was interestingly clean. A pair of luxurious leather recliners were bolted in against one wall, and a large flat-screen television hung opposite. The back doors were welded shut and had a small shelf containing various movies and an occasional book. He hadn't known that trolls could read. A stack of old comic books sat on the dashboard and in the middle console. Best of all was the Boba Fett bobble head glued to the dashboard.

The engine, specially modified for speed and power, roared to life, and the mismatched pair headed for the exit. Ogres roared in response and gave chase, but even their seemingly endless reserves of strength weren't enough to catch the truck. Xander and Bert were the last two to escape the battle of the fairgrounds. That fact gave the elf no peace of mind. It was all for naught if none of the others made it to the lake. He needed them if he had any chance of rescuing Gwen before dawn.

Cassandra stepped around a pile of shell casings and frowned. She hadn't been expecting human involvement on such a massive level. Holes pockmarked the parking lot, reminding her of the ruined ground after a heavy meteor strike. The surrounding damage was impressive considering the battle had lasted for less than a half hour. Her blood quickened with the thought of fighting again. She longed to test her steel against the greatest, just like in the warrior circles of old. Once, she had been a grand swordsman. Once. Now nothing more than dust on the shelf. Wars of glory and trophies were a thing of memory. Alvin deemed them barbaric and did his best to expunge the heroism from their deeds. She seethed at the thought of being forgotten. What worse death could a warrior suffer?

Closing her eyes, Cassandra titled her head back and inhaled deeply. The forged smells of cordite and sulfur danced in her nostrils in a heady bouquet. Battles were meant to be experienced. Enjoyed. This was much less, skulking in shadows and keeping away from human interferences. She was insulted. Lesser men celebrated greater deaths.

She carefully stepped over tiny rivers of drying blood. How long had it been since she'd last seen real blood? The question had no answer. The gravest insult was that her kind simply disappeared upon death. No bodies, no mess. Death became less glorious and stifled. Oh, how she longed for the days when they had held funerals, huge burning pyres stretching up to the skies in tribute to bravery. Now, there was nothingness, a vast blackness lacking remembrance and song.

This, however, wasn't the glory she sought. Too many of her kind had been killed here tonight but it was far worse than that. Human bodies littered the engagement area. Humans who shouldn't have been present. She stared down at the bloodstained uniforms and frowned. Rapid Response

Task Force, the RRTF, a clandestine part of the federal government who knew of the elves' existence. Xander had taken the game to a new level by involving the government's special killers.

After searching everywhere, she finally found what she was looking for. A pair of mangled boots stuck out, just enough to be spotted, from a rusted brown dumpster. She bent down and pulled the body out. Dead but still warm, it was enough to work with. Cassandra produced a slender vial of purple liquid and poured it down the corpse's throat. The body awakened, kicking violently with spasms. Lifeless eyes snapped open, and a strangled gasp passed his lips.

"What happened here? Where has Xander gone?" she asked, leaning close.

Those empty eyes shifted to her, and the corpse began to speak.

TWENTY-FIVE

Mile markers sped past, bright green blurs in an otherwise dark landscape. The car was deathly silent. No radio or conversation filled the cabin. Remarkable, considering the amount of questions Daniel knew Sara must be wrestling with. He glanced over to his wife and smiled. She was much tougher than her five-foot-one frame suggested, but then again he'd already known that. It was one of the main reasons he remained attracted to her. She was unlike any woman he'd ever met. Intense pride filled his heart and gave him strength.

Norman Guilt, on the other hand, was as stoic and immovable as his species implied. Daniel remembered the old stories about gargoyles, the silent stone protectors of church and cathedral. Much like the Jewish Golem, they watched and waited for wrong doers and evil. *How many buildings have I passed and ignored these grotesque statues, never knowing they were alive and watching back*?

Guilt hadn't spoken since he'd pulled his body from the ruined flesh of the ogre. His own form was broken and bleeding. Haunting echoes of past lifetimes twinkled just behind his eyes. What dark visions tormented him remained personal. Guilt felt pain the same as any other; he was just reluctant to show it. Gargoyles were private creatures, not prone to divulging more than necessary.

He briefly looked up to the rearview mirror as he guided the car down the off-ramp onto Highway 64 west. No one seemed to be following. His eyes drifted to the pair of humans in the backseat. Odd that he felt emotion for them. Hired to ensure Daniel followed instructions and didn't expose their dark secrets, Guilt wasn't supposed to feel anything. He had a job to do, nothing more. He was a soldier, a shadow figure best left to imagination and wonder. But the battle at the fairgrounds had shown him another facet of himself previously unknown.

Norman Guilt found passion deep within his granite heart. These two weak humans were the key to life or death for a great many beings and didn't even know it. Daniel had stood up to many difficult tasks tonight, so many that most never experienced the sensation. He'd stood up to Alvin and Morgen and refused to be cowed. The sheer gall of it left Guilt with budding admiration. It was enough to compel a level of loyalty. Guilt decided to see Daniel through to the end of the night.

"Are you alright?" Daniel asked Sara softly.

The wild deer in the headlights look subsided, if only just. "I don't know."

He nodded and pulled her close. The smell of her hair encouraged him, gave him strength when all else faded. "I feel the same. Believe me; this is almost too much for me to understand."

"Almost?" Sara asked, a hint of mirth dancing to her tone.

He shrugged. "I write about this kind of stuff, remember?"

"Writing and doing are two entirely different things, Daniel. We shouldn't be here. None of this should exist."

He agreed, but there was no point in voicing it. "I felt the same earlier, but, um, things have changed my mind. Elves and dwarves. Imagine it, Sara. I have been surrounded by creatures I thought I was only making up. I've talked with a dragon and was armed by a giant. The king of the high elves entrusted me with the task of getting his daughter back from the queen of the dark elves. I met a cab driver named Mort who is a gnome. Nothing I've seen or done makes sense, but it feels…well, it feels right. I can't explain it. God knows I want to."

She gripped his forearm. "Sometimes it doesn't matter what we want. I realize that I never believed in fairies and whatnot but I'm in the middle of a fairy tale now."

"Hold on. I don't write about fairies. That's ridiculous. There's nothing glamorous about little bird-sized people floating around sprinkling LSD," he defended. "I wrote about wars and epic quests. Never thought I'd be living one myself."

"Fate rarely takes our preferences into account when it calls upon us," Guilt said unexpectedly from the front seat.

Daniel had nearly forgotten about the gargoyle. "I'm finding that out. Does this sudden explosion of conversation mean you've had a change of heart?"

Guilt fell silent and continued driving.

Daniel chuckled softly. "Guess not. Sara, I'd feel more comfortable if you were home with the kids. What I'm about to do isn't going to be safe."

"We've had this discussion, and you know my answer. Besides," she added smugly, "you've been out of uniform for too long. Look at all that extra weight you're carrying around your waist."

"What is that supposed to mean?" he asked, sucking in his stomach.

"Just saying, you're not as spry as you used to be," she chided. "You need all the help you can get."

"As if a pair of disgruntled dwarves, a gargoyle, and a host of angry elves aren't enough," he snorted. "There's no changing your mind?"

"How long have you known me?" she replied.

He nodded, resigned to having his wife and companion at his side for the duration of this adventure. The idea didn't sit well. The very thought of losing her to the insanity unfolding around them sickened him. She deserved better, and he didn't know how to deliver. So far, nothing he had done had worked. Every additional action sucked her deeper into the mysterious world of the elves. Worse, she appeared to be enjoying it. *How strange*, he mused, *that she comes to enjoy what I have spent the last ten years writing about only through living it. Might make for a hell of an inflated readership if I could only get it out in print.*

Cutting through the sleepy town of Apex, Guilt drove on. Signs for Jordan Lake sprang up. They were almost at their destination, though far from final. Daniel hadn't been out this way in a while, not since his oldest son had insisted on going camping a few years back. Years since his time in the Army, and he still didn't enjoy sleeping on the cold ground with naught but a sleeping bag. Camping was meant for civilians who'd never had to enjoy the pleasures of field training exercises.

The constant orange drone of city lights faded to darkness, leaving them alone with nothing but the headlights and a hint of moon. Daniel took small comfort in the feeling of being alone. He preferred sitting in his favorite chair writing to being in a crowd. People and traffic made him nervous. Thank you, Operation Iraqi Freedom. The first finger of the lake came into view. Thin fabrics of mist hovered over the calm waters.

Another set of headlights broke the plain, miles in the distance. Daniel hoped it was the Schneiders. No one else enthused him. Xander's sudden appearance had left him more than a little dubious. The elf champion was supposedly dead. Perhaps Alvin had decided he couldn't trust Daniel and kept secrets. Unfortunately, secrets had a way of coming out at the most inopportune moments, and with drastic consequences.

"We are here," Guilt said, pulling off onto a dirt road.

Shutting the car off, Guilt flexed his sore hands on the steering wheel before exiting to stand watch at the edge of the road. The hoot of a great horned owl echoed across the water, reminding him of simpler times. The humans continued to perplex him.

Stepping out of the car, Guilt stretched, wishing he could expose his true form. Hiding behind the guise of humanity sickened him. He longed to be free again, to feel the wind caressing his face from atop the tallest tower, the breath of air over his wings as he soared across the skies. All Morgen offered were chains. Unmitigated sadness clung to him instead. The victim of depression too powerful for any human to understand, Norman Guilt stood guard and waited.

"Can we trust him?" Sara asked. She cast her gaze on the gargoyle.

Daniel wanted to laugh, finding the idea ridiculous. "Can we trust any of them? So far, the only one I enjoyed being around was Mort." He paused. "Sara, do me a favor. No matter what happens, don't trust Xander."

"Why?"

He frowned, not fully understanding the urge to ask the most pointless question in the middle of a conversation. "I thought he was dead. There was no possible way he could have survived the fight down in Ariel's office. We're being played for fools, babe. I'm beginning to think these elves are the real problem."

"This would be easier if I had a gun," she said.

He'd nearly forgotten insisting she learn how to shoot when they first started dating. She'd overcome her initial fears and now rivaled him in marksmanship. Almost. He decided it was time for both of them to get armed. Something bad was looming just out of view. He felt it and didn't relish the thought of jumping into the fight blind. Together, they got out and went to Guilt.

"We need weapons," Daniel said.

Guilt slowly craned his head, reluctant to take his eyes away from the approaching headlights. "There are some in the trunk, though the dwarves are bound to have a better selection."

Agreeing, Daniel popped the trunk and looked inside. Guilt was right. There wasn't much to choose from but enough to keep him and Sara alive for a while yet: random handguns and a double-barrel shotgun with a handful of loose rounds. Not that the dearth was surprising after what he'd witnessed back at the fairgrounds. The gargoyle was fiercer than any of the other races he'd encountered thus far.

He took a Sig Sauer 9 mm for himself and the shotgun for Sara and went back to Guilt. "Any idea who they are?"

The gargoyle shook his head. "They are still too far away. No scent carries on the wind, though I feel they are friends, for what that is worth."

"Shouldn't we get ready just in case?" Sara asked.

"Good idea. We don't need to get caught with our pants down," Daniel answered and handed over the shotgun.

She gave the heavy weapon in her hands a withering look. "Seriously? I want the nine."

"I shoot better," he said with a smile.

She wanted to debate the fact, but time and prudence were against them. Instead, she loaded her gun and dropped behind the car for cover. Daniel, wry grin on his face, locked and loaded the pistol and took up position at the back of the car.

"I never thought I'd be in a firefight with my wife," he commented. *Then again, I never thought I'd be in another firefight.*

"Just keep me alive," she whispered. Her heart wanted to say more, but the words wouldn't form. She finally recognized fear, and it numbed her to the bone.

Shivering suddenly from chill, Sara struggled to keep her knees from knocking. She wasn't a soldier. She lacked training and doctrinal tactics. She was the furthest thing from being an armed combatant, thrust into a spotlight she was unprepared for. The reluctance of her husband to talk about his wartime experiences started to make sense. She'd begged him endlessly at the beginning, all the while claiming not wanting to know. Now those fears and secret desires for forbidden knowledge threatened to consume her.

"Promise," he whispered back and took aim.

The car pulled up a non-threatening distance away and shut off. Hands came out first, empty and unassuming once the front doors opened. The rest of the Schneiders followed slowly. Neither particularly wanted to get killed by friendly fire this deep into the mission. Granted, a mission neither wanted to continue.

Guilt turned back to Daniel. "It appears your dwarves remain alive."

"I guess so," Daniel said and clicked the pistol back on safe. "Guilt, I need to know something before we continue."

Guilt blinked once.

"Whose side are you on?"

The gargoyle inhaled slowly. He'd been expecting such a question and, truthfully, had no idea how to answer. Morgen's promise of jewels and heavy salary kept him employed, and he'd amassed a great fortune through the decades. Hardly a dime was spent on more than normal day-to-day expenses. Norman Guilt was a survivor. He did so by being faster, smarter, stronger than those who would hunt him. Wealth was but an anchor weighing him down, chaining him to one place and one faction.

He took in Daniel again, slowly consuming every minor detail. The human continued to show great resilience against every obstacle thrown in his path. Many an elf would have given up and returned to their roost by now. There was an almost magical quality to Daniel that defied conventional wisdom. Humans weren't known for their ability to adapt well to uncomfortable situations. Every encounter throughout the past had ended with pain and bloodshed in the name of righteousness or misunderstanding. Confusingly, Daniel represented something else, something greater.

When he spoke, it came as a shock to them both. "I will ensure you remain safe for the duration of this quest. Morgen wishes you dead, as, I am sure, does Alvin. Elves do not take kindly to others interfering in their business. Perhaps your woman would be safer...elsewhere."

"You tell her that," Daniel snorted.

Not pretending to understand, Guilt turned back to the dwarves. He felt as if he'd explained enough. The less he said, the better off the world was. Gargoyles much preferred the cold, forgotten rooftops during a winter storm. They'd made the mistake of socializing once and never recovered.

"Don't shoot! It's us," Angus said. He gently chewed the tip of another cigar, swishing it to the opposite corner of his mouth much like Clint Eastwood in *The Good, the Bad, and the Ugly*.

Daniel nodded. "Angus. Fritz."

The animosity Fritz felt when they'd first met had returned. Time thinking inspired a deeper look into the way Daniel abandoned the brothers downtown. The dwarf didn't like being played and was starting to view Daniel as part of the problem. Angus, at least, appeared unaffected, leaving Daniel wishing his brother had the same quality.

"Daniel. Anyone else arrive?" The question was pointless considering theirs was only the second car, and none of the big players were around. Dwarven sight at night was impeccable and above compare, a byproduct of working long hours in the gloom of mines and caves but sometimes it was just plain difficult to accept harsh realities. Angus' eyes combed the nearby tree line and shore.

"Just you," Daniel replied. He studied the dwarf, wondering why they had settled on small talk instead of planning their next move. Daniel was inclined to act like Guilt. The less talk, the better, especially when more than one of those involved bore a grudge.

Angus offered a curt nod. "Think Xander made it?"

"I thought he was already dead. It seems like good old Alvin is playing a few cards close to the chest," Daniel replied more tersely than intended.

An uninterested shrug. "Alvin's the king of the high elves. How else would he play this? Would you do any different if your daughter was taken?"

"Yes, actually, I would. Morgen kidnapped my wife and brought her into the middle of all this shit," he snapped. "I haven't kept secrets or held anything back. And speaking of secrets, do you still have the box?"

Angus pulled the black box from a pocket and tossed it to him. "Have it. The damned thing is nothing but trouble. I don't mind dying, but not for her heart."

The beating rhythm of the heart felt oddly comforting. Relief eased his nerves. He couldn't be sure why, but the box felt like it belonged in his hands. And that was a dangerous thought. He controlled the destiny of another life. All he needed to do was keep it away from Morgen until dawn. That would effectively end any scheme she might be sitting on. Xander and the others could go find the princess on their own. As good as the idea felt, Daniel knew he could never follow through. He had given his word and liked to think he lived with a sense of honor. Besides, killing Morgen solved nothing and would only raise the price on his head. He very much wanted to be alive after the dawn.

"So what's our next move? We can't wait here all night for Xander, useful as he might be in a fight."

Fritz answered much too quickly. "We wait for Xander. This is his show. His girlfriend. We wait."

"Asheboro is over an hour away, and that's without getting pulled over by Barney Fife. We need to move now. They can follow." *If he made it away from those damned ogres. I would have sworn nothing so malevolent could exist.* "Every minute we waste here gets us closer to dawn and whatever plan Morgen is trying to hatch. Xander knows where the princess is being held, correct?"

Guilt nodded. He folded his arms across his chest and moved slightly to the right, partially blocking the path between Daniel and the dwarves. His clothes were torn and mostly in shreds. The primal urge to devolve into his original form beckoned ever stronger. Already, his skin took on the pale granite color of a statue. He seemed bulkier, more solid.

"I say we leave a message here and move out. Morgen will either know we escaped her trap at the fairgrounds or suspect we've all been killed. Either way, that doesn't give us much time before she heads to the zoo," Daniel insisted. "It's eleven now. We can be there just past midnight. That gives us seven hours to find the princess and stop Morgen."

Angus pulled the mangled cigar butt from his mouth and gave it a quick glance before tossing it down and getting a fresh stick. "What does it matter to you? Until tonight, we were nothing but figments of your imagination. What have any of us done to gain your trust and allegiance?"

Daniel opened and closed his mouth. Caught off guard, he struggled to find the right answer. "I don't think it really does matter, Angus. I could have turned around and gone home a dozen times, and, now that I have Sara back, I have no reason to stick around any longer. But the idea of an innocent girl being held against her will, even if it is by her own mother, and threatened with death or worse just doesn't sit right with me. My father used to say that a man wasn't any good unless he did something to try and make the world a better place. I guess this is my turn."

The answer seemed to satisfy the war-like dwarves. Even Guilt noted a stirring in his heart. He couldn't remember the last time a leader had inspired him. Reluctant as Daniel was, there was simply no denying his leadership ability. It bled through his actions and his words. Guilt started to feel the first bonds of loyalty.

Some of the anger lessened, though Fritz remained visibly disturbed. Pride certainly governed his emotions, but he left a healthy portion open to respect. Never given but earned, respect meant much to the dwarf. He didn't like having to place his trust in a human, especially one who hadn't actually done much since their meeting.

"I know you," Sara said, looking straight at him.

Fritz pointed to his chest.

"Yes. I bought a pair of diamond earrings from you last summer."

Fritz wasn't surprised. He'd sold millions of earrings over the years. Remembering one woman out of such a high number was next to impossible. He suspiciously wondered if

Sara buying from him was more than mere chance. Nothing could be taken for granted where Alvin was involved.

"Could be. I sell a lot of jewelry, though I don't recall seeing you," he replied. *And I damned sure wouldn't admit it if I did. You humans are nothing but trouble. Especially the two of you.*

Daniel looked from Fritz to Sara. Wheels could be seen turning, new ideas and theories springing to life. Fortunately, he was swift enough to keep them private. Mouthing off without getting the facts straight often ended badly. He already knew he'd been watched for years now. The thought of Sara being under surveillance shouldn't have been surprising, but it was. He decided that, when all of this was said and done, he and Alvin were going to have words.

Sara continued, slightly rushed and with purpose he didn't pick up on. "Oh, I wouldn't expect you to remember. I'm sure your shop is very busy. But I remember. You were very kind and professional, and I simply love the pieces."

He held out his hands. "I can't take credit for crafting the pieces, but I take pride in the quality of what I sell. So thank you."

"Thank you, and while I'm at it, thank you for taking care of my husband tonight. He's told me how important the two of you have been in keeping him alive for me," she finished innocently.

Daniel smiled, covering it quickly with a hand lest he give away her ploy. Fritz blustered and then blushed at the compliment. Dwarves were vain creatures, and his ego most enjoyed the kind words and accolades. Fritz scuffed a foot across the dirt, much like an embarrassed child.

"I guess we should get moving," he said softly.

"Right. Let's move out. Guilt and I will take point. It's a straight shot down 64," Daniel said.

"What do we do when we get there?" Angus asked.

Good question. "We'll figure that out when the time comes."

TWENTY-SIX

The annoying buzz of her cell phone ringing snapped Morgen out of her semi-daze. She hadn't taken her eyes off the Raleigh skyline since Guilt had left with Daniel. Centuries of plotting and scheming were finally coming to a close, and she found herself in the unenviable position of waiting. Morgen placed a hand on the chill window, relishing the feel of the cool glass. A light rain began to fall, more of a drizzle. She enjoyed foul weather. It gave her a sense of calmness otherwise impossible to achieve. So much had gone wrong since she and Alvin had parted ways. A world of promise lay shattered, discarded and abused, thanks to the foolishness of their actions.

A lamentable waste, but one of necessity. Humanity's unexpected rise as the planet's dominant species had forced the elves into seclusion. She regretted much; giving mankind fire, teaching them to hunt, and developing their societies. The initial joy of their efforts had rewarded them handsomely, at least until man had learned how to kill. The savage entertainment of such barbaric and cruel acts had propelled the species down an unending path of violence under which untold future generations continued to languish.

"Where did we go wrong?" she asked her reflection.

Presumably, the character flaw was not in the elves but in humanity. What manner of creature willfully engaged in the wholesale slaughter of its own kind, devoting immense resources and thought to better, more effective ways to kill? The thought process didn't make sense to her. She had once been a queen, as beautiful as the dawn's first kiss upon the horizon. Desperation had forced her hand, changing her, making her darker.

She answered the phone. "Yes?"

"Your ambush at the fairgrounds succeeded. Most of Xander's forces were killed. The others have fled."

"What about the humans?"

"Alive. But there is an…unexpected complication. Xander is alive."

Morgen tensed. Spies within Alvin's house had assured her the champion had been killed. "Alive? Are you positive?"

A brief pause. "Yes. He came with a platoon of government soldiers. I found one of the RRTF survivors and made him talk. They are en route to the zoo. It's only a matter of time before they learn where the princess is being held."

"It appears Mr. Guilt has betrayed me. Now the human government is involved. This is not what I expected when I sent you on this task, Cassandra."

"It's not too late."

"Find me Daniel and Mr. Guilt. I don't want any survivors. Take what you need. Do not contact me until you've successfully completed your mission. Has Alvin been informed about any of this?"

"Not that I know of. He's been kept out of the information loop thus far. I can't see why or how he'd learn about this battle," Cassandra replied.

"Good. Pursue them. Do not let them get to the zoo. Use any means necessary. I'll have air support dispatched to you shortly."

Morgen hung up and set the phone down. Brooding, she began to grind her teeth the way she did when severely irritated, which was too many times lately. *So close. I'm hours away from achieving my true destiny yet stand on the perilous ledge.* She contemplated contacting Alvin herself, but his obstinate attitude was as close to open hatred at imaginable. No. This task was too delicate for direct confrontation. Persuasion was necessary. Other means were required.

"Ma'am?" a young woman's voice called from the doorway.

Morgen sighed and turned. "What is it?"

"I'm sorry to bother you, but the club will be closing soon."

Morgen felt foolish for a brief moment before remembering who she was. There was no more powerful woman in the state, whether others chose to recognize it or not, yet not even she had the ability to keep establishments open longer than their stated hours of operation. Still, the thought of being reduced to following others' rules chafed her. A queen in title only. Fresh revulsion burned in her eyes.

Betraying none of her true emotions, Morgen gave a false smile. "Of course. How careless of me."

The attendant tried to brush off the awkwardness. "No worries, ma'am. We should have sent someone a little sooner. Please, take your time."

Morgen waited until the clicking of heels faded to nothing before dropping her smile and returning to the window. She took up the cell phone again. "This is Morgen. Have my personal helicopter fueled and ready to depart in the next twenty minutes."

"Absolutely not! I want Daniel found immediately. Am I understood?" Alvin roared into the phone. "Morgen cannot be allowed to succeed. Not tonight."

He slammed the phone and stormed off. News of the RRTF's involvement had pushed him way past the edge of infuriation. He'd taken every precaution to keep the government disengaged and, despite repeated assurances, was now faced with the unenviable task of dealing with the Department of Extra Species Affairs. Bogeymen and alien hunters were a special breed, but DESA specialized in the very real world of elves and dwarves.

DESA was a problem born out of necessity. Humans encroached on traditional elven lands at an alarming pace, forcing Alvin to make adjustments many others were disinclined to agree with. He saw the move as an extension of their rights and liberties. The opposition viewed it as confinement. Unethical restrictions were placed on their kind, forcing them underground and into hiding. All of the pride and glory of the elves was buried under bureaucratic administration. Monuments were methodically erased. Temples and statues moved to secure locations until eventually no visible sign of their civilization remained within sight of the human population.

He'd argued when Xander had first suggested bringing the RRTF into the picture. Most of the soldiers were hotheads with too much to prove. Too many times in the past, he had been forced to deal with friendly fire incidents. Nearly all of those had involved him getting an apology from the federal government the day after he was forced to explain to family members how their loved ones had died unexpectedly. Alvin hated the government.

Xander had been insistent, however. He was one of the new breed of leaders. Born amongst humans, there was no hesitation in garnering support for his causes. He pursued and engaged the dark elves at will, all under the complacent gaze of mother government. Alvin soon grew weary of the affair and left Xander to his work. Now that policy of non-involvement was circling around to nip him.

The infernal Xander had forced Alvin to move before he was ready. Alvin had little choice as to his next play. Dawn was approaching fast, and he'd struck out at every turn thus far. Daniel was a slender hope, a sliver of fractured reality he wanted to believe in but was never fully convinced. Humans were powerful, but only the ones who knew of the existence of the elves. Daniel was an anomaly at best. Alvin paged his chief of security and poured three fingers of cognac. The dark fluid contrasted with his pale skin.

Stern arrived promptly. The dark-haired elf rarely slept at night. He could almost always be found squirreled away in the command center watching recorded baseball games as well as the myriad security cameras, both inside and out. Some named him a worrier, but Stern knew better. He'd lost track of the number of times he and his teams had confronted and beat back threats to the families without any of them ever knowing. Only the king was privy to his work.

"There is work needs doing this night, Stern," he said gravely.

Stern nodded. "Dark night for work, my lord."

"Dark deeds are best done in the night," he countered. "A trick I learned from Morgen long ago."

Stern had no qualms about it. He'd merely been making conversation. Most of his family had broken away with the dark elves, leaving him a bitter shell of a man. He held no love for any of them, traitors all. As head of security, it fell upon Stern to ensure the prolonged safety and continuation of the line of high elf kings. He was ruthless about his task. That was how he got the nasty scar, permanently ruining his angelic features, on his neck and lower jaw.

He nodded again. Guessing had never been a strong suit. He hated riddles, much preferring a man to say what he meant. The world was filled with too many too weak to come right out and tell the truth the way they saw it. Instead, they sought to soothe fears and try to win minds over with subterfuge and gilded words. Pure rubbish. The true measure of a man came from his deeds, not his words.

Alvin swirled his cognac before taking a small drink. "How many men do you have available at the Citadel?"

"One hundred twenty-seven," Stern answered without hesitation. "Five are on sick leave, three off duty, and one going on emergency leave in the morning."

Alvin continued to be impressed with Stern's instant professionalism and attention to detail. Virtually nothing slipped past. "You may need to pull that man off leave. I need every available soldier to report for immediate deployment. Morgen has my daughter penned at the North Carolina Zoo — a favorite disposal place of hers. Hungry animals don't tend to be very choosy when it comes to their next meal. Take your men and secure Gwen. She is the only important target. Do you understand, Stern?"

Of course I do. "Yes, sire. Do you wish me to try and save any of the others once the princess is secure?"

Alvin paused to take another drink, giving Stern the impression he was contemplating the question. In truth, there was no thought. The fewer survivors of this debacle, the better for all parties involved. His war not only went through Morgen, but now he was forced to race against the humans. Time was running out, and he had only one card left to play.

Looking Stern dead in the eyes, he replied with a single word.

TWENTY-SEVEN

"Sir, there's no sign that anyone has been here," a faceless soldier said crisply.

The RRTF commander, rather the highest-ranking man left alive after the visceral ogre attack, was a fairly new sergeant with combat experience in Afghanistan and Iraq. Sergeant Torres cursed and spit. "Nothing at all? We were the last ones to leave the engagement area. Spread out and check again. There must be a clue."

They have two humans with them for Christ sake. Dwarves may be extraordinarily stealthy, but, in his experience, humans were just plain clumsy. Torres didn't have time to compare races. Much still needed to be done, and Washington was expecting his report within the hour. Compounding matters, he was down to nine men. The rest were either dead or wounded. An emergency evac bird had flown in to get rid of the bodies. All but one of his men was accounted for. The fact gnawed at him, forcing guilt to the surface until it threatened to consume him entirely. The thought of leaving a comrade behind galled him. Forget that the situation was unlike anything military service could have prepared him for or that the ogres had left him little choice but to displace in a hurry; he'd failed one of his men.

"Sergeant, what's the status?" Xander demanded impatiently.

"No tracks, no signs. Nothing. I don't think they managed to make it here."

"If they were dead, I'd know. The Schneiders are cunning and will have left some sign." He didn't mention the gargoyle or Daniel. In fact, he was more than worried that Guilt had stolen off with Daniel and his wife, leaving the rest on their own.

Xander paced off. He felt desperate, and it bothered him. The notion of not being in control haunted him deeply.

He was the sort accustomed to getting his way and knowing the game before it was played. Daniel changed that. He snuffed quietly. Humans were as unpredictable as the fickle wind, blowing one direction this moment and another the next. They were dangerous, cunning and manipulative. He hated them greatly, only suffering their company for selfish reasons.

Looking towards the lake, he found Bert slumped along the shore. The troll was but a shell of his former self. The loss of his brother had hit very hard, nearly as much as Xander's own sister. He understood the empty feeling but tackled it differently. Bert looked defeated, and, for the briefest of moments, Xander decided to be compassionate.

"You must look beyond the confines of your misery," he said softly after stopping just behind the troll.

"Whadda you know 'bout it?" Bert asked. His voice was thin, depressed.

The answer was surprisingly difficult to say. He'd been so focused on finding Gwen, the stark reality of Ariel's death hadn't sunk in. When he spoke, his words were thin and laden with regret. "My sister was killed earlier tonight. I haven't allowed myself to wallow in grief or guilt. I didn't kill her, Bert. Morgen did. She killed your brother as well. Don't stain his memory by wasting his death in misery."

Bert placed a finger to one nostril and blew. Huge ropes of mucus flew into the water. "I ain't you. Ain't no champion. Ma only ever wanted us to make a good life in this world. She left me and Lou with nothing but a dream. We never did no wrong, Xander. Swear. Just doesn't pay to be so big, I guess."

A comforting hand dropped onto his shoulder. "Fate is never kind. We are but a fraction of what once was. Our glories and triumphs are reduced to fading ink in dusty tomes. I don't know about you, but it burns a hole in my soul. Do you recall the feeling of being able to walk across the earth without fear of being hunted? This planet is infested with sickness, Bert."

The troll raised his head from his hands, giving Xander a suspicious look.

"Humans have turned our once majestic peoples into scraps of dignity, begging for the crumbs they drop. I want to change that," he said.

Bert took the bait. The grief of his loss blinded him. "How? You been working with them humans tonight. Seems like you and them is real good friends."

Xander flashed a toothy grin. "On the outside. In reality, they are nothing more than a tool to help me achieve my goals, but I can't rely on outside sources alone. I need help from within the clans."

"Help? From me?" Bert wasn't convinced.

Xander gave a soft nod. "The more of our kind that step forward to take a stand against the humans, the easier it will be for us to win back our vested rights. We can stand in the sunlight without cowering behind human guise or fear of reprisal simply because we dare to be different. Wouldn't it feel good to be a troll again? Not just some hired thug used for his size?"

"Being a troll is easy," Bert agreed. "All that smashing and grabbing. I like it. But the king would ne…."

"It's time for a new king." He paused to let the words sink in. "Alvin and Morgen have had their run, and look what they've done to us. The clans are in shambles. Most of the major families are broken, defeated. What little glory we retain is given to us. No, friend. The king and queen ruined our species and left us with this. They robbed me of my sister and your brother. Help me, Bert. Help me reclaim our kingdom and make us strong again."

Bert thought about it for a while. He wasn't a fighter or a great thinker for that matter. He was big, and that was about it. Trolls weren't hired for their quick wit or charm. They were big and pulled off being angry quite well. Very few of them were accepted into the ranks of the king's house guard. Fewer still applied. They much preferred a simpler life. A large community worked the warehouses and railroad shipping yards. Trolls were designed for manual labor. The heavier the load, the better they liked it. Bert knew there was nothing like the feeling of coming home exhausted after a hard day's work.

Only now, the workload failed to interest him. Lou's death hit hard, tearing down the walls of morality and integrity. He felt darkness creep into his soul. Anger and something he could only name mania stole him from his comforts and propelled him down roads he'd once feared to travel. Bert felt the blooming desire for revenge. Xander's words fueled him. He stood.

"I ain't no warrior, but I wouldn't mind taking a crack at that old bitch's head." He slammed his fists together.

Xander looked up into his nearly impenetrable eyes. "So you shall, my friend. So you shall. By the time this night is through, you and I will be back on top of the planetary food chain. The rightful rulers of Mother Earth."

"Sounds good to me, Boss," Bert said and slapped Xander on the shoulder, nearly driving him into the ground.

Doing his best to shake the numbing pain running down his spine, Xander feigned a grin and walked off. *One down. If only the others hadn't been so difficult to convert, my task might be easier. No matter. I haven't come this far by being unwilling to take risks.*

"I think we've got something," Sergeant Torres called out.

Xander stalked across the compacted sand. "What is it?"

"One of my men discovered a pair of footprints leading back from the shore. It appears whoever made them just missed cleaning these two."

"Show me."

Torres led Xander to the lake where they knelt down and examined the tracks. "Boots. These are not human. Look at the sole pattern." Xander ran a finger through one of the grooves. "This is standard dwarf combat issue. The Schneider brothers were here."

"Are you positive?" Torres asked.

"Absolutely. It may seem trivial to you, but dwarves take great pride in their perceived sense of originality. These boots were made by leather crofters in the western part of the country, or I'm a damned fool," he replied.

Torres scratched his chin, dubious of the elf's claim. "I can't deploy my men on a wild goose chase. I'm going to need more concrete evidence before committing further."

"These tracks were left uncovered for a reason. Dwarves are rarely so careless as to betray their movements. If I'm not mistaken, the Schneiders will have left a message for us, Sergeant," Xander said.

Torres gave a quick look around the beach. "Where? My men have combed every inch of the shoreline as well as about twenty meters into the trees. They've found nothing."

Typical human. You trust your senses too much and your instincts too little. "Follow me. There is a reason the tracks were left by the water."

Torres followed him to the lake's edge. Cold water lapped the shore tenderly. The sound soothed even the most hardened hearts. Xander couldn't have cared less. Water was necessary, but he found no appeal in lounging on the beach under the painfully blistering sun. It hadn't always been so. Once, long ago, he had enjoyed the kiss of sunlight, the feel of it caressing his flesh in intimate ways no woman ever could. The war against the dark elf clans had left him more comfortable in the unforgiving embrace of night.

He knelt at the very edge of the water, frowning as it sloshed up to wet his knees. Spreading his arms wide, palms turned up towards the sky and the judging sliver of moon, Xander uttered ancient words unheard in the world of men since the rise of the cavemen. Heavy winds drove water onto the beach. Torres stepped back before he got his boots soaked. Xander's eyes glazed over, momentarily closing, as the words drifted across the surface of the lake. Blue light shimmered, forming patterns Torres was unfamiliar with.

The strange symbols formed words as alien to him as Russian.

"What are those?" he asked.

"Dwarf runes. An ancient language when your kind was still infantile," Xander answered.

Torres frowned. He'd read of such things. DESA had a rather hefty mandatory reading list for recruits. Until now, he'd never put much stock in any of the stories. Odd men and women with fantastical minds putting the most inane and impossible thoughts to paper certainly weren't to be taken seriously. At least he'd thought so until now.

"What do they say?"

Xander rose and brushed the sand from his knees. "The others are already en route to Asheboro. We're behind schedule."

"What schedule? The agency sent us here to stop Morgen from finishing her plan. Anything else falls out of our jurisdiction," Torres argued.

"Morgen doesn't care about jurisdiction. There was an age when she ruled every continent without equal. Do you truly think she'll sit back and accept the instructions of your government? She's committed the entire strength of her house to tonight's endeavor and will stop at nothing to ensure success. War is coming, Sergeant Torres. What we do or fail to do tonight will shape both our worlds."

Torres looked back at his men, milling around their tactical trucks, smoking and deathly quiet. The sudden loss of so many friends left them in mute shock. Most were combat vets, the same as he, but not a one had ever been forced to go through such a destructive battle with so many friendly casualties. He doubted most of them would ever be the same again. Post-traumatic stress disorder was prevalent in many military circles, and the RRTF was no different. Torres knew, by committing them now, that more stood the risk of dying.

"Alright. I'll call it in." He left Xander on the shore. "Hey, mount up! We've got some dark elves to kill!"

TWENTY-EIGHT

"I can't believe that worked," Sara said excitedly as their car roared down state highway 64.

Daniel grinned and hugged her. "Me, either. Maybe I should have stayed home and sent you to Ariel's office."

"I wouldn't go that far. I'm no soldier, Daniel. I don't think my heart has slowed down since those two brutes took me from the house. Ugly monsters. What are they?"

"Trolls."

"Like *Lord of the Rings* type trolls? Gross."

He shook his head. "It's a little more complicated. Real trolls can speak and, at least according to Mort, hold their own in the work force. They like good, old-fashioned hard work."

"More than can be said for most people these days," she conceded. "What have you gotten me into, baby?"

She already knew the answer and was accepting it more easily than he had. Funnily enough, she had a complete distaste for anything fiction. Fantasy and science fiction did nothing for her. Biographies were stretching it. She was a mother with a part-time job (granted, one she immensely enjoyed doing) and grounded in reality. There was no escape from what her life had become. Until now.

The very thought that such beings existed among us was overpowering but exciting at the same time. Entire civilizations rose and collapsed back into dust, and these elves managed to outlive them all. Her only regret came from never paying much attention to her husband's books. Otherwise, she might have known a little more about the races she was dealing with.

In a way, Daniel was jealous. Writing was natural for him. Visions and plots came as easily as turning on the faucet. The true joy lay in creating memorable characters driven by some traumatic event. He especially enjoyed penciling life into the dour dwarves of the mountains, the lighthearted elves aloof in their forests, and the vindictive goblins ever raiding the worlds of men. They became his friends; echoes of his conscience capable of achieving deeds he could only dream.

Yet he'd initially found it difficult to come to terms with their reality. They simply weren't supposed to exist. Period. He wasn't precisely sure what calmed his fears and allowed belief to flow in, though seeing Guilt in his true form had certainly helped. Daniel knew that, as much as he wanted to give in to the fantasy and enjoy this newfound world, something deep down inside wouldn't allow it.

He noticed the wry grin etched on Sara's face and asked, "What's got you in such a cheerful mood?"

She gripped his forearm. "I'm riding in a car with a real live gargoyle! And I bought earrings from a dwarf!" She laughed. "Who would have ever believed?"

Seeing her mood cheerful considering the desperation of their circumstances left him in slightly less of a bad mood. Still, they were a hot minute away from being killed and dumped in a place where the bodies would never be found. Death had never offered much of a scare, not after his experiences in combat. He wasn't concerned for himself; he'd accepted the risks the moment Xander had convinced him to take the box of Carthantos. Sara, on the other hand, was neither prepared for nor expecting to meet her untimely demise at the hands of an imaginary being.

"I really wish you would have turned back. Something's been bothering me since I got involved at Ariel's, but I can't figure out what."

"Relax, I'm sure it will come to you," she consoled.

"You know that normally happens at the wrong moment," he countered. *I won't be able to live with myself if anything happened to you.* Of course, those were words he couldn't say. Thinking them was bad enough, and he was highly superstitious; risking ill will wasn't in his best interest.

She flashed a deep smile, the kind that always warmed his heart and helped him to forget the problems of the day. "This will work out, Daniel."

"What about the kids? I've met Morgen and Alvin. Neither is very compassionate towards us. She claims to have her people watching our house. What's to keep them from smashing their way in and…?"

He let the thought trail off into silence. Unable to bring himself to say killed, he struggled to wrap his mind around the different possibilities. There was one constant. He couldn't see any way out of the problem in which his family came out unharmed.

"Stop. You're going to work yourself up again. The kids will be fine." *I hope. Otherwise, there is one elf bitch I'm going to need to kill.*

Guilt occasionally looked in the rearview mirror. The humans fascinated him. Memories suddenly blossomed. He saw his people, his wife, and his family. He saw the great aeries in the mountains where the gargoyle race thrived. They filled him with hope for others more fortunate than his own doomed kind.

Daniel and Sara were nearly opposite. Whereas he was uptight and focused — too much, in Guilt's opinion — his wife was looser, more open to suggestion. Curious that she should seem stronger. It was her strength and courage that prompted him to finally speak.

"Your children will not be harmed," he ground out.

Daniel rolled his eyes, unwilling to trust the creature responsible for kidnapping him. Sara, however, perked up. "How can you tell us that when we're miles away from home? Even if you transformed and flew to our house, there's no way you'd get there in time to stop Morgen's hired guns."

Guilt smiled. "Morgen did not send anyone to your house. The trolls were dispatched to bring you to the queen. There were no others. Your children are much safer than you and your mate."

"I can deal with that. I think." She wasn't sure if his comment was good or bad, but at least the children were safe.

"Of course you're going to say that. We don't have any reason to believe you, Guilt," Daniel said quickly, letting his darkest thoughts get the better of him.

Guilt merely cocked his head. "No? I should have killed you and taken the box back to Morgen. This conversation should not be taking place. You asked me to help. I have. Do not insult my honor by suggesting I am untrustworthy."

Grasping the seriousness implied in his tone, Sara replied before Daniel could make matters worse. "Our apologies, Norman. You must understand this is all alien to us. My husband writes about you, but never did either of us believe you actually existed until tonight. I'm still in shock. You've had a decided advantage over us."

"Perhaps, but there is no pleasure in recognizing humanity for the villain it is. Yes, I know your kind, and it frightens me to no end. Your proclivity to make war rivals the worst heart amongst the elves."

The gargoyle fell silent and went back to the road. His old fears of being hunted, condemned simply for being born different from the rest, threatened to take control. For as fierce as he was, Guilt wanted nothing more than to return to the mountains and the freedoms of the wind and rock. He knew others still lived, hiding in long-forgotten mountain ranges and jungles. One day, he planned to abandon the corrupt worlds of men and elves and go off in search of the gargoyles. One day.

Curiously, he felt the need to protect the female. She had much strength, worthy of keeping alive even at the cost of his own life. The idea was oddly appealing, though he didn't know why. The natural protectiveness of the male gargoyle extended to the human. It was the first time he'd ever felt this way towards a different race.

"I shall get you to the zoo and, if it is in my power, keep you alive long enough to see you home again. Much of my strength is gone though. The ogre is a formidable enemy, but I will do what I can."

Sara leaned forward hesitantly to pat Guilt's shoulder. "Thank you."

Norman Guilt had never heard those words directed towards him before. The feeling was euphoric.

Another thirty minutes went by without much more than reflective mile markers passing in the window. Daniel drifted in and out of light sleep. Earlier events were finally catching up to him, and he reluctantly admitted he was exhausted. He chuckled. More than a few years had passed since he was in his prime. Army life had conditioned him well. He ate well, exercised regularly. But civilian life lacked the intensity, the hurry up and wait mentality the Army thrived on. There were days he felt absolutely lost. Today was not one of them.

Today, he was reminded what godhood felt like. Soldiers excelled when the odds were stacked against them. They walked the battlefield, impervious to bullets and the fear of death. All bowed down and respected them as they passed. Daniel sighed. He missed the days when civilians had stared up at him, whether in disdain or with admiration. It didn't matter. He'd felt like a god. Between the numerous accolades and medals for his deeds in combat, Sergeant Daniel Thomas could do no wrong. Mr. Daniel Thomas, however, was just another man in the middle of a sea of obscurity.

He'd already lost track of how many dark elves he'd killed tonight. The fact that the bodies disappeared without a trace upon death helped ease his mind. Truthfully, he didn't care either. They were in his way, an impediment keeping him from getting home safely to his wife and kids. And he gunned them down ruthlessly.

"Morgen won't have the princess unguarded. She's thrown everything at me but the kitchen sink so far. I can't see anything less than a company's worth waiting for us," Daniel theorized.

Guilt's nod was almost imperceptible. "Much of the local strength has been mobilized. The princess is very secure. It will take more than you and the Schneiders to free her."

"Wouldn't want to make anything easy," Daniel grunted. "Which enclosure is she in? It's been a while, but I remember the zoo being pretty big."

"There are over ten miles of trails. You are right to worry. Attack squads are emplaced at every intersection and strategic point. The princess is being held in the pavilion," Guilt explained.

"That's in the middle of the zoo," Sara said after some thought. "You mean to tell me we're going to have to fight our way through half of the zoo just to get there?"

"Nothing worth doing is ever easy. It is a fair assumption that the second half of Morgen's defense will arrive once they hear the gunfire. The odds are not in our favor."

Daniel winced and wiped his face, a gesture he'd seen his frustrated father perform hundreds of times when addressing his two sons. "I don't suppose you could change into a gargoyle and fly me to the enclosure?"

Guilt broke into laughter. "How uninteresting would the *Lord of the Rings* have been if they'd flown to the volcano and dropped the ring in? No. I cannot carry you. This must be done by foot."

Throughout the conversation, Daniel couldn't shake the feeling they were being followed. But every time he turned around, only darkness stared back. The Schneiders had gone on ahead, ranging a mile out to scout the area. This stretch of the highway was mostly farmland interspersed with the odd home here and there. Not a streetlight could be found. Even the city lights of downtown Raleigh were a distant haze. He yawned and rubbed his sore eyes. The slightest flicker of movement stole him from his stupor.

Daniel blinked rapidly. He wanted to believe his mind was playing tricks but knew better. Twin lines of lights stitched down from the object and headed straight for the car. They were under attack!

TWENTY-NINE

"Floor it!" Daniel shouted.

Sara gave him an odd look as Guilt didn't hesitate. The car raced forward, narrowly missing the ropes of machine gun fire pouring down from the assault helicopter trailing them. Chunks of concrete erupted in dust and debris. The superheated smell of gunpowder and lead melting into the road filled the cabin. Sara choked, trying to wave off the fumes.

"What is that?" she screamed over the roaring guns.

Daniel instinctively reached for his rifle but found only the shotgun and pistol. Both were useless against a helicopter. Worse, the highway was a straight and long road. There was no place to escape to. He hoped the pilots were elves; so far, none of those he'd encountered could shoot worth a damn. The sudden ping-ping-ping of rounds hitting the trunk confirmed they weren't.

"Guilt, get us off this fucking road!" he shouted right before the back window blew apart.

Glass slashed his hands and neck. Sara screamed. Hot blood trickled down Daniel's chest. Only Guilt remained unaffected. He drove the car for all it was worth, and the Challenger responded with all horses. No one thought for a moment that the Dodge had a shot at outrunning a helicopter gunship. Another salvo of 20 mm bullets tore up the pavement, narrowly missing the car only because of Guilt's quick thinking. He jerked the wheel hard right at the last moment, swerving the car out of the line of fire. Daniel popped up and fired back with the pistol.

Even if he did hit the gunship, he wasn't about to shoot it down with a few rounds from a pistol. He needed something bigger. *An RPG would be nice*, he thought grimly. *What I really need is that fancy wand Mort had me use against the wraiths.* The gunship roared overhead and disappeared in the night.

"Guilt, we need to move. They're coming back around to cut us off!"

The gargoyle searched the sky, failing to find the sleek, midnight black gunship. He snarled. His true form begged to be released. A metal gunship was no match for his stone body. Very few things matched a gargoyle's strength in battle, but even he wasn't strong enough for a chain gun cycling rounds at three thousand a minute. He'd be torn to shreds long before ever reaching the gunship.

Running silent, the gunship was undetectable to the naked eye. None of the normal lights were on, leaving the black aircraft perfectly camouflaged in the night sky. Daniel leaned over the front seat desperately searching the clouds. The thought of being ripped apart by angry red streaks of bullets sickened him. The worst feeling in the world was not knowing what would happen next.

"Cut the headlights," he ordered, knowing it more than likely wouldn't matter. The pilots were assuredly using night vision to fly, and the residual heat emanating from the engine would light them up like a Christmas tree.

Guilt was of the same mind. "We must find a place to hide. The pilots will not be fooled by your trick."

"No, but anything is better than waiting for them to swing around and kill us in the open," he replied.

Guilt, never taking his eyes from the road, swerved right suddenly and pulled off into a half-filled church parking lot. One thing Daniel always took for granted was just how many churches sprang up, and usually in the most inane places, around the south. Anything slightly larger than an outhouse became a house of the Lord, so many that he seldom paid attention anymore. That dedication to faith might save their lives, however. Miles away from anywhere, the fairly new church offered the promise of sanctuary, however momentary.

A handful of cars lined up next to the beige building. Daniel could see people moving inside. Unfortunately, they appeared to be getting ready to leave. He shrugged. Anything was better than being caught in the open. The gunship roared overhead suddenly, making each of them flinch. Ducking reflexively, Daniel raised the shotgun. Embarrassment flushed his cheeks when he noticed Guilt giving him that universal blank look that could only mean *idiot*.

"Inside quick!" he said and led the charge towards the church.

Bullets streaked down, ripping up the parking lot. A pair of minivans exploded, the concussion knocking Sara down. Cursing, Daniel turned back to get her. Death swooped down for another pass. Guilt stopped, and his body blurred as he changed into his true form. Wings spread, the gargoyle launched into the sky intent on doing battle with the gunship. Daniel knew he didn't have any time to waste.

"Get up, Sara. Run!" he shouted.

She ran as hard as she could on unsteady legs. Strength and pride were gone, absent mockeries of who she'd been before getting involved in this completely fictional world. She felt like she wanted to throw up. Her stomach clenched. Her eyes were sore and red. The very thought of death threatened to freeze her on the spot. Sara didn't want to die. Worse, she didn't want Daniel to die either. Everyone she'd met since being forced from her home wanted the opposite. Terrorized, she let Daniel drag her into the foyer.

Daniel kicked the door shut. People gasped and murmured at the sudden disturbance. The service was ended, and they were only trying to go home for the night. Unfortunately, anyone stepping outside was already dead. Daniel scanned the building, hoping to find concrete walls, anything capable of stopping the deadly fire raining down upon them. He was sorely disappointed. This was obviously not a wealthy congregation. The walls were plasterboard with only a half wall of red brick for decoration. Nothing to keep them safe.

"What's the meaning of this!" an elderly man demanded, red faced and angered.

Daniel waved him off. "Take cover, all of you! Get down!"

"How dare you come into our church and —"

He never finished his sentence. A tract of ceiling imploded in shrapnel and debris. Rounds dug into the wooden pews. Ripping the floor to splinters. A woman screamed. A baby cried. Panic gripped the crowd, and they cowered in fear of their lives. Death had come and meant to claim them all.

Daniel pushed Sara down, leaning over as a shield. A useless shield, to be sure, but it was all he could think of. Worst case scenario meant he'd die on top of her. The soft *whoomp* of rotors sped overhead. There was precious little time before the gunship circled and made another pass. He rose and began barking orders.

"Get these people to the back of the building, now! No one stays in the main hall. Chaplain, is there an office here? Something stronger than wood and plaster?"

The reverend nodded. His eyes were unfocused, hazed.

Daniel raced over and shook the man back to some semblance of sense. "Take everyone to your office and shut the door. Hurry, there isn't much time."

"We're going to die here," he stammered.

"Take a deep breath and do as I said." Daniel tried to smile. "Relax. They're not here to kill you. They want us."

Slow with shock, the civilians started herding towards the rear of the building. A few suffered from minor cuts and scrapes. One had a large splinter jutting from his forearm. Bright, red blood ran down his arm in brilliant streams. Old instincts sprang forth, but Daniel didn't have time to take care of the wounded. His prolonged presence only endangered these people unnecessarily.

"Daniel, we can't go back out there," Sara hissed.

"We don't have many options," he replied. "These bastards have us bracketed and trapped. It's only a matter of time before they get us. Duck!"

A steady stream of rounds tore another tract across the steepled ceiling a split second later. It took a great amount of self-control to keep from wasting most of his own ammo by firing back. Frustrated, he didn't see a way out. Perhaps the reverend had been right. Perhaps they were going to die tonight.

He crept towards the double door and cracked it slightly. More vehicles were either burning or mangled beyond repair. The Challenger was still intact, more or less. He dared to think they might stand a chance if he got behind the wheel. Only then did he realize Guilt was nowhere to be seen. Nor were the keys. He and Sara were trapped. The gargoyle had abandoned them to their fate.

"Can we make it?" she asked, suddenly at his side.

His mouth had barely opened when the Challenger exploded. A windshield wiper struck the door inches from his head, driving through the oak paneling with enough force to impale a man. Shell casings, white hot and sizzling, rained down in golden sheets. The gunship hovered, firing everything it had. Folding fin rockets left exhaust plumes across the sky, following them into the ground and trees where they exploded harmlessly. Another explosion, larger and more powerful, sent shock waves across the night.

Daniel shielded his eyes as jet fuel, burning hotly, poured down into the parking lot. Metal and plastic crashed down around them, some on vehicles and some inside the church. The rear propeller was buried halfway on the porch right before the rest of the gunship crashed hard in a great ball of flame. The concussion blew Daniel and Sara back with startled cries. He hit the back of his head hard on the tile floor. Blood trickled down his skull. Groaning, he pulled himself up in time to witness a large, bulky body slam into the already broken concrete. Smoke steamed from the unmoving mass.

Barely remembering his weapon, Daniel snatched up the shotgun and stalked back outside, sweeping the area for ground troops. He ignored the sound of the same door opening at his back. Satisfied the way was clear, he walked up to the body and looked down. Norman Guilt lay in a crumpled mess. Dark blood poured like sand from a hundred wounds. Great cuts ripped across his flesh. Smoke and steam continue to rise, wreathing him in a deathly shroud. The gargoyle had somehow found a way to bring down the gunship and save them. He had paid for it with his life.

Headlights, blindingly bright in the semi-dark, forced Daniel to throw up a hand and cover his eyes as another car roared into the parking lot. The deep mourn of a horn brayed once before the lights cut off.

"It's the dwarves!" Sara shouted as she emerged from the ruined church.

Angus and Fritz jumped out, weapons at the low ready, and surveyed the battlefield. Both seemed impressed by the increasing levels of random destruction. Daniel got the impression they were starved for adventure and overly enjoying every little bit of mayhem consuming central North Carolina this night. Regardless, he was glad to see them.

"Holy shit!" Fritz exclaimed. "We missed another one."

Angus grunted and nodded. "Yup. Looks like it was a good one, at that. You two alright, Daniel?"

Do we look alright, asshole? was what he wanted to say. Instead, he succumbed to rising exhaustion and shrugged. "We're alive. Which is more than I can say for him."

Angus knelt beside the gargoyle with a rueful grin. "Don't be so sure. These buggers can't be killed so easily."

He slapped Guilt's charred chest hard, forcing a tiny cloud of charcoaled clothes and baked flesh into the air. Guilt heaved suddenly, breathing deeply with a strenuous gasp. The dwarf edged back and gave him room to rise. Daniel and Sara could only stand with muted awe as what should have been a corpse struggled to his feet and shook free the coating of cinders. Guilt shimmered back into human form. His unreadable eyes looked first at the dwarves and then to the humans. The slightest hint of relief glimmered back at Sara. Her lower lip quivered, though from relief or regret remained unknown.

"How?" was all Daniel could say.

Guilt stared at the burning wreckage blankly. "That was good car."

"We need to move," Angus told them. "Fritz just picked up a transmission from the Citadel. Alvin's sending his entire contingent of troops our way. Time's running out."

THIRTY

The four-by-four roared down highway 64 like a tank, running red lights and passing slower vehicles without pause. Cramped despite the cabin size, dwarf, human and gargoyle managed to fit. And, much to Daniel's relief, there were plenty of guns. *Now I can fight properly*. The small group was as much contradiction as necessity. Sara couldn't stop talking, exclaiming how impressed she was with how the night continued to turn out and how much she enjoyed being a part of it, despite the danger. Guilt, on the other hand, hadn't uttered a word since his lament over the wreckage of his Challenger. Fritz continued to eye Daniel suspiciously and only barely tolerated the developing conversation between his brother and the human.

"Getting through Morgen's defenses won't be easy," Angus suggested. "She'll have her very best reserved for defending the princess. Just getting into the zoo is going to be a chore."

"I don't remember much of it. It's been a while since we last went," Daniel admitted, trying to recall anything at all about the layout.

"The zoo has two main entry points. Both are protected by natural obstacles. If we go through the Africa entrance, we'll be forced to traverse a long wooden bridge without much cover. The drop is considerable enough to keep us from jumping over. A small, man-made lake is underneath and wraps around the entrance."

Daniel yawned. "What about the other side? It has to be easier."

Angus shook his head and switched lanes. "Not by much. The ticket counters are right up on the sidewalk. We could always drive through them, but that only gets us into a courtyard with another, smaller bridge to cross. There's a natural swamp pushing left and a huge lake right. We're either going to have to swim or make a desperate charge across one of the bridges if there's any shot at getting to the princess." Angus fell silent, gloomy and brooding over the lack of choices.

Daniel felt the same. The odds continued to be stacked against him with little or no possibility of success. Victory was as much of an opponent as Morgen and her clans. Worse, he couldn't picture the layout of the zoo for anything. That left him with a decided tactical disadvantage. Enemy gun emplacements would be strategically set to cover all of the main avenues of approach with a healthy regard for crossfire and interlocking sectors of fire. He couldn't afford to underestimate their martial prowess based on the Schneiders' own military experience. Gangs had been infiltrating the military for decades in order to gain necessary medical and communications training. Why wouldn't the dark elves?

A twisted thought brought a low chuckle. He briefly wondered what Tavis would have done in the same situation. Of course, the elf hero was completely fictional and without compare to the real-life exploits of people like Xander and even Guilt. Shaking the thought loose, he refocused on the task at hand. Dark elves were anything but subtle, meaning they more than likely wouldn't have the major throughways mined or booby-trapped. He prayed they weren't keen on improvised explosive devices or suicide bombers. That might make for a quick end to a long night.

The heaviest weapon his team had rested comfortably in Fritz's hands: a portable .50 cal rifle. A single round could puncture concrete and blow a man to pieces of mangled flesh. He would have liked to have had a lot more, but the arsenal was as close to comprehensive as he could hope for. AKs and rapid-fire grenade launchers were stacked unceremoniously in the far back of the truck. He thought he spied a sack of hand grenades buried in there too.

For himself, he chose a short barrel M-4, standard US Army issue 5.56 mm rifle with laser sights and collapsible stock. The weapon was lightweight and easily maneuverable, especially made for close quarter combat. Three hundred rounds of ball ammunition in ten magazines filled the tactical vest. A secondary pair of Goran's wonderful night vision glasses sat atop his head.

Daniel was more anxious than nervous. So close to the end, he couldn't wait to get back on the ground and reach the princess. Getting her was his only objective. Safety and escape came only after retrieval. No doubt by that point Xander and his human goons, not to mention Stern and the high elves, would be pouring into the zoo. The scene would quickly devolve into utter chaos and, hopefully, provide him with an escape route unnoticed. With the princess in hand, he might be able to negotiate a ceasefire or better. If. He hated the word. Too many variables and not enough concrete facts often robbed people of victory but for the whim of chance. He'd seen it too many times.

"Any plans come to mind?" Angus asked. They blew through another red light, much to his amusement.

Daniel wanted to ask why none of the local law enforcement seemed to pay attention to any of their antics, especially after the intense firefights in downtown Raleigh. Not that it mattered much. He was in too deep to be forgiven any criminal acts now. The war between light and dark clans stood on the precipice. The slightest wind and the clans would tear themselves apart without reservation. The less law enforcement, the better. Each minute that passed meant one closer to him finding the princess and stopping a terrible fight.

"Not yet. I think I might remember parts of the zoo, but it's too hazy. I'm going in blind," he admitted.

Fritz snorted and spit out the window. "Figures. Never trust a human to do a dwarf's job. We've called in a few favors."

"What do you mean?" He ignored the barb, tired as he was of Fritz's prejudices.

Angus interrupted, seeing what was happening. "If it goes right, we should have about two dozen dwarves waiting just outside of the zoo by the time we get there."

Hope blossomed. "Reinforcements? This might not be so bad after all."

"Oh, it's going to be bad. Don't you fret about that. We're in for one nasty, bitching fight tonight," Angus said cheerfully. "I'm guessing Morgen will have around two hundred of her crack troops waiting for us. Should be fun."

Daniel blanched. "Two hundred is pretty steep, even with some of your friends."

"Not if they don't run away like you did to us in the park," Fritz snarled.

"Piss off, Fritz. I don't need it right now," Daniel snapped back.

The dwarf settled into a black silence.

"Isn't there anywhere you can sneak me in that doesn't have a natural barrier or electric fences?"

"Beats me, but I'd guess not. This is the only state-funded zoo, which means they can afford to have the very best for the animals and to keep poachers and damned fool people out. We should go in through the front door and kick the dark elves where it hurts most," Angus suggested.

"That will draw too much attention. Subtlety is best," Guilt finally spoke up.

"How do you propose we do that? Morgen will have the whole place bottled up tight. There is no easy way in."

"Nevertheless, any assault on the main gate should be a diversion. Our intent is not to kill all the defenders. We must get Daniel to the princess. That is our first and only priority."

The gargoyle fell silent again and resumed looking out the window. They sped past the Asheboro city limits sign. Only a few more miles and the speculation could end. Battle would be rejoined, leaving Daniel filled with sudden energy. He eyed Guilt with newfound respect. The gargoyle, once his kidnapper, continued to show devoted loyalty to the humans, and for that Daniel was immensely grateful.

"Norman, I need you to do something for me," he said suddenly.

Guilt turned.

"Look after Sara. Confusion will be everywhere once the battle begins. I don't want anything happening to her," he requested.

Guilt, having suffered the loss of his own wife, unable to protect her when she needed him the most, felt invigorated with newfound purpose. His word was given, and he was nothing without the convictions of his honor.

"I shall do my best to ensure your mate comes to no foul end," he confirmed.

Sara became incensed. "What? No. I don't need a babysitter, Daniel. I can take care of myself."

"Not this time. Those ogres back at the fairgrounds nearly killed us all, and nothing I did would have saved you. I need you to listen to me this time. If Morgen does what I'm guessing, we're in for one nasty fight. This is war, Sara. We'll be lucky if either of us makes it."

Her normally soft eyes hardened. "Daniel Thomas, I am not going to sit by and watch you kill yourself for some damned fairy princess!"

"Elf," Angus chimed in. "Fairies are nasty little shits. Wouldn't want to run into any of them tonight."

"Whatever! I don't care if she's an elf, a fairy or some goddamned mermaid trying to get back to the ocean! Daniel is my husband, and I'm not about to let him die for a cause he doesn't believe in if there's anything I can do about it."

She fell silent, arms folded across her chest. Daniel sat stunned. Her uncharacteristic outburst was oddly arousing and showed her in a new light. His respect for his wife rose greatly. She was made of stronger stuff than he'd imagined. War does funny things to people, and Sara was no different.

The fire had been stoked, and the determination to protect her family propelled her actions.

Angus watched them through the rearview mirror with unusual humor. "She's a keeper, Daniel. Good spirit is hard to find in a woman these days."

"Been with many women?" Daniel asked without thinking.

Angus chuckled. "A few, but never any human ones." He shifted the conversation back to the main topic. "Guilt might be right. If our friends are in place, we should be able to provide enough of a diversion to get you three past the initial defenses. They'll be heaviest at the entry points. Get past them, and it should be relatively easy to make it up the hill to the center."

"Getting past them is the hardest part. The zoo is all hills. Gunfire echoes a lot. The whole place will be alerted to our presence with the first shot. You're going to need to move fast," Fritz added, uncharacteristically taking an interest in their plight.

"You guys don't have any invisibility cloak, magic or anything do you?" Daniel half-joked.

"Magic is for sissies." Angus frowned. "We like to get work done with muscle and guns."

"Are all dwarves like you?" Sara asked.

Angus pretended to think. "Sure. We like beer and money. Most of our friends are either investment bankers or insurance agents."

"As long as they can fight, I don't care what they do," Daniel commented.

Angus slowed the truck and made a left turn onto the final road leading into the zoo. A trio of elephant statues watched as the headlights cut off. Five vehicles were pulled off just behind the statues. Smiling, Angus drove off the side of the road and cut the engine. Doors immediately opened, and fully two score dwarves emerged, armed and eager to being the hunt. Daniel took hope in the sight, though it proved fleeting. Much needed to be done before he'd feel comfortable again, no matter how many fighters arrived to help him.

One constant swirled through his thoughts. Many of these dwarves and, hopefully, most of the enemy would be dead before the dawn. He prayed he and Sara weren't on that list.

THIRTY-ONE

The four-by-four slammed into the ticket booth doing 80. Glass exploded into millions of fragments, some from the booth, some from the truck. Fritz howled with delight and shoved the long barrel of his heavy machine gun through the windshield. Incoming fire, slow to build at first until the initial shock of the dwarves' assault wore off, picked up at an alarming rate. Angus made out dozens of firing points, most concealed behind sandbag bunkers and concrete barriers.

Explosions rocked the convoy. Two RPGs struck the front of the second vehicle in line, reducing it to useless wreckage. Most of the dwarves managed to escape before the fuel tanks exploded. The driver rolled away and took three rounds to his chest the instant he tried to stand. He died with a strangled cry. Others were more fortunate, mostly thanks to the reactive thinking of Angus and the other drivers. Vehicles crunched and smashed through the ticket booths and into the small courtyard filled with a hotdog stand and gift shops.

Smoke grenades were tossed from every vehicle window, filling the courtyard with a rainbow of colors. Enemy fire continued to increase despite the sudden lack of visibility. The kill zone had been well marked, and the dark elves virtually couldn't miss, so confined was the space. Angus wheeled his truck hard left, wiping out a pair of picnic tables. He cursed, followed closely by a sharp chuckle, and drove the truck straight into the Nathan's hotdog stand. Unable to stop in time, the front end ran over a sharp cliff, leaving the vehicle stuck and exposed.

"Get out!" Angus commanded.

The handful of dwarves he'd picked up at the bottom of the hill jumped out and immediately began searching for targets. They needn't have worried. Dark elves were literally everywhere. Guilt's estimate of two hundred was far off the mark. There were at least that many defending the entrance point alone. *Ten-to-one odds. Just like the old days.* Angus gave up counting and started looking for an area they could take and hold long enough for Daniel to get deep into the zoo.

Their plan sounded simple enough. Drop Daniel, Sara and Guilt off in the trees far enough back from sight and attack. It was a distraction designed to cause maximum chaos and destruction, a feat dwarves excelled at once placed back in their natural environment. Nothing satisfied a dwarf as much as the thrill of combat. Perhaps money, but that was a matter of greed, not necessity.

What remained of the ticket booths was quickly secured. Any wounded elves were killed outright. Prisoners only got in the way, and the dwarves lacked the manpower necessary to keep any. Not to forget the long-standing enmity between the two races; the only thing a dwarf hated more than a goblin was a dark elf. They had a tradition of killing one another to the very last. This night would be no different.

Angus finished analyzing the defense, quickly developing his plan of attack. "Fritz, we need to secure that bridge as soon as this courtyard is cleared out. Set up firing points on both ends. I want fire teams in these buildings now. Heavy weapons to the front. Put suppressing fire on the elves on the far side of the bridge."

Mounted atop the frame of an old jeep, a dwarf raked the gift shop with a full belt of 40 mm grenades from his automatic launcher. Several elves tried to escape under covering fire, deciding it was better to face the dwarves than be shredded by shrapnel from a dozen grenades. None of them escaped alive. The berserker fury of the dwarves, once aroused, was next to impossible to quench.

Fritz whistled, a shrill sound capable of shattering glass. The gunner paused, read the hand signs and turned his weapon towards the trees in the zoo, emptying the ammo box attached to the mount. Behind them, the three remaining vehicles formed a loose semi-circle at the outer edge of the courtyard. Most of the dwarves had survived the initial push and were now gleefully going about dispatching their ancient enemy in the scattering of buildings.

Ten elves crawled up from under the bridge leading into the zoo and charged into the Schneiders. Fritz, taken off guard, was tackled to the ground and pummeled with cudgels. Bones snapped. Blood sprayed until finally he managed to get his hands free. He punched the nearest elf in the ribs as hard as he could and was rewarded with an audible snap. Three more kicked him, slamming with fist, foot and weapon.

Angus charged in, grabbing the nearest elf by the neck and snapping it quickly. His dagger plunged into the back of another before the first dissolved. Most of the pressure removed, Fritz was able to get up and give the dark elves a proper fight. The battle was over before any of the elves realized what was happening to them.

Others weren't as fortunate. Nine dwarves were already dead, gone like the passing of autumn leaves. The remaining drew closer and continued to fight without so much as a pause. Time would come to lament the dead, later when the sun rose and the smoke cleared. Tonight was time for killing. And killing was what dwarves did best. They hacked and slashed with axe and sword.

The battle quickly degenerated into mass chaos. Bodies struggled to stay alive in brutal hand-to-hand combat. The dark elves fought for everything they were worth. Their knives were sharp, tips coated in slow dissolving poisons. Physically, however, they were entirely outmatched. Most elves were thin, wiry. Their Dwarven opponents were bulked up and possessed immeasurable strength. The more elves were sucked into the melee, the more the tide of battle shifted to the outgunned dwarves. In the end, there was little contest.

"Clear!" echoed several times.

Angus nodded. *The easy part's done. Now time to secure the bridge.* "Olaf, push your teams up to the near side of the bridge. Interlace their fields of fire, but don't shoot unless you've got confirmed bad guys. I'm taking two teams to secure the far end."

Thick, red beard hanging down to his chest, Olaf growled and spit out a mouthful of chewing tobacco before complying. His dwarves moved soundlessly and emplaced their machine guns on either side of the bridge. Angus felt pride. No dwarf had been to war like this in years, yet they all performed their tasks as if it was yesterday.

"My teams, let's move!" he shouted and took off at a run.

The dwarf running to Angus's right cried out suddenly and pitched backwards. Blood spilled from his chest, right below the lung. Another round kicked up a puff of dust as it burrowed into the concrete nearby. A plastic trash can exploded, sending a ball of flame into the dwarves. Clearly, the enemy had more fight left in them. One of Olaf's gun teams began firing blindly into the tree line. Smaller trunks burst apart. Branches and the last few dead leaves crashed to the ground, but there were no bodies.

"Sniper!" Fritz warned as he took a knee and scanned the nearest trees with his night vision scope.

"Where is he? I don't see shit!" Angus shouted.

The older brother took cover behind a Dippin Dots cart, knowing full well the thin metal frame wasn't capable of saving his life if the enemy was using thermal sights. Worse, he hated feeling helpless. Not even during his stint in the first Gulf War had he run into any situations this paralyzing. There was that one time with the Djinn, but that was different. Angus wished for a proper shield, like the ones his kind had made before the invention of gunpowder. Back in the glory days of warfare and conquest, he'd charge into the trees and clear away the dark elf snipers without hesitation. One false move now, and his head was coming off.

Compounding his misery, the dark elves had booby-trapped the place with IEDs. The dwarves were trapped until Angus managed to secure the far side of the bridge. Remote detonations went off behind him, collapsing what remained of the buildings and sealing the dwarves in the courtyard. A few of the survivors looked back at the wreckage before redoubling their efforts at clearing out the enemy. The others buckled down and gave in to their inner berserker with abandon.

Another truck exploded, throwing several dwarves down. All but one immediately got back up. Frustrated, Olaf rose and roared an ancient dwarf challenge. Enemy fire shifted, seeking him out. Brandishing his family heirloom battle axe, Olaf pointed it at the cluster of dark elves seeking to regain full control of the bridge. Rounds from a dozen elves penetrated his body armor, killing him instantly. The axe fell in a cloud of ash and dust.

"Fritz, give me a target," he snarled over the sound of the suddenly renewed enemy fire.

Fritz shifted his gun, desperate to find the sniper before he and his brother were killed. Nothing. "They must be using some kind of heat blocking material. I don't see anyone."

I need a damned flamethrower. Burn the bastards out. Angus pulled the pin on a hand grenade and heaved it into a small clump of pine trees. He was rewarded by three smallish puffs of ash drifting up into the night sky. The detonation only served to infuriate the surviving elves. They charged under a withering barrage of small arms and rocket fire. Blood boiled, and the dwarves met the challenge.

Angus found the break he'd been waiting for and ordered all guns to open fire. Olaf's pair cut into the dark elves, savagely gunning them down. A dwarf caught a line of rounds across his throat. An RPG hit the already ruined hotdog stand. Hot shrapnel dug into Angus's right leg, sending immense pain up his hip. Shakily drawing down on the nearest elf, he squeezed the trigger. The elf's head exploded a split second before his body. And then the enemy was among them. Swords and axes were drawn and clashed once again.

More bodies fell. More disappeared. Blood pouring down his leg, Angus cleaved an elf from collarbone to hip with a nicked and dented axe. A pair of darts, slim and brilliant silver, dug into his shoulder and knocked him to the ground. Fritz shouted and cut a swath through the melee to kneel at his brother's side.

Angus pushed him away, but without strength. "You damned idiot! Don't worry about me. Stop the elves or we're all done for."

Fritz smacked him on the forehead. "Who's the dummy? We need you up for command and control. Get off your lazy ass."

Grimacing, Angus was pulled to his feet and leaned against the nearest vehicle. Slowly, the dwarves managed to regroup and push what little remained of the enemy defenders back. They secured both sides of the bridge, reinforcing the far end with Olaf's fire teams. Pushing deeper into the zoo was pointless, the sort of tactical blunder Morgen's forces were counting on. So few dwarves were combat effective, it would be a struggle just to hold the ground they'd taken.

Only when the gunfire stopped did he allow himself the luxury of worrying about Daniel. He wondered if the humans were safely within the zoo limits and en route to rescue the princess or if they were lying dead somewhere in the night. He wondered a lot of things as he looked around at what remained of his friends. *So few. So damned few, but, by god, it was a good fight!*

"Sir, what are your orders?" asked Hans, a short dwarf with coal black hair and eyes. Bright red blood stained his left arm.

"Ensure the bridge is properly secured. I want demo teams to sweep underneath just in case those little bastards in the trees left some nasty presents. Have the doc set up a triage area and see to the wounded. I have a feeling we're going to need everyone before the night is through," Angus said through the pain.

Fritz stopped beside him and set his rifle butt on the ground. "What about Daniel? Think he made it?"

Angus shrugged and reached into a pocket for a fresh cigar. "Beats me, but we'll sit and wait for as long as need be. It's a matter of principle now."

Somewhere up in the hills, a lion bellowed.

THIRTY-TWO

Breath coming rapidly now, Daniel watched the six vehicles gun their engines and race towards the North America entrance. Points of light blazed from the far side. The dark elves opened fire immediately. The dwarves almost relished the prospect of joining battle with their wiry cousins. The enemy knew they were coming. An outpost hidden behind the elephant statues was found and destroyed by the dwarves before his truck arrived but not before the dark elves managed to send word back.

RPGs flamed from the ticket booths, striking the second truck in the tires. Both tires blew, and the truck skidded to a stop in an administrative building. Angus floored his truck, seeking to punch through the flimsy materials at the gate. Glass and plywood exploded upon impact. There was a momentary pause as the truck strained to break free of the building, and then it was in the courtyard. The remaining vehicles streamed in after. Automatic weapon fire blazed from the windows as the vehicles overturned picnic tables and photo kiosks. A strange chant could be heard on the winds as the dwarves gleefully emerged from their vehicles to hunt down any dark elf they could get their hands on.

"That's our cue. Let's move," Daniel ordered.

Guilt took point, followed closely by Sara as Daniel pulled up the rear. They traversed the lightly wooded area and parking lot, coming up to the chain link fence surrounding the northern side of the zoo. The warning signs confirmed it was electrified but no obstacle to the rock-like gargoyle. Guilt grabbed the black painted links and pulled. Sparks danced off his flesh. The smell of burnt hair choked the air surrounding them. Guilt growled and tore the fence apart. A super blast of current flashed, and the fence went dead.

Smoke drifted from his face but Guilt seemed unaffected. "Come. There is little time. The distraction at the gate will soon be discovered for what it is."

Sara looked over her shoulder and mouthed a soft *wow* to Daniel before following Guilt into the zoo. The main gate was two hundred meters to their right, giving them enough room to maneuver without drawing attention. At least they hoped. The battle at the gate raged fiercely. Heavy weapons came into play. The loud reports as they fired reverberated through the surrounding valleys.

Guilt led them through lightly wooded terrain, stopping twice to help Sara over a small stream. Their path brought them to another fence, this time much smaller and easier to jump. The trio soon found themselves in the midst of a small cul-de-sac. Daniel dropped his night vision glasses to sweep the area. Only animal life registered. They were clear for the moment.

He pushed the glasses back up to the top of his head. "Where to now?"

Guilt pointed slightly left. "The pavilion is on the far side of this mountain. We must go close to two miles."

Not the news he wanted to hear. Daniel frowned and found himself staring into the eyes of a wary mountain lion. The big cat sat patiently, curiously studying him. Chills burrowed to his core. A prophecy of things to come. "There's no way we can make it that far unseen."

He glanced at his watch. It was nearly one o'clock in the morning. They still had six hours to work with, but he harbored no illusions about the ease of their task. Two miles, even at night, was a considerable distance. And uphill. He wanted to frown, to curse and shout his frustration, but knew doing so would only give away their position. He rechecked his weapon and waited for the others.

"I will do what I can, but I cannot make promises. Dark elves are treacherous and will be expecting such a maneuver. The quickest route is by using the employee trails.

They are direct and paved." Guilt looked at the mountain lion for a moment before marching off down the trail.

Daniel was left with a question on the tip of his tongue of the roads being mined. *Screw it. We're either going to make it or we're not.* He followed Guilt. Bugs chirped. Something large slithered across the ground and splashed into the water — an alligator, according to Guilt. They were in the cypress swamp area of the zoo heading towards the polar region. Off to the right, the sounds of battle subdued slightly. The harsh clang and clash of blades meeting drifted over the concrete bridge. Grunts and cries from the wounded intermingled with the horrific sounds of combat Sara had come to associate with these races. She couldn't understand how entire races, virtually concealed form humanity and struggling to stave off extinction, could so readily murder each other.

Light footfalls scuffed directly in front of them, forcing Guilt to freeze in place. Of them all, only he had true night vision. Daniel slid the glasses back down and watched as half a dozen dark elves raced towards the firefight. The moment passed swiftly, but Guilt kept them still until he was sure no more were coming. Waving them forward, he led them under a small bridge, down a curving path that took them into the sea lion enclosure. It also left them on the wrong side of the main walkway.

"How are we going to cross this?" Daniel asked, coming up directly behind Guilt and whispering in his ear. "We'll be exposed from both angles."

"Possibly, but the dark elves are distracted by the battle. We shall have one chance to get across. Our objective is the high road on the far side of the tram station."

Names and places meant nothing to Daniel. Nothing he'd seen so far was even remotely familiar, and the parts he remembered were long gone and changed. He was completely at Guilt's mercy. *This would be easier if I had a map.* No point in lamenting what couldn't be changed, he gestured for Guilt to continue.

They slipped through the shadows under a peregrine falcon, past the pair of sleeping sea lions, and into the foul smelling puffin house. Sara gagged at the stench, throwing a hand up to cover her nostrils. Several of the birds were startled awake and began squawking loudly. Her heart skipped at the sudden noise, and she fretted being discovered. Guilt took them out the far door and up a winding ramp leading back to ground level.

They were about to dash across the small open area when he stopped them abruptly. An enemy machine gun was emplaced in the viewing area to the polar bear pit. Three dark elves manned the position but were distracted by the firefight raging a few hundred meters away. Daniel's worst fear was confirmed. There was no possible way for them to cross without being spotted.

"Can you do anything about that?" Daniel whispered.

Guilt craned his neck, very slightly, as if mocking Daniel's absent memory. Instead of uttering a meaningless phrase to embarrass him, Guilt simply said, "Wait here."

In a move Daniel was becoming increasingly comfortable with, Guilt shimmered and became the gargoyle. Leathery wings bore him away without so much as a sound. Daniel forced Sara back so he had room to kneel down and take up a good firing position. She didn't protest, knowing too well how much her life depended on him. The hellish scenes of combat at the gates left her deeply shaken. Not even the fairgrounds nightmare had been so fierce, so contested. Her one saving grace rested in the fact that, in most cases, the bodies disappeared before they managed to touch the ground. That did little to assuage the violence playing out every time she closed her eyes. Dark thoughts congested her mind. She pictured Daniel being shot. Bleeding to death. In pain. Only his body would remain. It was all she could do to keep the tears at bay.

Oblivious to her inner turmoil, Daniel watched the enemy gun emplacement. The speed and veracity with which

Guilt attacked forced him back a step. He watched, amazed and suddenly afraid of his onetime abductor, as Guilt dropped onto the unsuspecting elves. The gargoyle moved fast. Granite-hard claws ripped out throats and plunged into hearts in a blur. He stood alone in less than ten seconds.

"Come on," Daniel said.

Sara followed him at a fast jog. They crossed the walkway, rounded an old storage building, and curved upwards towards the tram stop. This late at night, the trams were all parked in the zoo's motor pool. The animals were put away, most of them, at any rate, leaving the sprawling complex empty. A haunting miasma settled, turning shadows into lurking monsters. The sound of the wind delivered despicable intentions. Even the hint of moon bore ill will. A sudden noise in the bushes to the right broke Sara's concentration.

Daniel spun, raising his rifle simultaneously. The tiny red laser pierced the darkness even as he searched for a target. His heightened senses made him acutely aware of every minor detail. Latent heat signatures barely registered in the glasses, leaving him slightly bewildered and confused. No enemy could be seen. He'd already been through too much to leave anything to his senses. Stepping back to allow more room to maneuver, he gently laid his fingertip on the trigger.

"Come out slowly," he growled.

Branches cracked and waved. The dark shapes of leaves fell to the ground as Norman Guilt, transformed back into a man, emerged. "We must move swiftly. The enemy is no doubt aware of our presence and will be expecting a move on the princess. As you said, time is running out."

Daniel looked down the long, dark road winding up into the mountains. "We'll be exposed for most of the way."

"True, but we will be afforded the opportunity to move quickly. The roads are well maintained, and our enemy will not think that we would dare use them. This is the only chance you have, Daniel."

"Do you know the way?" he asked, reluctant to put all his trust in such an obvious avenue of approach.

Guilt blinked emotionlessly, and pointed towards the road.

Deep reservations convoluting his thoughts, Daniel decided there was nothing for it. The gargoyle had done them right since rescuing them from Morgen's ogre assault. He had no reason for doubt now.

As if sensing her husband's reluctance, Sara place a comforting hand on his forearm. She looked lovingly into his eyes and offered a tight smile. She didn't want to go any further, didn't want to take the chance of either of them being captured or killed or worse. This wasn't her war, and it damned sure wasn't his. They needed to get away and return to their quiet little world in the suburbs of Raleigh. Only there wasn't a return. How could they go back from what they'd seen and done this night? Men had died, lost to the seeds of the earth as their ashes scattered mirthlessly on the wind.

Returning her smile, Daniel gestured for Guilt to lead on. They had a princess to rescue, and time was indeed running out.

THIRTY-THREE

Thaddeus Blackmere yawned and rubbed his aching temple. The headache had come quickly and assaulted him with unrestrained fury. He'd taken aspirin about an hour ago and still waited through each agonizing minute for the medicine to kick in. Swiveling his chair around, Blackmere took in the view he never grew tired of. The dome of the Senate building rose above the trees, a majestic testament to what the idea of liberty was always supposed to be. If only people knew the truth of things, they might not be so fast to put their faith in their elected officials.

Blackmere was a lifelong servant of the people. He'd done a stint in the Navy in the early 80s before getting out and applying for the FBI. Ten years went by, ten eventful years in which he saw more than anyone should, before he was afforded the opportunity to do something unique with his life. Two men had approached him one evening after a particularly nasty kidnapping-murder case while he sat at a bar trying to drink the violent images away.

Neither had introduced himself, instead taking seats on either side. They wore nondescript suits, the kind of power clothes men in Washington liked to wear. Each had an easy look, too casual for Blackmere's liking. He'd entertained them for a while, provided they continued buying the drinks. One of them had left his business card and invited Blackmere to come visit their offices. He'd stared long and hard at that card before making up his mind. He'd seen enough of the violence mankind was capable of. It was time for a change.

Only the change he'd found far surpassed his expectations. Blackmere had quickly discovered a brand new world, a world he'd never imagined possible. Elves and dwarves, dragons and giants. Blackmere reveled in the newfound knowledge and voraciously took to his new line of work. The Department of Extra Species Affairs, DESA, fell far under the Department of Homeland Security, so far below congressional oversight it was practically negligent. Taxpayers unwittingly funded their budget, allowing DESA to do what its contract cited: protect the United States from the incursion of certain races defined as other than human. Over a decade had passed since that fateful night, and he still approached his job with zest. He liked what he was doing, and that was a rarity in Washington.

His close-cropped hair had gone from black to salt and pepper. He'd lost some weight, making him thinner than he wanted but still comfortably underweight. The sudden changes, perhaps not so sudden considering age and experience, accented his amber eyes. They were eyes that had seen too many things. Tired eyes in desperate need of rest, if only for a short while. Blackmere was considering putting in a leave packet for some much needed vacation. An island would do nicely. Warm sun, sand between his toes, scantily clad women with golden skin and a cold drink in his hand. He smiled.

The intercom buzzed. "Agent Blackmere, I have Field Director Bowman on the line requesting to speak with you."

He sighed, and the smile disappeared. Swiveling back around, he answered the phone. "Thank you, Eileen. Put him through."

"Thaddeus, I hope I'm not catching you at a bad time?" Bowman asked.

Blackmere smiled, knowing it didn't matter if it was a bad or good time. Few had the stones to say no to the Field Director. "Not at all, sir. What can I do for you?"

"We have a situation developing down in North Carolina. Reports are coming in from the local office of large-scale firefights. I think something pretty big is happening, and I need you to take your best team and head down there ASAP."

North Carolina? Damn it all. "That's where the king and queen are, correct?"

"Which makes it all the more important that you settle this immediately. We can't risk the two clans breaking into an all-out war. Not with the presidential election coming up. Can you imagine what would happen if any of this got out? Get down to Carolina and stop it, Thaddeus."

The line went dead, leaving Blackmere with dark suspicions brooding in his stomach. That tropical vacation was going to have to wait.

He looked out the side door window of the midnight black converted military helicopter. Eight others, two teams of four field agents, fully armed and armored, sat in the two benches behind him. They were his very best, men he'd trained and spent considerable time in the field with. Each was capable of leading the mission should he fall. He trusted them implicitly.

What was at least a five-hour drive was considerably shorter by air. It took less than two hours to get them into North Carolina airspace en route to the zoo. Blackmere poured over the limited intelligence passed down from Bowman. The agents in Raleigh provided little help. Most of their reports were speculation at best. There were no witnesses and nothing confirmed beyond a few wrecked vehicles. Most disturbing was the ruined church a half an hour west of Raleigh. Clearly, DESA agents were involved. Cleanup crews were busy recovering the bodies from the state fairgrounds as well as the helicopter wreckage on the side of the highway.

No one in Washington had authorized any action in North Carolina, or they were in flat-out denial if they had. Men were getting killed, and not a damned soul would admit why. Blackmere immediately became suspicious. Field teams were always combat ready, but that didn't make them expendable assets. It took a great deal of political red tape to authorize a field action, and he didn't remember seeing any recent requests. That meant either Bowman truly didn't know or was covering up information Blackmere needed to do his job properly. Either way, the situation here was beginning to smell.

"We'll be arriving over the target area in ten miles," the pilot announced over the headsets. "Where do you want us to put down?"

Blackmere picked up the map of the zoo. Not that it constituted a real map. It was more of a cartoonish follow-the-yellow-brick-road enclosure designed to entice children to keep going on what seemed to be a ridiculously long, circuitous route up into the mountains. He imagined his own children would remain enthused about to the center before they begged to either ride the tram or go home. Neither was an option for his team tonight.

The most current satellite images showed proof of a firefight raging at the nearest main entrance. No doubt the secondary entry points would be well guarded and perhaps mined, as well. Their best option was a large grazing field near the center, probably used for herd animals, he surmised. Regardless, it was the only true open area in the zoo capable of supporting a military-grade helicopter. They'd be exposed the very instant they arrived in the airspace, leaving them at a distinct disadvantage. The element of surprise would fade the moment the *whoomp-whoomp* of rotors washed through the valley.

Blackmere saw no choice. "Circle around to the east and put us down along the tree line. We'll take it on foot from there. Once we're clear, I want you to take off and circle. Provide air support on order and be ready to extract us."

"Yes, sir. Call when you need us."

Blackmere turned his gaze to his men, unsurprised to find each and every one of them watching him intently. "Ten minutes, boys. I want weapons locked and loaded. Alpha team takes points, Bravo flanks. We need to move fast across this open field. Don't stop to fire. Time is against us."

"What's the mission, sir?" one of them asked.

Good question. I wish I knew myself. "I don't know yet. Our objective is this domed building here in the center.

Whatever's happening will be centered close by. I'm sorry I don't have more to tell you, but Washington didn't give me many specifics. What I can tell you is that both the king of the high elves and the queen of the dark are involved. Our first priority should be to secure them if they are on scene. We'll figure out the rest as we go along. There might be civilians involved, so choose your targets carefully."

He didn't dare tell them other DESA teams were also in play, not until he knew on whose orders and why. Too many variables remained, keeping him uncomfortable. Bowman knew things he wasn't willing to divulge, things potentially devastating to Blackmere's mission. For a moment, he wished he'd never taken the job. The FBI had plenty of hiccups but at least dealt with matters openly. DESA had virtually no oversight, and that meant they could do anything at the Field Director's discretion. Blackmere wondered if they were walking into a trap.

Adjusting his front chest plate, Blackmere looked to each of his men. The chances of one being a mole were very slim, but not to the point he could rule it out. These men were all well known and trusted, in so much as he trusted anyone, but the federal government paid their bills, not him. They could easily be under the influence of Bowman — or anyone else, for that matter. He just didn't have enough information to be positive. And that led to mistakes.

"In fact," he added, "I want fire restrictions. Don't shoot unless you're shot at first. Standard rules of engagement apply. Noise and light discipline the instant this bird takes back off. Treat everyone as a hostile."

"One minute."

The pilot's voice was muffled, mechanical.

Blackmere unfastened his safety straps and slapped a magazine into his rifle. The *click-slam* of the charging handle going back and dropping forward as it chambered a round was nearly lost amidst the vibrations of the helicopter engines. Taking their cue, the two fire teams followed suit.

"Ten seconds."

The crew chief opened the side door. Cold air blasted the agents in a subtle reminder of their insignificance compared to the inexhaustible powers of Mother Nature. A quick glance at his watch made him groan. Dawn wasn't far off, and his wife was bound to be pissed when she figured out what had happened. The sad truth was that she ought to be used to unexpected departures and late nights. He'd never been able to tell her just what it was he really did, but she knew it dealt with the government and secrets of state, so she let it be. Now the secrets were on the opposite side, and Blackmere didn't like it.

The helicopter rocked briefly as the wheels touched down. Nine men rushed out into the cold dead of night with weapons ready and hearts pounding. The pilot counted to ten and jerked the stick back. Blackmere looked up and watched the sleek craft disappear back into the darkness. They had boots on the ground. It was time to go to work.

THIRTY-FOUR

Miles away, in the opposite direction and unknown to all but one other already at the zoo, Stern and his commandos hastened towards confrontation. While all were combat veterans of both elf and human wars, many of them felt a new form of trepidation. This was a different sort of war, one fought strictly in shadows without so much as a memory for the fallen. So many had already died this night. No one wanted to be the next on the list.

Stern himself held no reservations. He'd been the security chief for the king for nearly a millennium and was very good at his job. The high clans had won the War of the Schism, survived the death plague of Malgud the Mad, and endured the duration of the dwarf rebellion shortly after the recapture of Jerusalem by crusaders. Such a wealth of history rested in his mind and the dusty copies of scrolls and parchments waiting to be transcribed into digits.

Much in the world had changed since then. In fact, very little remained of the old ways. Obsolete forms of communication and modes of warfare nearly reduced him to a relic worthy of being shelved himself. Perseverance kept him in his position. Stern made sure to learn enough secrets to make him indispensable. Alvin *needed* him. Certain doors had opened suddenly. Stern's access to the deepest archives where scholars tirelessly poured over ancient history gave him insights into the current dilemma few others had.

The fools. Stern knew the truth, even if the others were less willing to admit it. There was no preventing it. The war must be embraced, accepted at the most savage level and met with untold ferociousness. Only through martial skill and the desire to survive would the high elf clans survive the coming darkness. Clenching his fist around his rifle stock, he watched the miles roll past.

"Sir, we're receiving reports that a dwarf war party has engaged the dark elves at the main entrance. Casualties are high and getting worse. Most of the initial defenses have been overrun."

Stern perked at the update. He'd shirked his human guise the moment Alvin had dispatched them. Better to meet this as an elf. Humans were a pathetic sort, unworthy of dominating the world. A plague of locusts, he'd once heard them called. They bred like insects but had an unfortunately long life span. The time had come to return the elves to their rightful thrones.

"What's our ETA?" he asked, living up to his name. The old sensations tickled his flesh. He wanted to get into the fight as quickly as possible. Damn the rest.

"Another thirty minutes at our present speed, Commander," the lieutenant answered after checking his equipment.

Not good enough. The battle will be over by the time we get there, and that human *will have the princess. Or they'll all be dead.* "Speed up. I want us there in half that. This is our fight, gentlemen. Inform all troops to be ready to disembark and engage the enemy the moment the vehicles stop. This is war."

The lieutenant nodded and relayed the instructions to the rest of the convoy. Stern turned his attention back to the road and the infuriating sea of darkness that seemed to stretch on into the depths of forever. His mind filled with ancient battles and deeds of untold greatness. Those days were gone now, faded into dust and ruin thanks to the gradual and steady decline of leadership and willingness to stand up for themselves.

People tended to forget the hard lessons when life became easy. Complacency was as bad a plague as mediocrity. Centuries of peace and prosperity made them forget, made them soft when they needed strength. His people were weak; of that, there was no doubt. They wallowed in their memories, all the while struggling off the scraps Alvin and Morgen begged from their human counterparts. Stern hated what his life had become. He hated the ineffectiveness of his station.

He was by no means a warmonger. True, violence invigorated him, quickened his blood, but only in controlled circumstances. Killing for the sake of killing wasn't honorable. There remained an immovable degree of honor in warfare; otherwise, what were they? Vulgar imitations of the purest form of life. That was an insult he wasn't prepared to allow his clan to suffer.

The miles sped by. The night deepened. Most of the rain had stopped falling, the clouds thinning and breaking altogether in places. He rolled his window down and took in the wet smell. It soothed him in ways nothing else could. He preferred individual challenge, a dual to the death in order to prove his worth. How many had fallen under his blade over the years? Certainly too many to count. His martial prowess was surpassed only by Xander, and that man had become a ghost. Stern didn't believe for a moment that Xander was dead. No doubt the princess was enticing him to abandon the clans and live among the humans. The idea galled him. *Perhaps one day we shall cross blades and see whom the better elf really is.*

Soon enough, they arrived at the outskirts of the zoo. Headlights went out, replaced by the small blackout drive lights. He listened to weapons being loaded, to equipment jostling as his men prepared to disembark for their assault. Truthfully, he didn't expect much resistance at the gates. The battle would be deep into the hills by now. The weak would have died first, leaving a disciplined, experienced cadre to root out of their bunkers and emplacements.

He wondered how many dwarves Daniel had convinced to join his foolish quest. The Schneiders were hotheads but retained a measure of practicality. They wouldn't be willing to risk too many lives for the princess. Elves and dwarves were great allies, but even that had limitations. Once great enmity had raged between them, and it was all either side could do to eliminate the other. Stern counted on some of that old feeling to carry through this night. The prospect of fighting a platoon of dwarves in full battle mode wasn't one he was willing to face unnecessarily.

"Lieutenant, what's the status of the battle?" he asked.

Their drones had deployed before their vehicles left the Citadel, giving him full battlefield access. Every movement, every action was recorded and relayed back to command headquarters for his use.

"Dwarves have secured the main gate and the bridge leading into the zoo proper. I'm not registering any weapons fire at all, though."

"Explain."

The lieutenant paused, fearful of inciting Stern's legendary wrath. "The drones aren't picking up any heat signatures in the zoo. We've known the dark elves possessed radar dampening technology, but that wouldn't translate to weapons fire. If there was a firefight going on, we'd know, Commander."

"Is it possible the humans have already reached the princess?" he asked quickly. Dangerous implications lurked in those words.

"Possibly, but I judge unlikely. It's nearly two miles from the gate to where we suspect she is being detained. They haven't been there long enough to reach her. Wait, I'm picking up new signatures!"

Stern punched the dashboard and cursed. Situational control slowly slipped from his grasp. "Who?"

"Humans, several of them. There's a government Blackhawk helicopter taking off on the far eastern side of the zoo."

"Show me." He switched on the imaging camera built into their helmets. What he found was less than pleasing. The helicopter roared out of sight, leaving nine clear heat signatures moving rapidly across a large field and directly towards the African pavilion. Stern was left with only one real choice.

"Lieutenant, broadcast our location and intentions to the dwarves on their battle channel. I want a clear path all the way to that pavilion. The princess is in there. We must arrive before DESA."

A few hundred meters behind the last truck in the convoy paced another vehicle running without lights. Cassandra remained the only variable unaccounted for in this sordid affair. Alvin knew she was out here, but he didn't know where or what her intent was. As far as the king was concerned, she merely tracked the movements of friend and foe. His ignorance continued to bring a smile to her face. What he didn't know, what he couldn't know, was that she intended to be the dagger that ended both his and Morgen's reign in the span of a single night.

After clearing the battlefield at the fairgrounds and ensuring no one would ever find the RRTF trooper already left for dead, she continued on to the rendezvous point at Jordan Lake. Again, she arrived late. The dwarf runes in the waters were miserably predictable, much as their makers. Dwarves lacked foresight. Fortunately, that rendered them a non-threat. She'd learned once from a master poisoner how best to deal with the dwarves' thick hides, and she came prepared for the eventuality. If everything worked the way she'd spent so long carefully planning, the dwarves would refuse to get involved.

The burning ruins of the church raised her curiosity but little else. Government agents and local law enforcement and fire were busy cleaning up the mess. By dawn, no one would ever know a federal helicopter had been shot down. Forced to slow because of the police roadblock, Cassandra smiled politely to the officer waving her through and left the scene. It held no interest. All of the parties involved were either already at the zoo or close enough for her not to worry.

The true prize awaited ahead, and that was still far enough away to keep her anxious.

Miles and minutes raced by, competing to see which ran out first. She hummed. The revenge of Cassandra Eveningshade drew close.

THIRTY-FIVE

"I don't like this," Daniel whispered into Sara's ear.

They'd just passed the red wolf enclosure and were heading down a slow, winding road towards what they guessed was the center junction. So far, they hadn't seen a single sign of their enemy. Vegas odds makers wouldn't have taken that bet.

"What's to like?" she replied with a grimace. "This whole thing stinks."

"Agreed. I almost feel like we're being allowed to get to her."

She cocked her head in thought. "A trap?"

He nodded. "After everything else that's happened tonight, I'm expecting it, but why? Morgen knows we're coming, and she's already made it clear she wants to stop us. That bitch is plain crazy."

"Don't start," Sara warned as playfully as she dared given the circumstances.

Daniel smiled, some of the tension draining thanks to her efforts. "I'm just saying."

"This is not the place for banter, Daniel Thomas," Guilt admonished. Even quiet, his voice rumbled across the darkness.

"I haven't seen a bad guy since we left the bridge. It's almost like they're gone," he countered.

Guilt marveled at the naivety behind those words. "No. Morgen herself is here, waiting for us. The dark elves have been given orders to allow us passage."

Daniel stopped, raising his weapon at the gargoyle. "Are you sure?"

The gargoyle halted and stretched his hands out in a submissive display. "The dark queen's intentions are well known. She is the mistress of trickery. Do not believe what she tells you. I was kept in the dark when she hired me, but my instructions were specific. I am to get you safely to the pavilion. The rest will take care of itself."

Daniel hesitantly lowered the weapon and circled off. He cursed his insistence at going down to Ariel's office to present his case. Otherwise, he'd be in bed with his wife right now, not marching deeper into a miserable situation he couldn't see a way out of. *Damn these elves and their secrets. Why can't any of them speak what they mean? No wonder the clans have fallen so far so fast.* He didn't know what to think anymore. The only one he actually trusted was Fritz Schneider. The dwarf hated him and made no qualms about showing it. Daniel could at least respect that. He knew exactly where he stood. These rest of those involved were too dubious to trust.

"Daniel, we're running out of time," Sara urged, hoping he made the right decision. The anticipation of something bad coming shook her confidence, and it was all she could do to keep a calm appearance. Inside, she was plain frightened.

"I know, but to tell the truth, I really think we need to turn around and go home. I've had enough of these people."

Guilt watched dispassionately. He didn't blame them for wanting to abandon a quest not of their own choosing, though heroes seldom got the chance to choose their destinies. Nor were heroes the mythical beings of virtue traditional fantasy wanted readers to believe. Heroes most often turned out to be those who were caught in the wrong situation at the wrong time. Daniel was such a hero whether he chose to recognize it or not.

When Sara spoke, it came as a shock to them all, herself included. "We've come so far. Giving up now just isn't right. That poor girl is all alone and facing who knows what kind of torments. Think if it was our daughter."

Daniel opened and closed his mouth quickly, the retort dying on his lips. He didn't know exactly what he'd do if Shelly ever came to harm, but the results would likely either land him in jail or find him dead in the middle of a large pile of bodies. They could hurt him all they wanted, though he'd rather not, but no one had better ever lay a finger on either of his children.

"What do you propose we do?" he asked them both.

Guilt replied, "This quest has been thrust upon your shoulders. I cannot tell you what must happen. You need to come to your own conclusion."

"I'm asking what you would do, damn it. Don't give me any lectures about trying to find myself and all that horseshit. Give it to me straight, Guilt. You owe me that much." Daniel trembled slightly with rising rage. His patience was gone. He wanted action, wanted to be done and back to his normal life. Everyone spoke in riddles and half-answers as if he was some sort of psychic reader. They were all worse than the worst conceived character in one of his books, and that was saying something; Daniel had crafted some of the most helpless, miserable characters in the hopes of connecting with readers. He'd never imagined those sorts actually existed and he'd one day be going to war alongside them.

"Go and see what she has to say," Guilt replied flatly.

Sara coughed. "Walk right into the trap? Are you trying to get us killed?"

"I merely answered his question."

Daniel winced. "He's got a point, babe."

"Seriously? He wants us to walk up to the same bitch that had me kidnapped from our house and say what? Hi, here we are! Look at the dumb humans."

"She already knows that," Guilt said with unusual levity in his tone. His shoulders shook slightly, jostling up and down.

"Did you just make a joke?" Daniel asked.

"I don't care if he made the Gettysburg Address! He wants to send us right back into her grasp," Sara protested. "I'm not going to do that, Daniel. I'm not."

"We're not going to give ourselves up," he replied quickly, pausing to glance around their surroundings. It wouldn't do to be caught bickering. "But his idea isn't altogether bad. She must already know we're here. Why not go storming in and do exactly that? No one in their right mind will think us dumb enough. It could be our perfect opportunity to break this wide open, get the princess and get the hell out of here."

"You know getting out isn't going to be that easy. We haven't done anything but skulk around in the dark like little lost children in some Grimm fairy tale," she countered. "Not that I'm ready to go through another battle like the one at the gate." *And we merely watched part of it. All those lives lost, and for what?*

Her point gave him doubt. All his focus had been on successfully getting into the zoo and finding the princess. Getting out with their prize intact hadn't even dawned on him yet. The night continued to get deeper, taking his concerns down with it. He frowned. Every time he thought he had it worked out and was ready to move on, something unexpected came rolling out to block the path. It felt like climbing up the Rocky Mountains again, only without the heavy firefighting gear.

"She makes a valid point, Daniel," Guilt added. "Morgen may not expect you to walk through the front door, as you humans say, but she will commit every element at her disposal to keep you from leaving. This is a...delicate matter."

"I know, I know. But this isn't helping me. We need a plan for getting out before we get in the middle of it," Daniel replied. "I've met Morgen. Guilt's right. She won't just let us walk out."

Sara didn't like the way he said Morgen's name. Clearly, the queen of the dark elves must be beautiful; otherwise, she wouldn't be worth mention. She felt a pang of jealousy deep inside and silently vowed to kill Morgen herself if it came down to it. Being part of this mystery wasn't so bad, she reminded herself, but she couldn't help but feel out of place by not knowing anything about, well, any of it. Elves and such. She wished she would have taken more of an interest in her husband's novels.

Sara had never read a single one of his books. The subject did nothing for her but elicit a few yawns and the occasional twirl of her hair while she waited for it to be over. She loved Daniel with all her heart but wouldn't lose a minute of sleep if she never had to read any of his fantasy for the rest of her life. She suffered through the movies and his retelling of his own plotlines and titles, pretended deep interest when a new subject came up. It wasn't anything to be proud of, but she thought it better to go along and humor him than risk another petty argument. She couldn't stand being asked what did you think about it. That never ended well. Her usual response was three deceptively simple and evil words. *I like it.* Daniel hated the answer so much he refused to talk about his work with her until he forgot and made the mistake of asking again. The cycle had already proved unbreakable.

Maybe it was time to fix that, after all of this was over of course.

"We need a few of those dwarves to come help," she speculated.

"There's been enough killing, Sara. I really don't want anyone else dying tonight. Not for the sake of a king and queen working behind everyone's backs." Daniel stifled an unexpected yawn. What he really wanted was to lie down and get some sleep. His emotions were running strong, but adrenalin was fading fast. His body ached, eyes burned. The amount of stress, mental and physical, he'd already endured would amaze most seasoned veterans. He hadn't worn a uniform in years and was admittedly out of shape; those factors helped contribute to his degrading fatigue.

"If it comes down to them or us, you know what I'm going to say," she replied fiercely. Thoughts of their children drifted through her mind.

He nodded. "I know. But we have to try and end this peacefully. Otherwise, they'll be after us for years, and I don't relish the prospect of looking over my shoulder for the rest of my life."

"There is movement down the hill to the right," Guilt interrupted.

"Where?" Daniel slipped the night vision over his eyes and followed where Guilt pointed. Nine figures, taller and bulkier than elves or dwarves, stalked through the planted bamboo grove running from the central plaza up to the aviary. Humans! He let the thought slide, finding it entirely too comfortable in making such a proclamation. Still, the question of what they were doing and who they were remained. "I didn't think there were any humans involved."

"Xander has a few remaining. The ogres took care of most of them. There should not be any others here," the gargoyle snarled. Unlike the other races, he could see perfectly at night, so he noticed their armor, their guns, and their distinct manner marking them as government agents. The temptation to fly away and not look back grew stronger. Dealing with the king and queen was one matter, one he had no qualms with facing, but the government took matters to new levels. Too many of his kind withered and died under federal interdiction while being blinded by false claims of protection. He had no trust in the men darting through the trees but didn't want to risk a confrontation with them either.

"It is DESA," he said, backing deeper into the shadows.

Sara asked, "What's DESA?"

"A clandestine government department answerable to no one," the gargoyle divulged. "The Department of Extra Species Affairs. They hunt us, contain us, and regulate everything our species does. They are very bad people."

Daniel had never heard of them, but that didn't really surprise him. In Afghanistan, he'd worked with more people that officially didn't exist than he could have imagined. There were government departments by the dozens he'd never heard of before the war, and that frightened him. People that don't exist can get away with anything. *No wonder these guys hate humans so much. We're still hunting them, still trying to be the overlords.*

"Do we engage, or will they ignore us?" he asked, suddenly more concerned with their chances of getting to the princess. Once again the tables had turned, leaving him with the wrong cards.

"It is bad enough they are here; do not risk open confrontation with them unnecessarily. It is a fight we cannot win."

Daniel could have sworn he heard fear in the gargoyle's voice, a tiny tremor just deep enough to be noticeable. *What could possibly scare one of these monsters? And do I really want to run into it?* The answer was no. "We need to find a way around them without being seen. The pavilion can't be far."

"About a quarter of a mile up this hill," Guilt guessed. "But it will take longer to circle around the humans."

"We're not being given much choice, Guilt. Lead us around behind them and get us to the pavilion. Time's running out."

Guilt took off, no more than a shadow amidst the greater darkness. Daniel almost wished he possessed similar attributes. His life would be infinitely easier as the long night drew towards the inevitable conclusion. Giving Sara's shoulder a reassuring squeeze, though whether for her strength or his he wasn't sure, he followed as best as he could.

THIRTY-SIX

The trap, while not overly clever, still managed to take them off guard. Dozens of black-clad elves popped up from behind rocks, dropped down from the ceiling and crept from behind impossibly thin trees. They were well armed and maintained tactical discipline suggesting years of military service. Daniel was instantly reminded of black ops teams in the desert. They'd terrified him then. The dark elves were worse. He couldn't be sure who would let their deep running prejudices take over and plunge a spear through his chest. The thought of being impaled sickened him, but none of the elves surrounding them carried the old weapons. *These bastards have the latest military tech and some sort of thermal dampening material built into their uniforms.*

Now prisoners, they were shuffled deeper into the pavilion. The smells of various primates and other interesting African animals assaulted his nostrils. Foreign plants tried to create the illusion of a sub-Saharan jungle but fell short amidst the rock and unnatural barriers designed to keep the animals isolated from human contact. A mandrill watched them with suspicious eyes. The pale blue stripes flanking its sharp red nose lent the primate a most sinister look and reminded Daniel of the foulness of what was to come.

He passed Sara a reassuring look but found her attention elsewhere. She hadn't met the queen, and her mind raced through different scenarios. Never much of a fighter, she continued to focus on punching the elf in the face. The plastic zip ties binding her wrists made that slightly more difficult.

A pair of dark elf guards blocked their path suddenly, forcing them to bump into one another clumsily. "Wait here," the leader ordered.

Daniel did as he was told. Only Guilt kept moving. His hands remained free, as if the dark elves viewed him as an ally. Daniel grew more suspicious. The gargoyle had given his word, but what did it matter given the admission of his hatred for humans? All of Daniel's plans, hastily wrought and not terribly well thought out, began to unravel, leaving him frustrated to the point where he couldn't think clearly.

The guard returned a moment later and nodded. "They are to come with me. Queen Morgen wishes to speak to the human."

Rough hands shoved him forward, eliciting a deep scowl from both Daniel and Sara. The thought of getting payback was mildly entertaining but ultimately a waste of time. Most of the elves looked alike, at least in his eyes, and even if he did stumble upon the guilty one, there was still the matter of getting through an untold number of others with weapons and advanced combat skills — skills he sorely lacked or had forgotten.

"What about Sara?" Daniel asked after noticing Sara being held in place.

The lead elf sneered. "She stays put. The queen wants to see you alone."

The idea of being separated from Sara after all they'd been through didn't sit well, but he wasn't in any position to take action on it. He struggled against his bonds, knowing all too well how effective they were. US forces used the same on detainees in Iraq. *At least I don't have a sandbag over my face. As long as I can see where I'm going, I'll know how to get out.*

"Wait here," the elf growled and jerked him to a stop.

Daniel bit back the curse immediately coming to mind. A trio of elves remained to guard him. Not that he could have managed much of anything to begin with. A few kicks would only result in him being beaten to the ground. What little strength he had remaining would be sorely needed soon enough. He chose to stand patiently while the elves went about playing their little game of who's in charge. The wait ended abruptly.

Morgen rounded the corner, emerging from behind a series of coffee trees. Her black pants, leather boots and loose-fitting, long-sleeved blouse complemented the pale tint of her flesh while making her appear more sinister, ominous. She was the reason dozens of her kind were nothing more than ash and dust, the reason behind so much unnecessary destruction and mayhem. *How could one person be responsible for so much casual violence?* The question left him stunned. He'd seen his share of combat, and very few commanders were willing to intentionally sacrifice so many for minimal to negligible gains, not to mention those soldiers lacked the discipline and blind submissiveness to follow orders to the death. His stomach rolled at Morgen's smile.

"Hello Daniel," she laughed. "I confess I hadn't planned on seeing you again tonight."

"Funny, I was hoping to be home and in bed by now myself," he fired back.

The smile faded quickly. "Dark times require sacrifice. Why didn't you do as you were told? All you had to do was give Mr. Guilt the box of Carthantos, and you and your lovely little wife could have left. This is your fault."

"My fault? You sent an army of fucking ogres to kill us all!"

"Ah, those. They were told not to harm either of you, but ogres are simple-minded creatures. Once their blood gets up from battle, anything goes."

Daniel shifted uncomfortably, angry and suspicious. "You expect me to believe you forgot that little bit of information? The queen of the dark elves? Bullshit. You knew exactly what you were doing when you deployed your thugs."

Morgen grinned savagely. "Very well, of course I did. I know everything that happens in my realm, no matter how small. The ogres were supposed to kill every last one of you and bring me my heart, but you pesky humans just don't play well with others. I should have had Mr. Guilt kill you from the beginning, but I let curiosity get the best of me. A weakness of mine, I'm afraid."

"You're weakness is getting a lot of people killed tonight," he frowned.

She waved a hand dismissively. "A small price for what is at stake. My armies know exactly what is expected of them. They give their lives freely for the greater cause. What better path to ascension than through becoming a martyr executing the holy crusade?"

Daniel realized then that she was insane, a despot queen who ruled atop piles of bones and empty chairs. When all light faded and the world cooled with death, she alone would remain in her insanity. He shivered at the image of her laughing once the last light died.

"You're mad!" he hissed.

"We're all different things to different people, Daniel. But I grow weary of this. Where is my heart?"

He stiffened. For most of the night, he'd thought of little else but rescuing the princess and keeping the box away from Morgen. Now that he stood before the dark queen with the opportunity to free both himself and Sara, he found he didn't want to. The heart was a powerful weapon that held great bargaining power. Forget the fact that he had it in his ammo vest pouch and the elves could easily relieve him of it if they bothered searching him.

"Let Sara go first," he countered.

Morgen shook her head, having already anticipated such a move. "Why would I do that? Let me make your position perfectly clear to you. The box of Carthantos is on your person. If I want to take it by force, I can, and there is nothing you can do to prevent it. You and your wife are entirely unnecessary."

Confused, he asked, "So why are we here? You could have taken it at any time and let us go. Do it now and save everyone the trouble."

She laughed again, direct and insulting. "Your naivety is refreshing, though somewhat misguided. The box is just a side item. I need you here, Daniel. You've become very important to the success of my task."

"Speak plainly. What is with you elves?"

Morgen stepped closer and told him everything.

Sara watched, helplessly, as he got dragged off around a winding corner and disappeared. Cold crept into her veins. A feeling of dread awakened and whispered that she'd never see him again. Shaking her head to clear the disturbing promises of paranoia, Sara once again fought against the tears. Deep down inside, she knew she wasn't half as strong as she pretended to be.

Realization set in, and she finally admitted to making the mistake of insisting Daniel take her along. *I should have taken my happy ass right back home, but no. Once again, I have to open my big mouth and push my way around. Look where that's landed me now. Up the creek without a paddle, as Daniel would say.* The only fear stronger than dying was her fear of leaving Daniel alone in this hive of villains.

The dark elves didn't seem to care much for her. They spoke their own language in hushed tones, seldom bothering to look her way. She presented no challenge and even less of a threat. Their focus lay on the dawn and the queen's promise of a new day, a new age of glory undreamed of by the clans for two thousand years. What was one lamenting human woman in the face of such glory?

A shadow moved quickly. The glint of silver reflected briefly in the orange glow of the dull overhead light. One of the guards stirred, jerking his head swiftly at some perceived threat. He was too late. The knife ripped across his throat, and he fell, hands clutching the wound in a desperate and ultimately futile attempt at staying alive. The second guard dropped just as quickly. The 9 mm round punched through the back of his head with ruthless precision. Silenced, the gun made no report as the assassin darted through the fauna.

The last guard, stepping over his dying comrade, looked wildly about. His weapon rattled in his trembling hands. More than once, he thought he saw his target, but it was gone before he tried to move on it. Death came swiftly. He never heard the shot, only felt the heated metal plunging into his chest, rupturing the heart, and out his back. His lips twisted in a queer smile as he fell to ash.

Trembling uncontrollably, Sara watched the scene unfold in a handful of seconds. Her fear of the elves dissolved upon seeing how easily they were dispatched. Her mind filled with all the terrible ways she was going to die before coming to understand the assassin wasn't here for her. Hope sparked, and she struggled against her bonds. Tender hands gripped her from behind as the knife cut the zip tie. Her wrists burned as circulation restored.

"Come with me," a woman hissed in her ear.

Rubbing her wrists, Sara asked, "Who are you?"

"My name is Cassandra, and I'm here to help."

"Why should I trust you?" Sara asked defiantly. Not a single soul she'd met on this strange adventure seemed overly interested in her wellbeing, and she had no reason to believe Cassandra did either.

"Because I am trying to save your lives. You and Daniel never should have gotten involved, but the Fates have different plans for us all. The high king sent me to watch over you, but I haven't been able to catch up with you until now. Your husband is in grave danger, Sara. We need to move quickly and quietly if there's any hope of rescuing him from the dark queen."

Cassandra emerged from the shadows, lowering her black facemask for Sara to see the sincerity in her eyes. It still wasn't enough to allay her suspicions. She'd been lied to enough already. "Why us? Your people have been trying to kill us since I was kidnapped from my own home. I don't have any reason to believe a word you've just said."

"Perhaps not," Cassandra answered quickly. There was a glimmer of something dangerous lurked behind her eyes. "Forget that I risked my own life to dispatch your captors. Or how I've been following you halfway across this state. None of this would be happening if Daniel had simply accepted the fact that no one was willing to touch his new book. Has he told you what happened at the agency? How he found Ariel dying? How her brother, the greatest champion the high elf clans has ever known, gave his life so that Daniel could escape with the box of Carthantos? We have all lost something dear tonight, Sara. Don't be the catalyst for more sorrow come the dawn."

That stern defiance weakened a little. Daniel had kept most of what had happened to himself, more likely to protect her from any unnecessary worry than to spare her the gory details. He'd never been one to share the bad stuff. Some things just didn't need to be shared. Most of his combat experiences remained secure in the vaults of his memory, unwilling and unable to accurately come out. For that, she was grateful. Tonight's events told her more than enough, and she knew she didn't want to know what had happened when her husband went to war.

Sara also gleaned one important bit of information. Cassandra had said that Xander was dead. Only Sara knew that wasn't true. She'd seen him with her own eyes back at the fairgrounds. Xander was alive and well, and deep in the conspiracy consuming them all. Games within games. Perhaps she wasn't as powerless as she'd thought.

Sara looked at Cassandra hard. The other woman had strength, but in the end, she was still an elf, and elves just couldn't be trusted. Still, she couldn't ignore the overpowering need to confront the queen and get some measure of restitution for the trauma she'd been forced to endure. Vengeance is a powerful motivator, and Sara's heart was filled with it.

"Very well," she finally relented. "Let's go see this queen and get my husband back."

Cassandra nodded and headed off. Sara followed the she-elf down the opposite path from where the dark elves had taken Daniel.

THIRTY-SEVEN

Daniel jerked back at the sudden revelation. His eyes widened in shock while he struggled to comprehend what Morgen had just told him. Once again, it didn't make sense. Everything he thought he knew was, at least according to her, a boldfaced lie meant to deceive him into working for the wrong forces. Unable to comprehend, he couldn't form the words to reply.

To her credit, the queen of the dark elves stepped back, folded her slender arms across her chest, and waited for the sudden information to process.

"My queen, I have dire news to report!" a scar-faced elf interrupted. He burst into the pavilion, red faced and breathing hard.

Morgen spun away from Daniel, anger flashing from her eyes. "This had better be worth my time, sergeant."

"Yes, your majesty. Our observation post overlooking the southern entrance just reported the king is here!"

Morgen's heart fluttered. Alvin! *He shouldn't have come. That fool is putting us all in jeopardy. I need to move quickly to preserve the night.* "Are you certain?" She winced, already knowing the futility of the question. "Double the guard around the pavilion. The king must not be allowed to interfere!"

"What about his house guard? Surely he's brought Stern and a heavy compliment of troops with him."

"Kill Stern if he gets in the way but stop the king!"

"Yes, your majesty!"

The elf raced off. Morgen felt time slipping through her fingers. Desperation compelled her actions, forcing her hand in ways she wasn't wholly prepared to accept without grave consequences. The threat of war echoed in everything she did. Never before had such a helpless feeling engulfed her to the point of abject terror.

Morgen turned back to Daniel. "My estranged husband seems to have a mind of his own. If I cut your bonds, will you behave?"

Daniel raised his hands. "As long as I can get my gun back. I don't want to get caught in what's coming unarmed."

"You may have your weapon once my heart is safely back in my possession," the Queen countered and gestured for one of the guards to cut the zip tie.

Freed, Daniel rubbed his wrists and pulled the box of Carthantos out of his ammo pouch. The ebony material drew in his gaze in, mesmerizing him with its enchantments. Shaking his head, Daniel held the box up. "On one condition."

"Be careful. Your next words may be your last."

The threat held no sting, and they both knew it. She'd already told him everything he needed to know, and it was all grim. Still, the promise of extreme violence loomed on the horizon should he overstep his bounds. That much had been made clear the moment she'd whispered her secrets.

Daniel didn't have any other choice but to keep going and lay out his hand. "Once all of this is finished, I want out. To go home and never hear from any of you again."

"Agreed. Now, the box."

His gaze went from the alluring wizard's box to her impatient palm. Turning over the heart proved more difficult than he'd imagined, and the slightest hesitancy gripped him like paranoia. He couldn't say why, but the box whispered to him, warned him not to turn it over to her. For reasons he'd never know, Daniel ignored the dire warnings protecting the box and gently began to hand it over.

The box hummed. Tiny jolts of electricity stretched between them. Morgen gasped, a quiet, imperceptible sound. Her eyes fluttered, though Daniel didn't notice. Voltage burned through his body, threatening to drop him to the ground. Reluctantly, the box slipped from his grasp and landed firmly in Morgen's hand. Vivid yellow light, the color of a dying sun, filled the pavilion. Explosions echoed around the dome. Morgen collapsed.

Elves rushed to her side before she managed to wave them away. She was a queen, not some mongrel-serving wench. Pushing up off the ground with as much dignity as she could muster given the situation, Morgen's eyes shined brightly. "At last! Alvin has kept this from me for so long. I am whole!"

Having staggered back, Daniel blinked rapidly, wiping the sparkling flashes from his vision. The box was gone. "What happened?"

Smiling for the first true time in decades, the queen of the dark elves stretched out her hands in unfiltered joy. "You have undone that which was promised to never be undone. You've helped me shatter the wizard's curse and returned my heart. Never again will my husband or any other hold dominion over me. I am once again the true queen of darkness."

There were very few *oh, shit* moments in Daniel's life, but this certainly classified as one of them. He wasn't sure if his involvement had been planned from the beginning or simply a poorly played ruse intended to keep him guessing long enough for Morgen to get her way and begin the war everyone seemed so intent on fighting.

"You shouldn't have done that!" a stern voice warned.

Everyone but Morgen turned, weapons rising. They were too late. Eight human soldiers in black armor armed with assault rifles were already in firing positions and ready to fire once the order was given. A ninth stood behind them, hands resting comfortably on the rifle slung over his chest.

"Your government has no business here, human!" Morgen seethed. Shadows gathered around her.

Agent Blackmere shrugged her concerns off. "Because of you, I've had to clean up downtown Raleigh, a ruined church in the middle of nowhere, complete with the wreckage of one of my helicopters, and now here. We have an agreement, Morgen. You mind your affairs, and we look the other way. Too many people witnessed this insanity."

"You will address me as your majesty, human. Remember your place."

Daniel started taking tiny side steps to get clear of the line of fire in case the heated exchange led to a firefight. Blackmere, to his credit, didn't rise to the bait. He'd dealt with both king and queen enough times to recognize bluster. "Morgen, we don't have time for games. You've got a mess of trouble streaming this way and no time to stop it."

"Fool. What could possibly go wrong now? Everything has led us to this very point. Shall I tell you what's going to happen?" Morgen slipped in front of her guards. "The high elf king is desperately trying to get inside this very building under the auspices of beginning an ancient ritual intended to reunite our two great houses and bring the elf race back to our rightful place in the world. The fool always was brash when it came to dealing with family. Unfortunately, our dear daughter will suffer for it, for it is her blood alone that can enact the magic. A small price don't you think?"

Blackmere squinted in frustration. "You're going to sacrifice your only child just so you can get back in power? You're one sick bitch, lady."

"Apples and oranges, Agent Blackmere."

"As the senior representative of DESA and the United States government I hereby order you to desist your actions and return to your home. No further measures will be taken against you if you comply imm…"

"Enough, you insipid little worm! I am queen and goddess, one who roamed these lands centuries before your kind slithered their way from the deepest ponds. Who are you to give me orders? Guards! Kill them!"

Two quick explosions rocked the pavilion. Windows shattered. A scream suddenly cut off. Bodies blew through the trees, crashing into stone and water. Branches and leaves drifted back down from the ceiling. A wall of smoke stormed inside. The air grew thick, choking. Men and elves picked themselves back up and searched for the new threat. Frantic orders were shouted over the ringing in ears. The tiny red beams of tracking lasers crisscrossed the interior.

Morgen was rushed to safety, leaving Daniel, the DESA teams, and the remaining dark elves exposed and bewildered. Heavy footsteps echoed down the cold concrete. Daniel watched the queen leave and knew it was time to do the same. Picking up his rifle from the ground where the guards had left it, he sprinted for cover back the way he'd been brought. Hopefully, Sara would still be in the same area, and they had the chance to escape before all hell broke loose.

Sixty high elves quickly filled the small area, each armed and ready to fight. The dark elf lines bristled with barely contained hatred. Generations of strife left no love between the clans. It was only through the steel discipline of commanders on both sides that the firing didn't begin. No one was in a position to willingly throw away lives unnecessarily. Not with the king and queen so closely involved.

Blackmere directed his fire teams to take up a tactical position in the empty meerkat pit. They formed a strong line perfectly covered by the plastered low wall. He briefly considered radioing for help, but none would arrive in time to save anyone if it came to battle. His small team of eight was outmanned, outgunned and outmatched by incredible odds. He'd never seen so many elves together at one time, and that frightened him.

"Orders, sir?" one of the sergeants asked.

Orders? What good are those going to do? "Hold position and maintain situational awareness. No one fires unless we have to. Let's let these pointy-eared bastards figure out what they're going to do first. If it comes to a fight, standard protocols apply. Take out the leadership and neutralize the rest."

"We can't take on that many," the youngest member said, shaking visibly.

"Sure, we can," Blackmere confided. *We just won't win.*

"Lay down your weapons immediately!" Stern's voice echoed through the pavilion. The high elf moved with authority, claiming the battlefield as his own without regard for anyone else. He knew as well as the dark elves that neither side was prepared to go head to head in such an enclosed space with the king and queen nearby. Any stray round could be lethal, the effects catastrophic. Stern was more than willing to risk battle. Honor demanded it, but at the cost of his king.

A dark elf called back, "Lower yours, high elf scum. You're surrounded and outnumbered."

"Is that so?" Stern smirked. "Dwarves in my employ hold the main gate. Your southern guards simply let us walk in unchallenged. What advantage do you think you have, I wonder?"

As head of security, Stern threw himself into his work with ruthless passion. He became hatred untamed when the cool grip of a rifle settled into his hands. Battle offered him the opportunity to lose himself to baser, more animalistic impulses. He'd never felt more alive than after taking another life. The first set of guards had proved little more than an appetizer for his bloodlust.

He counted enemy numbers, satisfied with the ratio despite being outnumbered three to one. The dark elves weren't the problem. Their tactics and attack patterns were so well known, he could execute them with little trouble. It was the human contingent that sparked worry. He'd known, through contact with Cassandra, that Xander had his own band of RRTF agents operating with him. The ones digging in a few meters back weren't it, presenting him with a totally different problem.

Government involvement brought matters to an entirely new level of action he didn't immediately commit to. Losses suffered at the fairgrounds by Xander were acceptable — laudable, even — in Stern's eyes. Humans had no business in elf affairs. Like everything else, once the government became involved, the game changed. More demands. More oversight. The scourge of the world continued to force itself upon those deemed less than equal. He contemplated moving against the RRTF first in order to neutralize their contact with the outside. It was a temporary measure at best, one that wouldn't keep more from arriving in force to bring Alvin's house down brick by brick.

Any decision was ripped from his control moments later when a pair of pickup trucks crashed through the opposite doors. Dwarves poured out, immediately taking up good firing positions with interlocking fields of fire. Cigar smoke plumed from Angus's nostrils. Beside him stood Xander, the remaining handful of RRTF agents and Bert, the troll. Stern scowled deeply, already recalculating his odds of success. Four factions, each with individual objectives. *This should prove an interesting fight.*

THIRTY-EIGHT

Princess Gwen resented the squalor of captivity in which she'd been kept for the last twelve hours. The indignity of it insulted her gravely. She was the heir to the throne of the high elves, now no more than a caged animal for others to view with passing amusement. Worse, her own mother had been responsible for her kidnapping and imprisonment. The foul deeds forced her to reexamine her position with both parents. Tied ankle and wrist to an old wooden chair, Gwen could do nothing but stare out the large-frame windows on the bottom level and reflect.

There are times in everyone's life when fate interferes. Grand designs fall short. A peasant becomes a king. Rivers flood and the earth goes barren. Every so often, fate takes an unexpected twist, throwing all conventional knowledge and wisdom to the wolves. Gwen could feel such an event. It electrified her skin, ached deep in her skeleton. She couldn't be certain, but an unprecedented moment flickered on the edges of reality, moving closer to engulf her and countless others converging on her position. All she needed to do was sit and wait.

The wait proved far shorter than she imagined. Cassandra and Sara were the first to arrive. The human woman was out of breath, trembling from fright, causing Gwen to sneer. Ever were humans trying to prove their lack of worth. Gwen grew confused upon seeing her. Whatever question she readied to ask died on her lips after Cassandra shook her head in a nearly imperceptible move.

"Princess, are you injured?" she asked, moving in to cut the ropes.

Gwen offered her best face. "No, but they will be back soon. We must hurry."

Sara, her breath normal, could only stare. After so much talk and mental conjuring, she stood before the princess of the high elf clans. Strange disappointment clashed with awe and a surprisingly minor amount of interest. *So this is the cause of our trouble. She doesn't look like much.*

"You seem concerned, human," Gwen said, angered at the lack of respect.

"I expected more," Sara replied tartly.

Even Cassandra paused, the knife halfway through the ropes.

To her credit, Gwen maintained her composure. "At one time, I was. Your people have reduced me to this."

Fair enough, but it's not like I actually care. I never dreamed you existed until a few hours ago. The thought sounded good in her head, though Sara doubted it would translate very well, especially considering how her husband was expected to save the princess. An awkward silence settled between them.

"Where is Xander?" Gwen asked sharply. That a human had arrived as part of the rescue party could only mean matters had gone horribly wrong. There was no other way her father would have dared involve them. She feared the worst.

Cassandra finished the last rope around her wrists and moved to the ankles. "Princess, I..."

"Oh, I imagine he'll show up shortly," Sara interrupted.

"Is he alright?" She couldn't keep the desperation from bleeding through her tone.

"Many have died this night. Ariel was the first casualty. Absolutely everything that could have gone wrong has." Cassandra fell silent and continued to cut.

Sadness gripped her heart, but Gwen lacked the words to voice it. Ariel had been her best friend for centuries. And now she was dead. Nothing, but ash and already fading memories. How cruel life became when no one was looking. Too many opposing thoughts clashed to give her a clear mind. Revenge. Sorrow. The unnecessary need to know why.

Why didn't matter. It rarely did. Ariel was gone, and that was that.

"What is the meaning of this?" Morgen raged upon entering the room.

The women stopped and turned. Guards flanked the dark queen, though she proved a daunting enough figure without them. Sara had never seen a woman so wholly consumed by evil. Waves of hatred poured from her body in sheets. Violence shone brightly in her eyes, the promise of eternal damnation itching to be set free.

"Mother, your time is ended!" Gwen screamed. Pent up emotions drained her, leaving her a wreck when she needed to be strong.

Hands on her hips, Morgen seethed, "How dare you! What would you be without me? I gave you life, you miserable little bitch."

"This is the worst family reunion I've ever seen," a new voice called from the shadows surrounding the stairwell.

Sara grinned despite the uncertainty of the moment. The voice was the sweetest, most comforting she'd heard. Daniel came into view, weapon aimed at Morgen's heart. The look in his eyes spoke volumes. His intentions were perfectly clear; one small mistake, and the queen of the dark elves died.

"You again," Morgen said snidely. "You've become quite the persistent thorn in my side, Daniel. I'm impressed. How about a job?"

"I'm done with you psychos. There was a time when I held the idea of what you are in adoration. Every word I wrote was one of love. The truth is far less than what I had hoped. There's a reason your race fell from the top of the food chain," he answered.

Thick, dark veins protruded across her forehead. "Do tell, *human*."

"You're so self-centered you've ruined everything. You're not a queen," Daniel accused. "You're just a puppet lost in the past. Give it up and realize where you are, lady.

The world doesn't need your kind anymore, not like this. You are obsolete."

Her guards moved as one, bringing their weapons up. Daniel was faster. He shot the first in the stomach and trained his rifle on the second. The survivor halted, suddenly less sure about defending his queen. Many promises had been made, but death seemed the only relevant one at the moment. He lowered his weapon and slowly raised empty hands.

"Seems your people don't share your convictions, your highness," Daniel said. "There are two ways we can end this. Peacefully: we all walk away and try to forget it ever happened. Or I make a lot of little piles of dirt for the janitors to clean up tomorrow."

"What makes you so confident that you have the upper hand? Or perhaps you are showing off in front of your lovely little wife?"

"Lower your weapons and move against the wall," Xander interrupted. The cold steel of his sword glowed in the near dark. He'd had enough. So much violence and death had changed him. He'd expected casualties in order to bring his meticulous plans to fruition, but nothing on the level seen tonight. Many friends were gone and, while he was more than willing to sacrifice a few more in order to succeed, he wanted it to end.

Bert loomed just behind; the troll was still visibly distraught at the loss of his brother. A handful of RRTF soldiers fanned out to take up defensive positions around the lower stairwell. Hidden behind reflective face visors, they were a mixture of scared and nervous. Too many had already been killed by ogres to leave them with much confidence.

Morgen seemed most unsurprised by Xander's sudden appearance. "The paladin of the light. You're supposed to be dead, Xander."

"I would have been if you'd have sent better men. As it is, they work for me," he replied coolly.

She narrowed her eyes. Crimson flashed hotly in her cheeks. "What do you mean?"

"Mother, you're a fool," Gwen interrupted and, finally free, marched to stand beside her betrothed. "Between your meddling and Father's procrastination, it's a wonder the pair of you haven't sunk the clans into total ruin. The time has come for new leadership."

"What blasphemy is this?" Morgen asked, slowly realizing what was happening.

Gwen smiled sweetly, hands on her slender hips. "We're taking over. Your time is finished. It is time for the clans to rise again. This world once belonged to us; it's time to reclaim it for the glory of our species!"

"That's what this has all been about?" Daniel demanded, angered at the deception. "A fucking coup?"

"Don't be so crass, Daniel," Gwen scolded. "No one asked you to get involved in the first place."

"But now that you have, there isn't any way we can just let you walk away. You've seen too much. Know too much," Xander added.

"You aren't keeping me," Daniel snarled, briefly considering raising his rifle.

"Don't," one of the RRTF warned.

Xander shook his head. "I'm afraid your death will be more appropriate. You've proven a major pain tonight. Much too dangerous to be allowed free."

"That's murder!" Sara exclaimed.

"Of course it is. Now, weapons down and hands up," Xander ordered.

Reluctantly, Daniel did as instructed and backed towards Sara. If he had to die, he wanted to be at her side. The frightened look on her face spoke volumes, but, to her credit, she refused to look away from the cold steel weapons pointed at her. Daniel had never felt more love or adoration than at that moment. He tried to find the right words to say, anything before the violence of death tore through them, but nothing came to mind. Now that the end had arrived, he was rendered speechless, impotent.

The explosion shook the pavilion a moment before the concussion threw many of them to the floor. Black smoke flowed in along the ceiling. Dust and bits of plaster drifted down in showers. Someone coughed. Another groaned from a broken ankle. Heavy footsteps echoed down the stairwell. Daniel looked through the haze and spotted the unrepentant figure of Stern marching towards them. Directly behind strode Alvin. Daniel didn't know whether to laugh or weep.

"What is the meaning of this?" Alvin roared.

Cassandra, picking herself up, slid through the stunned crowd. Her eyes focused. Intensity radiated from her body. Alvin started to smile when he saw her coming to him, thinking he was about to get answers. Cassandra's arm rose slowly. The dark pistol was all but un-seeable in the fractured light. His grin dissolved. She fired once. Twice. Three times before his body burst apart in a cloud of dust and ash. The high king of the elves was dead.

She flung two grenades towards the combined guard force and ran. Morgen screamed, her world shattered down around her. Those guards not stunned by the assassination opened fire. Cassandra fled for her life a split second before the grenades exploded.

THIRTY-NINE

Daniel lifted his head up. His ears rang from the dual explosions. His vision drifted in and out. Sara groaned under his weight. He'd thrown himself down on top of her to protect her from the blasts, bruising her ribs in the process.

"Are you all right?" he asked.

Sara nodded slowly. "Get us out of here."

"Where is she?" Stern bellowed.

Most of his guards were back on their feet and beginning the search for the assassin. Morgen, stunned, sat in a crumpled heap cloaked in her misery. Sobs racked her body. Tears flowed down her cheeks unchecked. Despite their irreconcilable differences, she did still love Alvin, though would never admit it.

"I want Cassandra found immediately! Do not harm her," Stern ordered. "I want to do that myself."

"What about the others?"

Stern looked at the survivors. He despised the humans but didn't view them as a threat. They were too stunned to pose much of a problem. Besides, they only wanted to go home, making them a non-factor. The queen was a mess, much too bereaved to put up much of a fight. Her soldiers, rightfully so, clustered around to protect the fallen matriarch. That left Xander, Gwen and his RRTF. They were the real threats.

Xander made the decision for him. "Kill the high elves!"

RRTF soldiers opened fire. Three elves died in the first salvo. Stern fired and was rewarded by watching the armored soldier drop. Blood fountained from his exposed throat. The elves gathered their wits and counterattacked. Stern led the charge into the small ranks of men with swords drawn. Rifles were used as clubs. Men fell stabbed. Elves dropped under crushing blows to their heads. The clash of bodies and weapons was frighteningly loud, evidence of the bitter hatred between races. Very soon, the floor ran red with blood and bodies.

Stunned at the ferocity of the battle, Bert shook his head sorrowfully and backed away. Dying wasn't going to bring Lou back or make his dead ma proud. The troll decided it was time to look out for himself for the first time since being sent by Morgen to Daniel's house.

Daniel noticed the troll disappear and, refocusing his attention on his wife, decided to follow suit. It was past time that they leave. "Come on, we're getting out of here."

"What about her?" she asked, gesturing to the queen.

Daniel frowned. "What about her? She's got what she deserved."

"Daniel, we can't just leave her like this. She'll be killed!"

"And?"

Pursing her lips in an angry move he recognized too well, Sara said, "What would you do if I died in front of you?"

He sighed, knowing the decision had been made for him. "Fine, but if she causes any trouble it's on your head."

Sara smiled and headed towards the queen.

"Your highness, we're going to take you out of this mess," Daniel said, reaching down to help her up.

Morgen pushed him away. "Go on, leave me! Alvin is dead. It has all been pointless. Millennia of plotting, waiting and for what? Death truly does claim us in the end. Now those dreams are just dust. Let me die with some dignity."

"I don't have time for your self-pity bullshit. Everything that has happened tonight is your damned fault. Now get up off your ass and follow me," Daniel barked.

Morgen allowed him to help her up and did as she was told. A great weight slipped from her shoulders as she relinquished all responsibility. Grand dreams of reunification fell to ash, much like her husband, leaving her a hollow shell.

She fled from her life, knowing she'd never be able to escape. She was still the queen of the dark elf clans. Too many looked to her for decisions.

They made it back to the stairs when another group of RRTF stopped them. Unlike the men under Xander's influence, which Daniel noticed were wearing singular red bands around their right arms, these were less apt to shoot first. Their leader waved their weapons down after he recognized Morgen and stepped forward to introduce himself.

"I'm Agent Blackmere of DESA. What's going on down here?"

Daniel regarded the man carefully. Without knowing which side who was on he decided to keep it simple. "The king is dead, murdered by one of his own. The princess and her boyfriend are trying to take over, and we're getting the queen to safety."

"Don't forget the battle between the elves and humans," Sara added.

Blackmere's face darkened. "What humans?"

"There's a bunch of guys dressed like you fighting with Xander. They have red identification markings on their arms. You didn't know?"

"Take four of my men and make your way back to the main entrance. I hear there's a pack of dwarves waiting for you," Blackmere said and turned to his teams. "The rest of you, with me. We're going to put a stop to this."

The battle ended quickly. Much of the fight had gone from the elves after seeing the king die and the queen disappear. Blackmere's DESA team attacked from the rear, dropping as many targets as possible with specially designed rounds that penetrated the central nervous system. Elves and humans fell immobile yet fully coherent. Making sense of it was something else entirely. Three RRTF soldiers were down, one dead. Light and dark elves suffered similarly. Who knew how many had already died? A few managed to escape but wouldn't get far before being captured.

Blackmere strode through the prone bodies, searching for the familiar faces of any leadership. He stumbled upon Stern first and knelt beside the chief of security. Raw hatred poured from the elf's eyes. Blackmere knew Stern was fighting the chemicals, trying to win free and escape. Unfortunately for him, the more he struggled, the deeper the chemicals took root in his bloodstream.

"Mr. Stern, I am Blackmere, senior field agent," he said. "The chemicals in our rounds have rendered your muscles useless, temporarily of course, but you can still speak. I need to know exactly what happened here."

"Why should I tell you anything?" Stern growled.

Blackmere set his helmet down and ran a hand through his hair. "There's the question, eh? Because I represent the federal government, and I can promise that you'll never see the light of day again if you fail to cooperate. So how about it, sport?"

Stern knew Blackmere's reputation and that of the special prison located on a tiny island in the middle of the Hudson River. No one who went in ever came out. He gave in. "This has been brewing for a while, but we didn't know how deep it went. Xander and the princess tried to overthrow the king and queen even as the clans were trying to reunite. Then some humans got involved."

"We have the humans and queen secure. Where is the king?" Blackmere asked.

"Dead. Cassandra killed him."

Shit. Blackmere rocked back on his heels as if slapped in the face. News of this would turn Washington on its head. "Get this man the antidote. All of them but these two right here and our rogue friends. They're going to jail."

Xander and Gwen were arrested for their crimes. Xander maintained innocence even as Gwen railed against their capture and the righteousness of their cause. Blackmere had heard it all before. The last rant of the condemned. He frowned down on her prone figure, amazed at how low the second highest-ranking member of the high elf clans had reduced herself.

Those RRTF members working for Xander were led off in custody. DESA frowned upon extracurricular activities, especially when it came to regicide. The rogues would stand trial for treason and conspiracy to commit insurrection, but their actions would leave a stain on DESA's reputation. Regardless, Blackmere had done his job. His only problem lay in what to do with the human couple involved. He left the mop-up to Stern and his revived elves, under careful watch of his fire team, and went to find Daniel.

"Is it over?" Sara asked, spotting him coming up the stairs first.

Blackmere gazed at her a moment before shifting to the queen. His heart slowed upon seeing Morgen. The queen looked decidedly less regal than he had imagined. Never having met either of them, Blackmere wasn't quite sure what to expect. She was broken and wore a bewildered look.

"Your majesty, my name is Thaddeus Blackmere with DESA. Please accept my condolences for your loss. I'll dispatch a team to ensure you return home safely once this is cleaned up. Is there anything else I can do for you?"

Morgen shook her head, a fresh stream of tears breaking free. "Where is my daughter?"

"She's secure. We're moving her to a nearby holding facility," Blackmere replied.

"He's dead. Gone. It's finished because of her."

"She's had a rough day," Daniel cut in. "We all have."

"I agree, and I'm sorry you got involved with this. The elves usually have better sense than that."

"You mean the government knows?" Sara asked in surprise.

Blackmere smiled. "Of course we do. I work for the Department of Extra Species Affairs. We're assigned to keep an eye on these folks and ensure nothing terrible leaks out into the general public. Until now, it's worked out fine."

Daniel shrugged. Nothing surprised him anymore. "You could have showed up sooner. A lot of people died tonight."

"Unfortunate, but my hands were tied," Blackmere added. "I've heard you gave a good accounting of yourself tonight. I could use an extra hand, someone who knows their way around a gun."

"You're the second person to offer me a job tonight. I have one. I'm an author," Daniel answered.

"Last time I checked, an M-4 isn't a pen," Blackmere countered. "Just think about it. I don't need an answer now."

Sara cut in. "Agent Blackmere, is there anything you can do to keep these people from harassing us further?"

"I believe so. We are the government, after all," he said with a deceptive smile.

FORTY

Sara yawned and stretched. The towel wrapped around her torso slipped just enough to produce a smile out of Daniel. Wet hair dangling around her face, she pouted and waggled her finger. He tossed a wet washcloth at her and laughed.

"Can you believe it's been a week already?" he asked while applying toothpaste to his brush.

Sara finished drying off. "The longest week of my life. I can't help but think more of those pesky elves are lurking in our hedges, despite Agent Blackmere's promise of protection."

Truth be told, they'd only had one further incident. Bert had showed up two days after the affair ended. Unusually humble, he'd sincerely apologized for his part in the business and vowed to help them if they ever needed it. The troll refuted being a fighter, unlike his elf counterparts, and still wallowed in the misery of losing his brother. Daniel had nearly cried himself with the admission and pledge. Some things in life continued to amaze.

He spit. "I think a week of nothing happening means the elves are going to leave us alone. They've got bigger issues. The light clans need a new leader. Morgen hasn't been heard from since her husband died. We should be fine."

"Hmm, I still feel like I need some protection," she said and walked out into the bedroom.

Daniel looked down at the wet towel heaped on the floor. "Oh, I think I can be all the protection you need."

Whistling softly, he strode into the bedroom, expecting to find her naked and waiting. He opened his mouth to speak but fell short as his gaze fell upon his wife. Sara was indeed naked but with a knife held to her throat. Daniel's heart froze, eyes following the slender arm up to Cassandra's face. The blond elf stared daggers at him.

"Don't do it," Cassandra warned. "I'll enjoy ripping her throat open."

Daniel slowly raised his empty hands. "What are you doing here?"

"You spoiled my revenge; now I'm here to spoil something of yours," she replied. "Unless you can think of a better way to pay me back."

"Get your hands off of her, bitch," Daniel seethed.

Cassandra laughed and pushed Sara down onto her face. "Relax, lover boy. I didn't come here for her. I came to kill you."

"What did I ever do to you?"

"Your interference kept me from killing Morgen," Cassandra answered. "I got Alvin, but you helped her escape back to her fortress."

"Cassandra, it's over. Xander and his girlfriend are going to prison. Whatever you owed them is null."

"Owed them? I used them! They wanted to take over the clans. I only wanted Alvin and Morgen dead for killing my parents. This is all about revenge, Daniel."

"I am sick of you fucking elv—"

As Cassandra lunged, Sara snatched the lamp on the nightstand, smashing it into the back of the elf's head. Glass shattered. The knife skittered out of Cassandra's hand. Blood ran down the back of her head. Sara didn't relent. She tackled Cassandra, raining blows on her face and stomach. Another time, Daniel might have been aroused at the sight of his naked wife on top of another woman, but now he feared for her life. Sara didn't pay him any attention. She was defending her home and her husband.

Cassandra managed to bring her knee up and kick Sara off. She rolled over, trying to get up. The bar of soap caught her in the temple, and she fell with a sharp gasp. Sara, winded, pulled herself to where the dagger had landed and grasped the cold weapon. Cassandra hit her a second later, landing on top of her and driving the wind from both in the process. They punched and slapped, desperately tried to push each other away. A cross blow split Cassandra's lip. Bright, red blood trickled from Sara's nose.

Daniel jumped in, snatching Cassandra's golden hair and flinging her away. The elf was surprisingly strong and a trained killer. She tucked into the roll and popped up on a knee, using her right hand to brace her slide. The vehement look in her eyes told Daniel all he needed to know. She wasn't going to stop until someone was dead. She charged again, too fast for him to react. A pair of blows caught him on the side of his head. Dazed, he swayed groggily before she delivered a roundhouse kick to his temple. He dropped unconscious.

"It's just you and me now, pretty," Cassandra growled through quickened breath. "Looks like I get to kill you after all."

Sara stared at Daniel's body, searching for the rise and fall of his chest.

"He'll be fine, which is more than I can say for you," the elf threatened and advanced again.

Speed and the force of her impact made a perfect combination. She'd hoped to catch Sara off guard and finish the fight quickly. Instead, she staggered backwards a few steps and clutched at the dagger buried to the hilt in her stomach. Blood poured down her legs. Her lips blued. Confusion twisted her features. She dropped to her knees, mouth opening and closing uselessly.

"You should have stayed in hiding," Sara said.

Cassandra died with a strangled rattle. Her body broke apart in ash and dust, only the memory of her confusion vivid in Sara's mind. The dagger hit the floor with a loud clang, bringing her back to reality. Sara knelt beside her husband and cradled him in her arms. Fresh tears flowed down her cheeks as all the pent up emotions and rush of adrenaline flushed out of her system. She was left with the feeling of finality.

His eyes fluttered open, dazed and unfocused. "Is she?"

She nodded. "Yes. It's over."

Groaning in pain, Daniel stared up into his wife's soft eyes. "We're going to need to take another shower."

She laughed, melodious and light. "Can you get up?"

Truthfully, he didn't want to. Her embrace felt too good to abandon. "I think so."

Sara helped him, sitting him on the edge of the bed while she went to slip into her housecoat. She carefully stepped over what remained of the elf assassin and broken glass.

"Mommy, what was all that noise?" their son asked from their doorway, rubbing his tired eyes.

Tightening the sash on her housecoat, Sara went over and hugged him. "Nothing hunny. Everything is all right."

Daniel watched her lead their son back to his room. The pile of ash at his feet was a grim reminder that their life was anything but normal anymore. He looked down at the small notepad and pen he always kept beside the bed for when inspiration struck. Half of his life had been spent pretending to be a great warrior in one of his fantasy novels. Reality proved disheartening. He'd gotten to live that dream, at the cost of his sins and now was left feeling…empty. *How am I ever going to get back to writing?* Grinning, he hurried to follow Sara to the shower. Cassandra's ashes were beginning to stink.

Watching from the shadows beneath a large maple tree, Norman Guilt quietly processed what had just happened. His initial desire to help the human woman had faded as quickly as it sprung to life. He couldn't figure out why, but the woman had a unique aura surrounding her. She was special. More so than her husband. The gargoyle was impressed with the ease with which she'd killed Cassandra — impressed and worried. He had a sinking suspicion that the world of elves and men were going to collide soon, and there'd be hell to pay when it did.

Whistling, Norman Guilt stuffed his hands in the outer pockets of his overcoat and strode off into the night.

Preview of the Lazarus Men

"Once you agree to this you can never go back. Your life will change forever and not necessarily for the best," Mr. Shine said, his thin hands clasped behind his back.

Carter Gaetis paused to glance at the odd man. Grave doubts plagued him. It had been months since their first meeting and he still didn't wholly trust Mr. Shine. Several qualities making him human were missing in Carter's opinion. Shine was tall, lightly built and possessing a permanent sneer. His pale complexion and dark hair lent a cadaverous presence Carter found acutely disturbing. The perpetual rasp in his voice was due to an injury sustained in the line of fire long before Carter was born.

Mr. Shine continued, "Are you prepared to commit yourself, your life and your dedication, to our cause, Mr. Gaetis?"

Carter tensed. He was torn. Born to believe there was no escaping the past, Carter spent years languishing under the effects of being convicted of murder in a court of law. Penniless. Branded a villain by the rigid constrictors of society, he contemplated suicide. Darkness crept into all corners of his life, all but his wife and daughter. They'd stood beside him through the worst of it, but even that wasn't enough. The longer he failed to act the more they suffered. His sad tale dragged them down right along beside him, furthering his compounded misery.

"Once you say the word all of your pain will be erased. Your debts to society will be paid in full and you will be free. Born again into a new life, a new purpose."

For a price. Nothing comes without a price. The real question is am I willing to pay it so blindly? There must be another way.

But there wasn't. All his options were exhausted. He'd tried finding work but convicts were mostly shunned. Mr. Shine offered him an escape but the cost, the cost threatened the security of his very soul. Carter wasn't a violent man, or so he told himself. He'd tried to live a good life, to matter in the eyes of god and his peers. A drunken moment of indecision stripped it all away and brought him to this point. He clenched his jaw, teeth grinding.

Mr. Shine, for his part, had done this innumerable times before. Each was unique but the candidates all acted similarly. He'd come to the quaint living hab expecting Carter's indecisiveness. After all, it was no easy thing to accept the forceful removal of one's past life without grave concerns. Shine rolled the stiffness from his right shoulder, the lingering effects of an old injury, and viewed the street. The sleepy village along the Hudson River would have gone unnoticed if not for human expansionism. Linking Canada to old New York City via the major train hubs, the Hudson River maintained the prominence it once held during the colonization of the New World some six hundred years earlier.

Shine inhaled the early autumn smells of changing foliage and the dampness of the river. He briefly considered retiring to this part of the world before chastising himself. There was no way a man like Shine could ever retire in any fashion save one: an assassin's kiss. He exhaled mild disappointment. This forgotten stretch of the world was one of the few peaceful places he'd ever been.

Carter finally asked, "Will they suffer?"

Mr. Shine smiled in the dark. "No. Their part in this sad tale will finally be over. They will be free, Mr. Gaetis, much as you will be."

Carter sighed. He wished there was another way. Anything but this. Sadly there wasn't. He was as much a victim of circumstance as his family. With grave reluctance, Carter nodded curtly. There was no other option.

"Please Mr. Gaetis, I need to hear you say it," Shine insisted. His eyes took on a wicked glow.

"Yes, Mr. Shine. I accept your offer."

His words lacked the conviction with which they were meant. Carter was a strong man but even the severity of the moment left him weak in more ways than he was willing to admit to any man, especially Shine. He didn't like the thin man at all. Carter imagined there'd come a time for reckoning before the end. He only had to wait until that day.

Shine nodded back and clapped his hands in front of his waist twice. "Good! I knew you'd make the logical decision. Very smart of you, Mr. Gaetis. Now, if you'd please follow me inside, we can conclude tonight's business and be off."

"You can't be serious!" Carter all but exploded. Making the decision was one matter, having to participate entirely another. He wasn't prepared to endure the endless stream of nightmares from what came next. No man should.

Mr. Shine fixed him with a withering glare. "Oh but I am. This is not a game, Carter. The only way I can be assured of your commitment is by having you participate. Anything less is inexcusable. Our employers demand unconditional obedience." He paused, letting Carter stew. "Perhaps I was mistaken. Perhaps you are not the proper candidate for this position. Good night, Mr. Gaetis. I wish you the best of fortune in the future."

He'd never know what spurred the following words, but Carter grasped at the tiny rope Mr. Shine dangled before him. "No, wait. I'll do it. It's just going to be…"

"Hard? I understand. We have all gone through similar." Shine pat him gently on the back. "Consider it being part of a brotherhood."

Pulling the lapels of his black, trench coat tighter around his neck to keep the harsh wind coming off the river from creeping down his back, Shine started across the street.

Mr. Shine peeled the bloodstained, leather gloves off and tossed them down on the flower pattern comforter. He wasn't smiling but lacked the seriousness Carter expected after murdering two people in their sleep. Instead he wore the look of grim satisfaction that only a man trapped in such a profession could produce. And professional he was. Only a single speck of blood escaped the bed, landing squarely on his right cheek. He looked down to where Carter had collapsed in a pile of vomit and tears.

"It's done, Mr. Gaetis," he announced quietly. "As far as anyone knows you and your family died here tonight in a regrettable gas fire. Welcome to the Lazarus Men."

The hab exploded in flames as Mr. Shine and Carter across the street to the waiting hover car.

ARMIES
of the
SILVER MAGE
CHRISTIAN WARREN
FREED

Malweir was once governed by the order of Mages, bringers of peace and light. Centuries past and the lands prospered. But all was not well. Unknown to most, one mage desired power above all else. He turned his will to the banished Dark Gods and brought war to the free lands. Only a handful of mages survived the betrayal and the Silver Mage was left free to twist the darker races to his bidding. The only thing he needs to complete his plan and rule the world forever are the four shards of the crystal of Tol Shere.

Having spent most of their lives dreaming about leaving their sleepy village and travelling the world, Delin Kerny and Fennic Attleford never thought that one day they would be forced to flee their town to save their lives. Everything changes when they discover the fabled Star Silver sword and learn that there are some who want the weapon for themselves. Hunted by a ruthless mercenary, the boys run from Fel Darrins and are forced into the adventure they only dreamed about.

Ever ashamed of the horrors his kind let loose on the world the last mage, Dakeb, lives his life in shadows. The only thing keeping him alive is his quest to stop the Silver Mage from reassembling the crystal. His chance finally comes through the hearts and wills of Delin and Fennic. Dakeb bestows upon them the crystal shard, entrusting them with the one thing capable of restoring peace to Malweir.

the Dragon Hunters

CHRISTIAN WARREN FREED

The Mage Wars are a fading memory. The kingdoms of Malweir focus on rebuilding what was lost and moving beyond the vast amounts of death and devastation. For some it is easy, others far worse. Some men are made in battle. Grelic of Thrae is one. A seasoned veteran of numerous campaigns and raids, Grelic is a warrior without a war. He languishes under mugs of ale and poor choices that eventually find him locked in the dungeons of King Rentor. His only chance at redemption is an offer tantamount to suicide: travel north with a misfit band of adventurers and learn the truth of what happened in the village of Gend.

Grelic, suddenly tired of his life, reluctantly agrees and meets the only survivor of the horrible massacre: Fitch Iane. Broken, mentally and physically, Fitch babbles about demons stalking through the mists and a terrible monster prowling the skies, breathing fire and death.

What begins as a simple reconnaissance mission quickly turns into a quest to stop Sidian, the Silver Mage from accomplishing his goals in the Deadlands. The last of the dark mages seeks to recover the four shards of the crystal of Tol Shere and open the gateway to release the dark gods from their eternal prison.

Grelic and his team are sorely outnumbered and ill-prepared to deal with the combined threats of a dark mage and one of the great dragons from the west. Not even the might of the Aeldruin, high elf mercenaries, and Dakeb, the last of the mages, promises to be enough to stop evil and restore peace to Thrae.

THE FRACTURED UNIVERSE I
DREAMS OF WINTER
CHRISTIAN
WARREN FREED

It is a troubled time, for the old gods are returning and they want the universe back…

Under the rigid guidance of the Conclave, the seven hundred known worlds carve out a new empire with the compassion and wisdom the gods once offered. But a terrible secret, known only to the most powerful, threatens to undo three millennia of progress. The gods are not dead at all. They merely sleep. And they are being hunted.

Senior Inquisitor Tolde Breed is sent to the planet Crimeat to investigate the escape of one of the deadliest beings in the history of the universe: Amongeratix, one of the fabled THREE, sons of the god-king. Tolde arrives on a world where heresy breeds insurrection and war is only a matter of time. Aided by Sister Abigail of the Order of Blood Witches, and a company of Prekhauten Guards, Tolde hurries to find Amongeratix and return him to Conclave custody before he can restart his reign of terror.

What he doesn't know is that the Three are already operating on Crimeat.

BIO

Christian W. Freed was born in Buffalo, N.Y. more years ago than he would like to remember. After spending more than 20 years in the active duty US Army he has turned his talents to writing. Since retiring, he has gone on to publish more than 20 science fiction and fantasy novels as well as his combat memoirs from his time in Iraq and Afghanistan. His first book, Hammers in the Wind, has been the #1 free book on Kindle 4 times and he holds a fancy certificate from the L Ron Hubbard Writers of the Future Contest.

Passionate about history, he combines his knowledge of the past with modern military tactics to create an engaging, quasi-realistic world for the readers. He graduated from Campbell University with a degree in history and a Masters of Arts degree in Digital Communications from the University of North Carolina at Chapel Hill. He currently lives outside of Raleigh, N.C. and devotes his time to writing, his family, and their two Bernese Mountain Dogs. If you drive by you might just find him on the porch with a cigar in one hand and a pen in the other. You can find out more about his work by clicking on any one of the social media icons listed below. You can find out more about his work by following him on:

Facebook: @https://www.facebook.com/ChristianFreed
Twitter: @ChristianWFreed
Instagram: @ christianwarrenfreed

Like what you read? Let him know with an email or review.

warfighterbooks@gmail.com